Jiggered BY GIN

Bohemia Bartenders Mysteries
Book Four

LUCY LAKESTONE

Velvet Petal Press
Florida

Cover design: Sky Diary Productions

Hardback ISBN: 978-1-943134-37-3

First edition

Velvet Petal Press, P.O. Box 922, Cocoa, Florida 32923

Learn more about the author at LucyLakestone.com

About the Book

A ROYAL PAIN IN THE PALACE ...

Mixologist Pepper Revelle and the Bohemia Bartenders land in London for a UK adventure—a gin festival sponsored by dashing distiller Mark Fairman, who wants them to do more than make cocktails. As valuable books mysteriously vanish from his mansion's luxe library, Mark asks Pepper and her colleague Neil to track down the thief.

But there's another olive in this martini of mischief. At their frenemy Alastair's bar, a storied gin palace from Dickens's time, bizarre break-ins add another mystery to the mix. Pepper and Neil's sleuthing takes them on a wild ride from the city's swank watering holes to a fascinating real-life palace as they face deception, devilry and danger.

While Pepper's tempted by Mark's extravagant flirting and charmed by his loaner dog, she wonders if hot nerd Neil will stop playing hard to get. But thoughts of love in London seem trivial when murder is poured into the punch. Can they solve multiple mysteries before they're juiced like a lime in a gin and tonic?

Jiggered by Gin is the fourth book in the Bohemia Bartenders Mysteries, funny whodunits with a dash of romance set in a convivial collective of cocktail lovers, eccentrics and mixologists. These quasi-cozy culinary comedies contain a hint of heat, a splash of cursing and shots of laughter, served over hand-carved ice.

For Karen,
my dear friend and fellow Anglophile,
who can quote Monty Python with me
all day long.

Chapter One

I had no idea where the Dickens I was. It seemed appropriate to invoke the Victorian novelist, given this bustling London bar might've come right out of one of his books.

Even if I didn't know where I was, exactly, I felt right at home. This was a bar, after all—with its faux gaslight sconces, tiny old prints of racehorses and carved-wood trim. As a mixologist, I found the faint aroma of centuries of gin-swilling and beer-drinking—and the racket of a boisterous crowd—comforting and happy, especially after the dreary trans-Atlantic flight and all that fuss at the hotel.

And this place looked so cozy, and the soccer team—I mean, football team was so glad to see me, and they kept buying rounds.

"Pepper! One more, love!" shouted a barrel-chested footballer with floppy blond hair whom I'd taken to calling Blue Eyes after missing his name early on. "You're not getting squiffy, are you?"

If *squiffy* meant tipsy, well ... "Maybe? Not sure I should have another one, guys," I said, even as an amused server set a laden tray on the round table and doled out half a dozen pints. "Don't you have a game or something?" I knew less than nothing about English football.

"First match of the season is Saturday," said another player, dark-skinned and lanky with a beautiful smile and a theatrical wink, his shirt sporting the same colorful shield all of theirs did. "Plenty of time to drink before then."

"Besides, drinking just makes us better," said the blond guy, handing me the cool glass while not so subtly glancing down at the cleavage revealed by my poufy tropical dress.

"I don't need beer to make *me* better," I joked in a Mae West kind of way. They roared and held up their glasses.

I blinked at the full pint and pushed aside a wave of wooziness. I chose to blame the jet lag. My bladder sent me another warning sign. And my phone buzzed again in my canvas messenger bag, which leaned against my foot under the table.

"Come on! Pep-per! Pep-per! Pep-per!"

I had my pride. And it wasn't *that* late. I lifted my beer, pushed my cat's-eye glasses higher on my nose, and started chugging to their cheers.

I wasn't a beer drinker, usually. I liked good beer, but I was a cocktail gal. I made delicious drinks at my bar back in Bohemia, on Florida's east coast. And with the Bohemia Bartenders, a team of mixologists from a handful of bars in my town, I mixed top-notch craft cocktails at premier events. We'd arrived here in London this morning for a gin festival.

The opening party was set for this evening, so we had a few hours for tourism, especially when our hotel couldn't check us in because of a computer failure. And despite the very proper clerk's horror at having Americans in loud tropical clothes in his foyer, he held our luggage so we could explore.

But my tourist dreams didn't quite work out. My good friend Melody, a bodacious blonde, bailed on me when Luke, who was handsome in a teenage vampire kind of way, convinced her to visit Harrods by appealing to her love of shopping. Luke didn't love shopping, but he'd do anything to spend time with Melody. Barclay had gone off with our friend Gina—not a bartender but his new sweetheart. And they'd all vanished before I finished my conversation with Neil.

Neil couldn't be seduced into going with me—just like he couldn't be seduced any other time, apparently. He had a meeting with the festival's organizers.

Neil led the Bohemia Bartenders and owned a fabulous bar back home. He was a total cocktail nerd and author of a book that would be featured in a seminar at the festival. He had stunning gray eyes rimmed in dark blue, rusty-brown hair, a close-cropped beard, and an impressive bow-tie collection. I crushed on him hard when we first met, but since then, I'd been a little crushed by his retreat, even as we'd become good friends.

I still had a thing for him, but the more Neil pushed me away, the more I was pulled toward another source of attraction— London distiller Mark Fairman. I was eager to see Mark, and not just because he was the hottest redhead on either side of the Atlantic. He'd told me he needed help but had yet to reveal why. Mark brought out all my worst instincts, but hey, sometimes bad instincts led to good fun.

Like drinking with a London football club in the Rod and Wimple, after losing myself in a maze of cobbled lanes because my phone's fuggled data plan made my map app about as useful as a cocktail fork in a punch bowl.

In spite of the charming company, this latest chugalug added up to one beer too far. I got only halfway before I had to put the glass down. The guys had downed theirs by then and laughed and joked and then shouted out to a couple more logo'd friends who'd entered the bar.

I suppressed a burp, leaned down to grab my gray canvas bag, and extracted my phone to see a flurry of texts.

At least my texts still worked.

Neil's was the latest in a series of messages that mostly consisted of "Where are you?" He wrote: "Change of plans. We're going to pick you up. Need an address."

Hell, I didn't know where I was. That was the whole reason I'd sat here drinking through the middle of the day. Well, that and the friendly company and the scrumptious fish and chips I'd had for lunch.

"I'm at the Rod and Wimple," I texted back. Let him figure out the address.

"OK," Neil finally sent back. "Mark knows where it is. Be outside in ten."

Well, wasn't he bossy today.

I kind of liked the idea of Neil being bossy. Ahem.

And what was that about Mark?

"I've got to go, boys," I told the guys, standing unsteadily and slinging my bag over my shoulder. I pulled out my wallet, but Blue Eyes waved it away.

"I've got this, darlin'. And you're breaking my heart," he said in his delicious accent as the others chimed in with sorrowful "Aws." "Here, let me give you a souvenir."

He stood next to me and then, with all the timing of an exotic dancer, slowly drew his team jersey over his head, leaving him with nothing but skin underneath. He handed the shirt to me with an irresistible grin as I unsuccessfully tried not to ogle the quilt of muscles that rippled across his torso.

"Crapnoodles," I murmured, and the guys laughed in delight. I dragged my lichen-green eyes (yes, they have been compared to a lovely symbiotic fungus-algae life form) back up to my benefactor's sapphire ones, then opened my bag. First I pulled out a Sharpie and waved it at him, and he smiled and signed the jersey. Then I stuffed the shirt in my bag and pulled out a card. "Here. If you're ever in Bohemia, Florida, look me up."

"Pepper Revelle—Mixologist—Nola," he said, reading the card with a wrinkled brow.

"Nola's my bar. New Orleans-themed. I'll make you a Sazerac."

"It's a date, Pepper."

I waved and backed away from the table, tripped over someone else's purse, then made my way to the bathroom. After relieving myself of excess beer, brushing my longish caramel-colored hair and applying fresh cinnamon-red lipstick, I emerged a happier woman. I eased through the crowd and slipped out the door.

And blinked in the bright light of a breezy, cool, September afternoon.

It was easy to forget it was daytime in a pub like that. And such a pleasant daytime, too. I sighed in relief and surveyed the pale blue sky. When we'd left home, Florida marinated in the soupiest of hot temperatures with a tropical storm offshore threatening torrential rain. Here, all was uncharacteristically fair.

And all was Fairman.

Mark Fairman.

A sleek black Jaguar had stopped at the curb, and I looked through an open window to see a familiar face peering out at me.

"Hot Pepper," he growled with a roguish grin. "Get in."

Chapter Two

"So what have you done with Neil and the others?" I asked Mark once I was settled into the soft leather seat and he'd accelerated into traffic.

"Always on about Neil," he chided in his irresistible accent. "Aren't you pleased to see me?"

"I think so?" I smiled at him, reacquainting myself with his thick, dark red hair, golden-brown eyes, scruff and mischievous expression. "Why are you picking me up?" *And how much trouble am I willing to get into?*

"One, I sent a mini bus for the others. And two, I wanted to bring you to my place personally."

"*Your* place?"

"The hotel had—issues, which they realized when their system came back online. They'd double-booked the rooms. I came to the rescue."

"How did you know about the hotel issues?"

"I ran into Neil at the festival meeting and was privy to the anguished phone call," he said dryly.

I eyed him as he athletically maneuvered through traffic, driving on what my brain was convinced was the wrong side of the road. "Did you have anything to do with this?"

"You wound me, dear Pepper. I happen to have enough space for you all, and I'm on the board of the festival. It's the least I can do. Besides"—he shot me a warm glance—"this will be fun."

Why was I nervous? I pictured this weekend turning into one of those country house parties in the historical romance novels I liked to read. But it wouldn't be like that. We had plenty to do for the festival, and I wanted to spend my spare time playing tourist. I'd never been to London. Glimpses of tantalizing sights dazzled me along the way, as castles and cathedrals competed with glittering sci-fi skyscrapers in the crowded skyline.

As we crossed the Thames over the Blackfriars Bridge, I texted Millie, our team's Girl Friday back home in Florida, to see if she could sort out my phone's data. I wanted to get my maps working. I was still lost. Or maybe Mark just made me feel that way.

"How far out is your place?" I asked.

"That depends on what you mean by 'far out.' I consider it totally groovy," he said, doing a hilarious Austin Powers imitation.

I rolled my eyes, but I couldn't help but smile. "I mean, how long till we get there?"

"Not long now."

"Does our staying with you have to do with that problem you mentioned when you were in Bohemia for the film festival?" I asked him.

"Ah-ha. I knew you had an analytical mind under all that deliciousness. But not entirely, no. I genuinely wanted to help."

"So ... do you still have your little problem, whatever it is?"

"I do," Mark said, a tad more grimly.

"Are you going to tell me what it is?"

"Patience, Pepper. I'd rather give you the lay of the land first and show you."

Hmm. Show and tell with Mark Fairman. Maybe from there, we'd progress to truth or dare.

Stop it, Pepper. You have work to do! And judging by how quiet Mark had become, he really did have something bothering him.

I knew Mark had an estate or, at the very least, a large house. It had to be, to hold our entire crew. But I wasn't prepared for the three-story brick mansion trimmed in white stone that greeted us behind a screen of trees and a gate in a secluded property plunked in the middle of a busy suburb.

One might call it a modern suburb, but it's all relative. What looked modern to a Londoner seemed antique to someone from Florida, where a house from the 1930s was considered historic. Still, his sprawling pile of bricks was clearly older than its surroundings, perhaps by centuries.

Mark hit the gate code on the keypad, and we pulled up in the curved drive behind a large, white passenger van labeled *Fairyland Distillery* disgorging my bartender crew. I let out a little sigh of relief to see them, even though Neil raised an eyebrow at Mark's black Jag when it purred to a stop. I popped out, slung my bag strap over my head and waved at Neil, and he granted me a worried little smile.

While Mark dispensed directions to a couple of guys extracting luggage from the van, I walked over to the group: Luke, Barclay and a smiling Gina, all wearing shirts in tropical prints; Neil in his vest and bow tie; and Melody.

"There you are!" Melody exclaimed and gave me a hug. My tall, blond friend wore skin-tight black pants and a wild shirt-dress sporting parrots, including a bright blue bird that matched her eyes. "Wait till you see what I bought."

"Only half the store," said Luke, pushing his longish brown hair away from his face. "I have no idea how you do that on a bartender's salary."

"I scrimp and save and have more than one pot simmering on the stove," Melody said mysteriously.

"And did you find any rum?" I asked Barclay.

Always handsome, with his light-brown complexion and unusual green eyes, Barclay positively glowed as he put an arm around Gina. "Oh, we found some. I pulled some strings and got us a distillery tour."

"It was fantastic!" Gina said, her brown eyes sparkling. She seemed a little tipsy already. Gina was a lightweight, and she needed

to pace herself, or I'd have to answer to her brother—Jorge Listo
was my business partner in my bar back home. Actually, it was fair
to call Nola a restaurant since we'd expanded the food menu, but I
would always think of it as my bar.

"Where were you?" Melody asked.

"Um ..." I hesitated as Neil listened in. "Just walking around. I
ended up in a pub. Some nice soccer players bought me a beer." Or
three.

"Soccer players?" Melody grinned. "I'm proud of you, Pepper.
Did you get their numbers?"

While Neil grimaced, I pulled the jersey out of my bag. "Just
this."

Mark had stepped up to us. "You were drinking with these
fellows? That's my favorite club. I should've come in and joined
you!"

"No time," Neil said, a bit curt.

"Just so," Mark agreed, still shaking his head as I put the shirt
away. "Pepper, you have a way of charming your way into ... well. At
any rate, here's Ben and Albert. They'll show you to your rooms and
get you settled."

Albert, a stocky man with short brown hair, a graying beard and
a tweed driving cap who I figured to be in his fifties, grunted a
greeting and turned back to the luggage.

But the other man, slender with tousled straw-blond hair and
pale blue eyes, in his mid-twenties, I guessed—a few years younger
than me—smiled and shook our hands. "Hi. Ben Burton. I help
Mark with whatever needs doing, here and in the distillery."

"Nice to meet you," I said.

"Where's the distillery?" Neil asked, looking around.

"In the old dairy," Ben said. "It's quite something."

Neil nodded. "I hope we get a tour. I want to see the magic
behind the award-winning Fairyland Distillery." Was it just me, or
did I detect an edge of sarcasm? Fairyland produced stellar craft
liquors. So what was Neil in a snit about?

"Oh, you'll get a tour!" Mark said, oblivious to Neil's tone. "Pepper, which bag is yours?"

"That one." I pointed to a big blue suitcase, and to my embarrassment, Mark started rolling it toward the house. I looked at Neil and shrugged, still feeling awkward at Mark's attentions.

Neil just quirked his mouth and slung his big leather bar bag over his shoulder, and our group moved toward the house. Ben and Albert followed with the groaning luggage cart.

House was an inadequate word, of course. Mark led us through a large, high-ceilinged entrance hall with four comfy leather chairs in front of a grand fireplace big enough to hold a horse. We followed him up an intricately carved staircase and through elegant wood-paneled hallways past seemingly endless rooms until we reached what he called the East Wing.

Out of the shadows, a figure emerged, and I twitched in surprise. The thin, tall woman wore a severe black skirt and starched white shirt, her gray-threaded brown hair coiffed in a perfect bun.

She looked with disapproval at Mark, who still hauled my suitcase. "Sir," the woman said in a way that was more scolding than respectful.

"Ah, Mrs. Pidgeon," Mark said. "Would you show these fine people to their rooms? I'll take care of the Garden Bedroom."

He smiled at me, and Mrs. Pidgeon turned her pale gray eyes in my direction like a couple of space lasers and frowned.

Note to self: Do not cross Mrs. Pidgeon.

"Here come the boys." Mark gestured behind us, where Albert pushed the luggage-laden cart and Ben carried an armful of shopping bags labeled *Harrods*.

Must be an elevator, I thought.

While the bartenders sorted out their stuff and Mrs. Pidgeon moved off down the hall, allocating lodgings, Mark spoke softly in my ear. "She's the house manager and my assistant and general keeper. A bit stuffy but sterling, absolutely sterling. This place

would be a pile of rubbish and liquor bottles if it weren't for her."
He straightened and talked in a more normal voice. "Come along,
then. I've put this room aside for you."

I tried not to think about how he could have put a room aside
for me when he didn't know until maybe an hour ago that we'd all
be piling into his mansion, but I followed him. He set my suitcase
down in the middle of a large room that smelled of wood polish and
flowers, no doubt from the enormous bouquet on the mantel of the
elaborate marble-framed fireplace. Heavy, dark green drapes framed
huge paned-glass windows complemented by pale green walls. The
view encompassed terraced gardens and pretty outbuildings. And
the luxuriously appointed canopy bed was nothing short of royal.

I set down my messenger bag in shock. "Are you serious?"

"Oh, they're all pretty much like this," Mark said offhandedly,
though he waggled his eyebrows as he saw me gape at the bed.
Through the open door, I could hear my friends exclaiming over
their rooms, too. "Except yours has the biggest fireplace and one
more thing. Come on in, Albert."

Albert entered, cradling something in his arms. When I realized
what it was, I let out a coo.

"A puppy!" I held out my arms for the floppy-eared thing. She
was what I'd call an older puppy. An adolescent? She was still
babyish around the face but starting to get leggy. With her caramel
and white fur, she looked a lot like my darling Cavapoo Astra, who
was at home with my Aunt Celestine at our duplex in Florida.
"What? How? I mean, what am I going to do with a puppy?"

"Consider her on loan," Mark said, obviously delighted at my
reaction. Even Albert, who'd come across as grumpy earlier, smiled.
"Cavalier King Charles Spaniel," Mark continued. "I thought you
might miss your little dog, so she'll keep you company. She's house-
trained, more or less, and Albert or Mrs. Pidgeon will keep an eye
on her while you're out and about. But while you're here ..."

"Oh, Mark." This was a weird gesture, if generous, and having a
dog right now, even on loan, was ridiculously impractical, but I held

the soft little Cavalier close anyway and looked into her big, brown eyes. She licked my face. "Does she have a name?"

"Victoria. Unless you have other ideas."

I laughed. "No. Victoria is fine, if kind of a mouthful."

"Let Mrs. Pidgeon know if you lack anything. Wifi password is *drink me*. No spaces." He grinned.

"Thanks," I said, trying to ignore his flirty tone. As I cradled Victoria and rubbed her belly, Neil appeared in the doorway. He saw the dog, swallowed the questions he obviously had and said, "The party is at eight. I suppose we should plan to grab something to eat beforehand."

"All taken care of," Mark said. "You'll have a hearty tea here, and Albert and Ben will drive us all to The Dandy Tipple. There'll be food there as well. Take an hour and relax and get ready. And if you don't mind, I'd like to show both of you something before teatime." He nodded at me, and I realized he was looking for an opportunity to tell us about his mysterious problem.

"That sounds fine. Neil?"

"Of course." Neil looked relieved that Mark wasn't going to squirrel me away in the wine cellar, which he'd threatened to show me the last time I saw him.

"Excellent," our host said. "Meet me by the big fireplace. Can you find your way back downstairs?"

I shrugged. "Maybe?" This place was a warren of dark hallways.

"I'll get us there." Neil shot me a reassuring smile, a sexy smile, and my heart beat a little faster.

Oh, geez. This trip was going to be complicated, wasn't it?

Chapter Three

Victoria made a wonderful companion for my twenty-minute nap, curling up in my armpit and snoring adorably. Naps with dogs counted double, but this snooze only served to emphasize my jet lag as my phone alarm dragged me awake.

After my quick shower in the fully modernized en suite bathroom, the little dog wasn't much help as I tried to get dressed. She hopped up on the bench where I'd put my suitcase and jumped inside, sniffing avidly, no doubt smelling Astra. And Astra would surely notice the smell of strange dog when I got home. I hoped she would forgive me.

Finally, Victoria let me extract a retro-style black dress with a deep V neckline, hot pink trim and a pink crinoline to fluff out the skirt. I brushed off the dog hair and pulled out black heels; they were fairly comfy but not something I'd ever wear behind the bar. Fortunately, I didn't have to work tonight, so I didn't anticipate standing for hours.

Last, I donned my cat's-eye glasses—the sparkly pair. Eyeglasses didn't help me see any better, though I supposed someday I might need them for that. They were occasionally useful during citrus-squeezing. But more than anything, they were just part of my identity now, and I felt naked without them.

I added chunky vintage jewelry, along with the leather necklace-turned-bracelet, adorned with beads and an alligator tooth, that I'd acquired from a voodoo priestess in New Orleans. I figured the good-luck charm worked because I was still alive despite a few unpleasant encounters with some very bad people.

I was gazing into a gilt-framed mirror like some kind of princess and pinning up my hair when a soft knock came at the door. "Come in," I called, finishing the job with a rhinestone brooch as the door opened.

I turned to see Neil, looking devastatingly dapper in black pants, dark silver-gray vest, black shirt and patterned gray and black bow tie. We both just stood there dumbstruck for a second, drinking in our mutual finery, until Victoria barked.

Neil grinned and looked down at her. "You were saying?" Then at me. "What are you going to do with her?"

"Mark said someone would take care of her when we're out and about. Isn't she adorable?" I pulled the strap of my canvas bag over my head, cross-body, then picked up the puppy. "Admit it. She's a love."

"I didn't think it was possible, but you're actually even cuter *with* the puppy," he joked.

"I'm not sure whether to take that remark as an insult, so I'll ignore it." Still, my heart did a little flutter. Victoria squirmed, so I put her down, and she trotted after us as we headed out of the room. "You remember how to get there?"

"The fireplace downstairs? I think so. I have a pretty good sense of direction."

Fifteen minutes later, after we'd bumbled through endless hallways and into a grand dining room, then a lofty glass conservatory filled with tropical plants that reminded me of home—where we lost Victoria in the jungle for five minutes while she found something to pee on and I crossed my fingers that Mrs. Pidgeon wouldn't catch us—we got to the fireplace. Mark was there chatting with Ben, whom he sent off to oversee the final preparations for tea. Victoria ran up to Mark and put her little paws on his legs.

"You're impossible to resist." Mark looked at me when he spoke, but then he scooped the puppy into his arms and scratched behind her ears. The puppy was surely more irresistible than I—with Mark a close second, in his open-collar white shirt, expensive-looking nut-brown sport jacket and close-fitting trousers.

"Thank you for meeting me," Mark said to Neil and me.

Neil nodded. "The least we can do, given you're putting us up."

"My pleasure." Mark set Victoria down, and she stood, her fringed tail wagging, ready for action. Or possibly dinner. "But I plan to take full advantage of your presence. I have a mystery on my hands, and I'm hoping you can help me figure it out. I've confided only in Mrs. Pidgeon, given I'm not sure who's involved, and the staff love to gossip. But I'm getting ahead of myself." He gestured, and we followed.

I had a vague sense we headed in the opposite direction of the east wing, where we were staying. The west wing? I was sure we were in new territory when Mark took us into a cavernous picture gallery lit by an elegant, metal-framed skylight two stories above that ran nearly the length of the room. A couple of tufted benches sat in the center, like in a real art gallery. Victoria took off running toward the other end and came back with a miniature tennis ball in her mouth, which Mark threw. She bounded after it, her long ears flapping. Obviously not her first rodeo.

I wandered, scanning the art that filled the walls, one framed picture above another. Then I screeched to a halt by a portrait of a handsome red-haired man in a nineteenth-century suit, surrounded by a pack of spaniels that looked like Victoria. "Mark, this one looks just like you."

He stopped with us and chuckled. "It *is* me. One of my friends had it done as a birthday present, quite without my knowledge. It looks like a painting, but it's actually a Photoshop job done up on canvas. I had to hang it. It makes me laugh. It's bloody pretentious, but it inspired me to get Victoria." The little dog was back with the ball, and Mark had her drop it in his palm before he threw it again.

"Are there family portraits in here?" Neil asked.

"Yes and no. I'd like to say these are all my ancestors, but some of them came with the house. I have a few of my own, of course." Mark nodded at an oil painting of a fellow with big sideburns in a fancy coat and hair as red as his. "And this is some of my art collection as well."

"So this is a family house?" Neil asked.

"Goodness, no. Well, yes, someone's family but not mine. I brought in the Fairman portraits. My family has money, which I've turned into more money, but we were never as posh as all this."

"If I may ask a rude question," I said, "what is your family history?"

Mark smiled. "You might say I've come full circle. We made our fortune with gin."

"Now this is a story I want to hear," said Neil, always up for a history lesson.

"They were early adopters, as it were," Mark said as we strolled slowly along the gallery. "They started with wine, then transitioned to gin back when it was truly disreputable in the 1700s, when the well-off were still drinking genever. I'm embarrassed to say it was the crack of its day, though our family's was better than most. By the mid-1800s, they were settled in Clerkenwell and doing a fine business with quality London Dry gin. For reasons beyond me, they sold out and diversified. I had no interest in becoming a grocer, but I was keen on reviving the family legacy. I always liked that naughty part of our history, and I liked gin. So I started Fairyland Distillery, and this place had a perfect spot for the work. Plus I get to live in this house. It's a bit much, I'll grant you, but there's plenty of room for my collections."

"Your family is—are—grocers?" I asked.

"They own supermarkets and other retail. Still do. Well, and the odd energy and tech company. I'm still a bit involved there."

I looked at him curiously. "Who's 'they'?"

Mark shrugged. "My parents. My brothers."

Oh, dear. This goofy hunk of English manhood had *brothers?*

Hubba-hubba. Neil gave me the side-eye, as if he could read my mind, and I pretended not to notice.

"Here we are." Mark turned and leaned over the handle of a dark, beautiful wooden door. In a moment, he pushed it open.

He hit a switch as we stepped into the room, with Victoria on our heels, and chandeliers sprang to life above us.

I gasped. "A library! Did they film *My Fair Lady* here?"

He laughed. "No, Professor Higgins's library was modeled after a library in a castle in France. But when this one was renovated in the 1800s, I believe they may have taken some inspiration from the same spot. At least when they built the spiral staircase. Isn't it wonderful?"

A tightly spiraled staircase of dark, carved wood was centered on the left-hand wall, leading to a bookcase-lined balcony that ran the length of the deep two-story room and bent back behind me and over the door. A wrought-iron railing guarded its edge.

On the far wall, a large Palladian window let in light from the garden.

Opposite the staircase was an ornate fireplace, above which hung a tranquil Impressionist painting of a water scene. "Giuseppe De Nittis," Mark said when Neil asked who'd painted it. There were a few comfy chairs and a suitably old desk. One table held open books; another small one held a tray with full decanters and glasses and a bottle of Mark's Frilly Fairy Gin.

Otherwise, shelves lined every square inch of wall, and all of those shelves were crammed with books. I felt like I'd died and gone to book heaven.

"You actually read?" I exclaimed.

Mark grinned. "Pepper, Pepper, Pepper. Do you think the only thing I do is lure mixologist minxes to their doom? Though some ladies do seem to like the library."

My face heated. "Uh, I didn't—"

"I *do* read." Mark pointed to the second story. "You may be surprised to know I have an excellent seventeenth-century poetry collection."

"Really?" Now Neil looked skeptical. "Society is all but rude to this delicious solitude."

"Testing me?" Mark raised a devilish eyebrow. "Andrew Marvell." Then he looked at me. "Though I prefer 'To His Coy Mistress.'"

I gulped. I didn't remember all the details from English class, but I knew it was a seduction poem.

"So what's the deal here?" I asked. "What did you want to show us?"

"Well, what's rather interesting to me about this library is that I acquired it pretty much intact. The previous owners had no interest in it or assumed it lacked value because they'd talked to some collector or another who said this place wasn't known for its books. But I thought otherwise when I saw what was here and took a few books to a dealer in town to assess."

I picked up Victoria, who was trying to chew the buckle on my shoe. "Valuable books?"

"Remarkably valuable. He was surprised as well. The thing about really valuable antique books is that most dealers have an idea of where they are and who owns them. It's unusual for rare books to simply turn up out of nowhere. He suggested I hire him or someone else to do an inventory."

"And what did you find out when he did the inventory?" asked Neil, who'd settled into one of the comfy chairs with a leather-bound volume he'd pulled from a shelf.

Now Mark looked embarrassed. "I'm afraid I didn't hire him. I just put it off, you know, and I was having a good time going through the collection myself, taking notes. I'm keeping a journal of what I find. It's a pleasurable way to unwind when I need a quiet night. But one evening when I was going through the illustrated books, I noticed one was missing. *Ulysses.*"

"James Joyce?" Neil asked. "There's an illustrated version?"

"Oh, yes. Illustrated by Henri Matisse." Neil and I exchanged a look as Mark continued. "I didn't realize how limited an edition it was. I intended to go through it in detail later. But it's quite a distinctive volume, and it was clearly missing. I asked my book dealer friend if he'd ever heard of it, and he almost fainted. He showed me pictures of a comparable copy. It was definitely the Matisse version from 1935, signed by Joyce *and* Matisse. Only two hundred fifty were signed by both, and the entire edition consisted of just fifteen hundred copies."

"Good God," Neil said.

"You think it was stolen?" I asked.

"That seems likely, doesn't it?" Mark shook his head. "But it hasn't shown up on the market. My friend has his ear to the ground. And that's not all. After I realized it was gone, I did a quick photographic survey of all the bookshelves and am keeping a list that I'm fleshing out as I have time. Now that I'm paying attention, I've noticed other volumes have gone missing, and not all at once. I could probably handle this the normal way and report it to the police, but the truth is, while all the books are valuable, there's one in particular I really want to get back. And I don't think they'll see these thefts as anything more than someone taking advantage of a rich collector who couldn't care less."

"But you do care about this book?" I asked. "What is it?

"I care about *all* of them but this one in particular. You'll think it corny, but I've always loved Arthurian legends."

"I love them too!" I piped up.

Mark smiled. "Well, my father knew I loved Arthur. Fancied myself a knight errant and all that when I was a boy. I suppose I should add that my brothers and I are all overachievers because my father is a hard bastard to please. When I graduated from Cambridge, he gave me this special book to congratulate me, and I just about fell out of my chair. It's an extremely rare edition of T.H. White's *The Sword in the Stone* from 1938, hand-colored and signed by the author, with a magnificent jeweled leather binding. It really started me on my collecting. It's like nothing you've ever seen."

"And worth quite a bit, I expect," Neil said.

"Indeed. Close to thirty thousand pounds. But as you might imagine, it's really valuable to me because it was a present from my father. I haven't always been successful. I was a fool a lot of the time in school, and I do enjoy my pleasures. But this book meant that my father saw something in me and appreciated me. I feel like I've let him down by letting it slip through my fingers. I must have it back."

Mark's earnestness surprised me, but it also touched me. I knew what it was like to disappoint a parent. I still didn't fully understand why my mother thought I was such a disaster, why she consistently pushed me away, though I thought it was because my choices represented everything she'd rejected in life. At least Mark's father was proud of him.

"We'll do our best," I told him. "We need as much information as possible."

"How many books have you lost, do you think?" Neil asked.

"Perhaps ten, fifteen books I know of and possibly more. The shelves in here are a bit dusty, so it's not difficult to tell when something's been moved."

"I suppose we can't blame the maid if it's dusty," I joked.

A corner of Mark's mouth lifted. "I haven't had any house-keeping in here until I can determine the value and needs of the collection. The room is always locked. Mrs. Pidgeon has the keys to everything, and she guards them with her life. I trust her absolutely. But even she doesn't have the code. No one should be able to get in here."

"I mean, couldn't they just pick the lock?" I said, drawing on my extensive knowledge of TV crime shows. "This room doesn't look very high-tech."

"Then you weren't paying attention when you walked in." Mark pointed behind me, and I turned back toward the door. Above the modern silver-toned handle was a keypad.

Neil stood, put the book down and walked over to look at it. "Alarm system?"

Mark nodded. "I had that installed as soon as I purchased the house. I had a feeling this library might hold a few treasures."

"Windows?" I asked as I stroked Victoria's silky ears.

"Also alarmed," Mark said.

"Any other way in?" Neil asked.

"I've looked. I mean, I have an imagination as much as the next fellow. I don't think there are any secret doorways. These bookcases are solid. No tomfoolery with the fireplace or anything."

"Very strange," I said. "Have you tried cameras?"

"I have," Mark said. "One on the second story aimed at the door. One hidden by the fireplace, aimed at the window. Between them, they see pretty much the entire room. They record continuously, so I check the footage whenever I see something's missing. They've revealed nothing yet. It's baffling."

"Has anyone else been in this room ever?" I asked.

"Well, we had a reception for Fairyland in here once, early on, before the cameras. It's such a terrific room. Everyone loved it. So the whole staff, distillery and household, and several guests were here."

I quirked my mouth. "And nothing went missing then?"

"No. At least I'm fairly certain it didn't. Only much later. Do you think you can help me?"

Neil had circled the room and ended up next to me. "We'll give it some thought. It would help to have a list of the missing titles."

"Can you give us the door code?" I added.

"Can I trust you?" Mark showed me one dimple. A Mark Fairman dimple could power all of Florida's air-conditioning for a month.

"You'll have to take that chance," I said. "Cough up."

Chapter Four

My brain whirred like a blender as Mark escorted Neil and me and the happily following Victoria to what he called the drawing room. "I'll take Victoria to get her supper. Enjoy yourselves, and I'll join you shortly."

He melted away with the pup on his heels, and we entered the large room to find our whole crew and a bunch of others milling about, munching on delicacies. I couldn't help pausing to gawk at the slate-blue walls, high ceiling carved with cream-colored figures and golden garlands, expensive-looking antique carpet, a chandelier and ornate old furniture.

Neil mumbled something, and I turned to him. "What?"

"Nothing," he said. But I could've sworn he said, *I can't compete with this.*

Hmmm. Was he competing? Was Neil finally interested in me? Was I interested in Mark? Truth was, Mark was hotter than a forest fire, but the sheer excess of this place was as daunting as it was seductive. And then there was Neil—solid, smart, kind, and for me, as irresistible as a Manhattan, perfect, straight up with a Luxardo cherry.

I put all those thoughts aside and sniffed. The food smelled fantastic. A uniformed woman walked around with a tray, offering tiny sandwiches. More dishes were piled on an elegant sideboard— ham, breads, piles of cheese and fruit, quiches, pastries, petit fours. A man in formal wear by the buffet handed teacups to guests. But I

heard a familiar sound and looked around to see a classy old bar at
the end of the room. There, another man stirred the contents of a
crystal cocktail beaker with a long bar spoon, then poured what I
was sure were gin martinis into coupe glasses. He popped a three-
olive pick into each before handing them to Barclay, Gina and Luke.

"Sandwich?" came a voice at my ear. It was the woman with the
tray. I took a napkin and peered at the pretty little things, crusts
trimmed, unidentifiable innards in mostly pastels. She started
pointing. "Egg salad, cucumber salad, roast beef, chicken salad—"

"Yes," I said. "One of each of those."

Neil chuckled. "Let me grab a couple of plates."

He was back in a jiffy, and we loaded the plates with tiny sandwiches, then went by the buffet and added more goodies.

Ben approached us, looking more dressed up than earlier, with a
skinny black tie, black jacket and white shirt. "Would you like
anything else? Tea, perhaps?"

"Tea would be perfect," I said, and Neil nodded agreement.

"Sugar?"

"Yes." "No." Neil and I answered at the same time. You can
guess who wanted the sugar. We both said no to milk.

Ben hustled off. The cocktails were tempting, but I sorely
needed caffeine if I wanted to survive this evening and get on
London time.

"Isn't this fabulous?" Melody trilled, coming our way and
steering us to a grouping of chairs around a low table where we
could set our bounty. Her blond hair curled around her shoulders in
waves, and her black wiggle dress with crisscross straps was to
die for.

The others came over and joined us, Barclay in gray pants and a
pale green shirt, Gina in a killer bright green dress, and Luke in
black pants, light blue shirt and suspenders. Or as the Brits might
say, trousers and braces? I needed to work on my lingo. We all
looked good and ready for the party at Alastair's bar.

Ben swung by with our cups of tea, and I took a long, hot, sweet sip. Sugar. Caffeine. Delicious. This was the kind of tea that made me understand the British obsession.

As Ben went off to greet some other folks who'd come in, I scanned the crowd. A couple of them looked vaguely familiar—from the staff of Fairyland Distillery, I was pretty sure. I'd seen them in New Orleans at Cocktailia. And there were a few other people who looked like friends of Mark's I'd also seen at the cocktail convention. Meanwhile, there were enough servants running around to staff the *Titanic*.

As the others chattered, I leaned toward Neil, who sat in the chair next to me. "No shortage of suspects," I murmured in his ear.

"If all of these people are around all the time, that's for sure. The food's good, though." He smiled at me around a bite of tiny roast beef sandwich.

"You might as well fuel up." I popped a petit fours into my mouth, moaned with pleasure and made short work of it as Neil's eyes darkened. "You're going to have to deal with Alastair's crap at The Dandy Tipple."

THE FESTIVAL OPENER at The Dandy Tipple was well under way when we arrived, crowded and noisy and happy under the glittering chandeliers and patterned ceilings—made of intricately stamped tin tiles, I thought, painted cream. The antique decor, all carved wood, mirrors, marble and etched glass, struck a wild contrast with the thumping party music pumping through the speakers.

The bar's proprietor, Alastair Markham, once went to school with Neil. Oxford, to be precise. Neil dropped out to follow his true calling as a mixologist, and Alastair never let him forget it. Come to think of it, I had no idea what Alastair had studied. I'd have to ask Neil sometime.

The truth was, Alastair had an inferiority complex and could be extremely unpleasant to Neil as a result. At least that was my theory. So I was as surprised as Neil when Alastair greeted us with enthusiasm, shaking Neil's hand firmly and leaning in to give me a quick kiss on the cheek.

"The Bohemia Bartenders!" Alastair exclaimed, pushing back the golden, floppy boy-band bangs that always seemed to be falling into his brown eyes. "I'm so pleased you could come tonight."

"Really?" I asked, looking around for the criminal mastermind who was holding Alastair hostage. I did spot the rest of our crew— we'd all arrived in Mark's personal shuttle, and they'd scattered to sample the delights of the party. Mark had come separately with friends and staff in another passenger van, and he held court by the dark red marble fireplace.

Neil and I exchanged a glance before replying to Alastair. "We appreciate the invitation," Neil said. "Beautiful bar."

"It's a pre-Victorian treasure." Alastair seemed genuinely pleased, his cheeks a touch pink. His slender figure was clad in tweed trousers, creamy shirt and matching vest, complemented by a skinny caramel tie close to the color of my hair, and he appeared to be trying very hard to be friendly. "Let me show you around."

I was glad he volunteered, because the truth was, The Dandy Tipple stunned me. Sure, I had a cool New Orleans-themed bar back in Florida, and it was plush and beautiful, but it was difficult to compare it to this gorgeous, sparkling, elegant bonbon of history.

"So this is a gin palace?" I asked, thinking back to the festival website's description of Alastair's bar.

He shot me an *Are you an idiot?* look that was more like the old Alastair, and then he recovered his civility. "Um, yes. Back when gin was the plague of London, several drinking establishments popped up to put a pretty shine on all the ugliness associated with the poor, cheap gin that flowed in the 1800s."

"Dickens called them 'perfectly dazzling' even as he bemoaned the filth that surrounded them," came a familiar Southern drawl at my shoulder.

I whirled. "Mr. Cray!" I gave the old New Orleans rum collector a hug. Over a blue collared shirt, he wore a white sweater that matched his flyaway hair.

"Kayanne Pepper, my dear, it's lovely to see you." He was probably the only person who ever used my given first name. Then again, I was about the only one who called him Mr. Cray.

"Cray!" Neil grinned, demonstrating the point, and shook his hand.

Alastair nodded politely, though he seemed annoyed that his little tour was interrupted. "Dickens drank here, you know."

"Didn't Dickens drink everywhere?" Neil asked dryly.

Alastair snorted. "Perhaps, but very few pubs of that era are left, and certainly not many gin palaces. And he spent a *lot* of time here, or so I'm told. So this place is doubly rare. Between the Blitz in World War II and the latter twentieth century's obsession with everything modern, not many gin palaces survived. But now they're protected by heritage laws. We're very careful about any improvements we make."

"It's absolutely beautiful." Cray looked around in appreciation, the starry points of the chandeliers reflecting in his blue eyes.

"We've restored the dining room to its original glory," Alastair said, pointing to an open set of doors paned with beveled glass, beyond which several more tables were visible. "And we've kept the bar as close to its original condition as possible, barring the modern improvements we need to make drinks. The wooden floor has been restored. The bar is mahogany, with a marble top. All original glass. We've electrified the gaslights, of course."

He gestured to the dark, carved wood. The intricate wooden back bar extended almost to the high ceiling, embedded with wooden arches framing etched glass panels, backing niches full of high-end booze. At the center, atop this structure, a large square clock looked over the bar. To either side of the clock were racks that held antique-looking barrels labeled "Old Tom" and so on.

"Original barrels?" I asked.

"A couple of them," Alastair said. "Mostly reproductions. Empty, of course. There was all sorts of rubbish in our cellar when I took over the place, and I salvaged what I could for decor. Like that copper coal bucket over by the fireplace and a few lanterns for color. I use the space for storage now." He got a funny look on his face, as if he was biting his tongue. His eyes darted furtively around the increasingly crowded room. "I'll show you later. Here, come to the bar. I'll have Ari make you something. She's almost as good as I am."

There was the Alastair I knew. Unconsciously arrogant. He led us to the bar, where four bartenders were hard at work keeping the crowd lubricated.

"Everyone, this is Ari Fernsby, my right-hand woman. She can make anything for you, on or off menu. I need to make the rounds." And then, as we said our hellos, Alastair was off. In fact, he went straight to Mark, spoke in his ear, and both of them looked back toward us before stepping aside and talking quietly again. What was up?

"What can I get you?" asked the willowy woman behind the bar. Ari's dark blond hair was pinned up in charming disarray around a heart-shaped face. Her eyes were ice blue, her lips dusky rose, her makeup subtle. She wore a short, tight, light blue brocade halter vest, along with a white blouse and clingy dark gray trousers.

"Let's see what you have." Neil picked up a printed card from the bar, one of the menus for tonight's special event. "How about a gin fizz?"

"I'll have one of those," Cray added.

"On its way. And you, love?" Ari asked me in her lovely English accent, with a smile that I returned.

"I'm Pepper. Thanks. Surprise me," I said. "I always like to see what a fellow mixologist is working on."

Ari's smile broadened. "No pressure, then," she joked, but she went to work on the fizzes first, adding the ingredients—including egg whites—to a tin and shaking the mixture well to get its signature foam.

She presented those to the boys, complete with Dandy Tipple swizzle sticks with their little top hats, then started in on something for me. My supernose picked out interesting spices, along with Campari. Gin was involved, of course, and bubbly Prosecco, as well as orange juice. She garnished the highball glass that held the pretty pale orange concoction with an orange twist.

"My twist on a Garibaldi Sbagliato," she said as I took a deep sniff and then a sip.

"Oh, nice. Clove and cinnamon?"

"Right on. I infused the Campari." She smiled. "Do you like it?"

"It's delicious. Not sweet—balanced perfectly. I'm always so impressed at how versatile gin can be."

"Absolutely. Are you making cocktails for the festival?"

"Yes, I'm with the Bohemia Bartenders—Neil Rockaway here is our fearless leader."

"Love the drink," Neil said.

"I love your book!" Ari answered. "I'll be helping with your seminar. So pleased to meet you."

"Thanks." Neil gave her a warm glance, and I almost spit out my cocktail. But that would've been rude. Plus, it was really good.

"Hey, Ari!" Ben bounced up to the bar. "Hit me!"

She rolled her eyes. "I'll hit you, all right. Thirsty?"

"Parched! I've been lugging swag for Mark and driving all his louts about."

"He works you too hard. G&T?"

"Of course."

"He's so boring," Ari said, tipping her head at Ben, and we laughed as Ben shook his head and smiled.

"Sometimes a gin and tonic is the perfect solution," I said.

"Especially the way she makes it," said Ben. Clearly they had a friendly acquaintance. Or more. Good. I wasn't prepared to watch Ari flirt with Neil.

A minute or two later, and Ben was off. Neil and I thanked Ari and started circulating. Cray wandered away to talk with friends. We ran into Nigel and Lottie Dashwood, professional bon vivants who traveled the world blogging about cocktail events.

"So nice to have an event at home for once," said Lottie, sipping on some sort of gin and lemon cocktail. She wore a sage-green pantsuit. A few tendrils of her bouncy dark curls escaped a cute little matching Fedora-style hat, and her brown skin glowed under the pretty lights.

Nigel looked pale and doughy as usual, but a tad flushed, already a few drinks in, I guessed. He slurred his words slightly. "Don't you like traveling, darling?"

"Of course I do. But I have to go to the dentist sometime."

We laughed.

"Well, don't leave the Tipple without twisting Alastair's arm," Nigel said. "He's got the really good stuff stowed away, and lord knows he rarely has such an appreciative audience. Lovely collection of rums and whiskeys." He leaned unsteadily into Lottie, who took him by the elbow, grinned at us and shrugged, and led him away.

"Oh, crap!" I grabbed Neil and ducked behind him.

"What?"

"Mr. Mixy. Dionysus preserve us."

Neil laughed. "I thought you were rid of him."

"Is one ever really rid of Mr. Mixy? He's like heat rash in Florida. Always poised to itch and burn."

"That might fall under the category of too much information," Neil quipped as I peeked around him.

My big-bearded ex-boyfriend—his beard had fully regrown after its trials and tribulations during the film festival in Bohemia Beach —approached the bar with his entourage. Only one was lugging a video camera this time, but that meant he was still making his stupid TV show.

I tugged Neil to the end of the bar, where a door with a frosted glass window, slightly less ornate than everything else in the place, offered escape.

"Come with me," I said.

"That's not a public space." He gestured to the discreet *Staff Only* sign.

"Oh, don't be such a rule-follower. Besides, you give me the appearance of respectability." He laughed again as I pulled open the door, pushed him into the dark corridor and shut it behind us. Then I bent down and tried to see through the clear bits in the frosted-glass design in the door's window, hoping Mr. Mixy would move on to the buffet in the dining room. I took a nice, cool sip of my drink. This wasn't so bad. And I was here with Neil, who'd moved slightly closer to me as I peered through the glass. Maybe he was trying to get a peek, too. He put a hand on my shoulder, and my heartbeat sped up. I could feel his heat at my back and was just wondering what to do about it when a voice from behind me made me jump.

"Are we interrupting something?" came the deliciously deep, gruff English tones I was starting to know so well.

We spun around to see Mark. And Alastair.

"Well, they're here now," Alastair said. "Might as well show them."

Chapter Five

"Show us what?" I asked. It appeared Alastair and Mark had emerged from a door marked "Office" off this dim hallway. The music was slightly less loud in here.

Mark shrugged. "I told Alastair that you two were helping me sleuth something, and he's had a bit of an issue he thought you might help solve."

"Me? Don't you mean we?" Alastair snapped, glowering at Mark. We?

Mark rolled his eyes. "I'm the silent partner, remember?"

"It doesn't matter," Alastair said. "They need to know everything."

Ah, so Mark was at least some of the money behind The Dandy Tipple. That partially explained how Alastair could afford his globe-trotting among the cocktailians; even if this glitzy place did well, I doubted it afforded a jetsetter salary.

The Bohemia Bartenders were paid just enough to travel. At the very least, our fees covered our expenses and time, we had fun, and our cocktails made us look good.

"So what's going on?" Neil asked.

"Someone's been in our vaults," Alastair answered.

"You have a vault?" I asked. "Like a bank?"

"Of course not," Alastair huffed.

"Not like a bank. But a vault, yes. Or vaults. Either way." Mark smiled. "Underground storage, like my wine cellar. That's where they used to hold the gin barrels."

I cocked my head. "And what's in there now?"

"Bottles, mostly," Alastair said. "Stock. Some wine. A few rare liquors. A few dusty old bits from over the years that haven't been worth cleaning out."

"Anything interesting or historical?" Neil asked.

"I suppose," Alastair said tartly, "if you find wooden boxes and broken chairs interesting."

I didn't appreciate his attitude. "Well, if you want to be hostile about it—"

"Now, now, Hot Pepper, please don't be cross," Mark said. "We'd just like you to take a look. We don't like the idea of someone stealing from the bar, though to be honest, we haven't noticed anything missing."

"My inventory is a bit out of date," Alastair admitted. "But the really valuable bottles are intact."

"Then how do you know someone is breaking in?" Neil asked.

Alastair pushed back his bangs with a sigh. "I came in one morning some months ago and found the vault gate ajar, the lock broken. I had it replaced, and a few weeks later, the same thing. It happened once more. Finally, I gave up on the old gate latch and put a new padlock on it. No one's been in since, that I can tell."

"Come on down and have a look. You can leave your drinks here." Mark pointed to a low table outside the office door.

We deposited our glasses, and Alastair led us to a closed door. He opened it to reveal a stone staircase that wound down into the dark. As we descended, a basement smell overwhelmed my nose—musty, damp, with the added funk of age.

Just when it was getting too dark to see, Alastair hit a switch, and a bare electric bulb lit a small space in front of a cage. No, not a cage. Vertical, black iron bars blocked off an opening in the shape of a pointed arch, with a dark area beyond. A rectangular gate with the same vertical bars hung in the middle of the arch. It was in pretty good shape, though its lower half had brown spots where the paint was flaking.

A shiny silver padlock secured it—an add-on, not an update to the old lock built into the gate. The shackle looped through the bars of the gate and the cage.

Alastair pulled a set of keys from his pocket.

"Wait a second." I eased past him and leaned in to look at the lock. "I'm no expert, but this looks pretty scratched up. Do you think someone tried to get in again?"

"Let me see!" Alastair said in alarm. He looked closely, then Mark and Neil took their turns.

"Maybe from regular use?" I asked.

"I don't think so," Mark said. "Looks dodgy to me."

"Can we see inside?" Neil asked.

"I'm getting to that." Alastair seemed to be in a constant state of fluster. He used a key to open the lock and pushed the gate wide. Then he hit another switch, and a series of bulbs came on in the vaults.

"Wow." I couldn't help a little thrill. This looked like something out of a medieval fantasy, a series of small rooms with low, arched stone ceilings connected by wide pointed arches. I only had to duck a little as we moved inside, but the guys walked gingerly to avoid banging their heads.

We wandered through rows of wine racks and shelves sporting high-end bottles, but mostly there were liquor boxes stacked on pallets and all the sorts of things bars had in their storage space. In one dark niche, wooden boxes and junk lay in a dusty pile. I didn't want to get too deep into the mess and spoil my dress, but it didn't look like anything worthwhile. And there were puddles on the stone floor.

"Did you spill something?" I asked, gesturing to the water. In fact, the whole floor looked wet.

"It rained," Alastair said. "Whenever there's a good rain, we get puddles. Just before we bought the place, there was a real flood down here."

"It's happening more and more across the city," Mark said.

"It's why anything valuable I want to keep dry is stored up high on shelves or racks," Alastair added.

"How did they get gin barrels in here?" It was possible to haul them up and down the stairs, but it wouldn't be fun.

Mark pointed into the shadowy recesses of the vaults. "There used to be access to the outside where they'd load them in. It's been bricked up since."

"So no one is getting in that way," Neil concluded.

"Maybe no one is getting in at all, anymore," I suggested. "You don't think anything is missing, and you haven't seen evidence that they broke in again, right? Problem solved?"

"Maybe so," Mark said, "but I just don't like it."

Neil loitered by the shelves of high-end booze, examining the bottles. "You might want to see this."

Uh-oh. We crowded around him as he held out a bottle of what looked like vintage rum. "See the top? The seal is broken. Maybe they didn't take the bottle, but I wonder if they tampered with the rum."

"You have an obsession with rum," Alastair said.

"Only a slight one." Neil smiled.

"Shall we get it tested or—" Mark began.

Alastair rolled his eyes. "Oh, just pour some into a glass and see what we can see."

"Or sniff," I added.

Alastair dug around in a box and pulled out a clean Old-Fashioned glass. Neil worked out the bottle's stopper and poured a couple of fingers' worth into the glass.

"That doesn't look right," Mark said.

I took the glass from Neil and sniffed it. "It doesn't smell right either. I mean, it's rum, but I think it's really watered down." Before anyone could object, I took a sip. "Oh, yeah. I bet someone helped themselves and topped this off with water."

Neil glowered at me. "That wasn't very safe," he muttered.

I shrugged. At least we had an idea of what was happening. "So maybe you just have a happy drunk who found their way down here and helped themselves." I handed the glass to Alastair, who sipped and scrunched up his face like a desiccated apple.

"I hate to ask this," Neil said, "but could it have been one of the staff?"

"If the staff need to get in, they get the key from me," Alastair said. "And I'm always here. Anyway, they have access to all the good stuff whenever they want it, though I discourage too much sipping behind the bar. They have no *reason* to break in. Not if you're a barman who's soaking in booze already."

"Then I guess you need to keep an eye out for sneaky customers," I said. "At least you know what mischief they're up to."

"I suppose." Alastair still looked puzzled. "I'll have to go through all the bottles and see what else the duffers drank."

We exited through the gate, Alastair locked it, and we headed upstairs. Mark and I were first through the door at the top. I whispered to Mark, "If only your mystery were this easily solved."

He leaned over and murmured into my ear. "We'll have to wander around my wine cellar and sample a few bottles, just to make sure the answer's not down there." His breath on my neck made all the little hairs there rise up.

I straightened, looked back and caught Neil's raised eyebrow. I gave him a little smile, picked up our drinks from the table, handed him his and pretended my face wasn't hot.

My hormones were confused. Probably as jet-lagged as the rest of me.

But something else bugged me, too. What kind of drunk makes multiple visits to break into a liquor vault just to drink? I could see one case of impulse drinking, maybe on a dare—but two or three just for a dandy tipple?

Chapter Six

When we reentered the party, a ripple of energy shot through the crowd like a Bohemia Beach wave, but it wasn't on our account. Hollywood had made an entrance.

"Look, it's Oleanna!" I said to Neil. Oleanna Lee, a Chinese-American actress and star of the blockbuster *Keystroke and Dagger* movies, had entered the bar along with a few other attractive people who were probably actors too. They looked sort of familiar. We'd become friendly with Oleanna at the Bohemia Beach Film Festival, and I had to admit I felt kinda special when she saw us, waved and headed our way.

"How *are* you all?" she squealed, hugging us both. In a moment, the rest of the Bohemia Bartenders had surrounded us, too, getting their hugs in.

"It's great to see you!" I said. "Congrats on the *Dagger* movie." It had ripped up the box office this summer.

"It's good to go out with a bang," she admitted. "I'll miss that series, but it's fun to do something new."

"I'm so glad you made it. Can you come to Neil's seminar tomorrow?"

"Wouldn't miss it. I'm filming here, but I have a few days off and plan to make the most of them. I should be able to make Saturday's party too."

"That's going to be fabulous," Melody said. "At a real palace. Not just a gin palace."

"A palace full of art deco awesomeness," I added. I had a thing for art deco.

"Stay in touch," Oleanna said. "Let me know if you go shopping." She gave Melody and I a significant look.

"Melody already bought out Harrods," I said, "but I'm game for browsing some cool shops. Maybe the Notting Hill market Saturday?"

"I could do that. You have my number. Let's stay in touch!" And then she was off, only to be intercepted by Mark and Alastair, who positively glowed in her presence. Then again, Oleanna brought a glow with her everywhere.

"So where'd you two go?" Luke asked Neil and me, bringing me back to reality.

"What's back there?" Barclay pointed to the *Staff Only* door. Gina clung to his other arm. They were so cute together.

"Well, aren't you nosy?" I teased, but I shot a sidelong glance at Neil, who had his poker face on.

Melody just lifted her eyebrows at me and smiled. She'd known me for a while and had radar for whenever I was discomfited by a guy. Specifically Mark or Neil. I think she was rooting for Neil. But given the self-imposed dry spell I'd had ever since I met Neil, I think she was rooting for pretty much anyone just so long as I got laid.

"Just getting a tour of the back bar," Neil said. "You having fun?"

The other bartenders exchanged a look.

"They won't admit it because they're worried about their party cred," Gina said, "but they're tired, and so am I."

Barclay snorted. "She's right."

Neil smiled. "Let me guess—you want to go home? I mean, back to Mark's?"

"Yes, Dad," Luke said, and we all laughed.

"My partying energy is pooped," Melody added. "A couple of

drinks and no sleep are killing me."

"And we have my seminar in the morning." Neil suppressed a yawn, but it escaped and we all caught it and yawned, too. "Mark said we can use the shuttle. Albert will take us. You all want to go? Ten minutes, OK?"

Neil said a word to Mark. We finished our drinks, hit the loo (the bathroom was as spectacular as the rest of the place) and were back at the passenger van in five.

Neil sat next to me but didn't seem in the mood to chat as the van tootled through the city. He just looked out the window. So I checked my phone and found that Millie had texted me. She'd pinged the phone company, and my data plan should be updated if I restarted my gadget.

A few minutes later, I was able to pull in data again and checked the state of the tropical storm off Florida. The updated track looked ominous. I pushed down my nerves. It was only a tropical storm. It wasn't Hurricane Katrina, which had destroyed my child-hood home and basically exiled me from New Orleans when my parents sent me to live with Aunt Celestine and never invited me back. Still, I shot off an email to Jorge to make sure he had someone to help board up the windows at Nola in case it got stronger.

"You OK?" Neil asked. He'd seen what I was looking at, and he knew my history. "Worried?"

I looked up and tried to smile. "Just looking at the forecast."

"It'll be OK. This one doesn't look that bad."

"I hope not." My voice cracked a little. *Geez.* Just when I thought I'd gotten over that nightmare, it haunted me again.

"Take it easy." He put an arm around my shoulders.

I didn't question the gesture. Just leaned against him, sank into his warmth and let him comfort me. I drifted off thinking about New Orleans.

I woke with a start, jolted out of a chaotic dream where I was running through New Orleans's cemeteries. The van had arrived at

Mark's. Neil removed his arm without comment. And here we were, back to square one. But I felt a little better.

I grabbed my bag, and we all tumbled out. Mrs. Pidgeon waited for us in the foyer. I supposed Mark or Albert had given her a heads-up.

"Good evening." She glowered at us all. Was it my imagination, or did she look particularly askance at me? "This way, please."

At least she realized we might not find our way back to the guest wing by ourselves. She led our tired crew to our bedrooms. I entered mine alone but was delighted to find a lovely little Cavalier curled up in the middle of my ridiculously royal bed.

"Victoria!" I called out to the puppy. She jumped up, her tail wagging. She wasn't Astra, but she was awfully cute and licked my hand as I petted her. I donned my nightshirt printed with a cute dancing cocktail shaker and martini that said *Nightcap!* and curled up with her under the covers, sinking into a pile of pillows as soft as a cloud.

I woke up after a few hours, confused about where I was, especially with a little dog snoring next to me who reminded me of Astra. Then I remembered when I realized the bed was much softer than the one I had at home.

I picked up my phone, which was charging on the nightstand— 4 a.m. I put in the wifi password Mark had given me. *Drink me.* What a scamp. A look at the Hurricane Center site showed nothing much had changed with the forecast at home. I told myself to relax as I did some aimless scrolling. Then the phone froze, like the wifi had just stopped. Weird. I tapped for a few more minutes and gave up. No use in using my pricey international cellular data when I should be sleeping.

BECAUSE WE WERE HERE for a gin festival, Neil's workshop late Thursday morning focused on gin cocktails from his book *Cutting-*

Edge Classics: Cocktails With a Twist. It paired venerable old recipes with exciting updates. His seminar would focus on the history of gin drinks.

He had us making two versions of the Corpse Reviver No. 2—Savoy bartender Harry Craddock's 1930 version and a new one—and had pulled a punch recipe associated with Charles Dickens from somewhere. But not from Neil's book. I'd made pretty much all the cocktails in his book, so I knew it well.

The festival had scheduled seminars in venues across London. Since Neil's was scheduled for The Dandy Tipple, where Dickens reputedly drank, he'd figured a Dickens favorite wouldn't go wrong.

His plan added up to a lot of mixing (and drinking) for a morning session. Our crew had to make about a hundred each of the two Corpse Revivers as well as the Dickens punch, whose ingredients Neil had tweaked and recalculated.

We'd requested supplies in advance, and Alastair's crew had done their job beautifully. We hadn't seen Mark at all this morning during a hearty buffet breakfast in his mansion's huge dining room, and Alastair was noticeably absent for our first hour of prep once we arrived at The Dandy Tipple. But Ben brought in cases of Mark's Frilly Fairy Gin for the cocktails, and Ari showed us around and helped us set up in the surprisingly modern kitchen. She even squeezed lemons with me while Melody created fancy lemon twists and Luke worked on measuring out and mixing the Cointreau, absinthe and an aperitif for Harry Craddock's classic Corpse Reviver No. 2. Probably an appropriate choice, given how many hangovers there were after the party last night.

Neil hovered over the stove, creating a special hibiscus syrup for his modern variation, The Resurrectionist.

As time went by, Barclay, who'd shared the stove to create a raspberry syrup for the gin punch, moved next to me to start combining the ingredients. The lemon juice would go into the punch, too.

"Where's Gina this morning?" I asked him.

"She wanted to see the crown jewels at the Tower of London, so I told her to go ahead. We'll meet up later."

I elbowed him and smiled. "It's going well, eh?"

He quirked his mouth, trying not to give anything way, but his eyes twinkled. "I like her a lot."

"That's cool. Just don't break her heart. Jorge will kill me before he kills you."

"I don't think her brother is that violent," Barclay joked. "But don't worry. He's made it very clear that I need to treat her right. And I wouldn't consider anything else."

Alastair appeared in the kitchen. "The dining room is nearly full," he said in his crisp accent. "Are you ready to begin?"

"Just about," Neil said, looking at his vintage watch. Barclay used to wear one of those, too, but it appeared he'd gone over to the dark side and one of those smart watches that recorded your heartbeat and sleep patterns and bad decisions. I liked Neil's better.

Neil nodded at Barclay. "Your punch is up first. How's it going?"

"Great. It's a perfect light starter."

"Excellent," Neil said. "Pepper and Luke, you'll shake and pour the Corpse Reviver No. 2. Melody will garnish. You can switch up for the Resurrectionist. Are you ready?"

"It's delicious," Luke said, toasting Neil with a glass of the No. 2 he'd already mixed up.

"It better be," Neil said to our chuckles. "Make sure you shake those with the big ice cubes to avoid over-dilution." He nodded at Luke. "And remember, four of these taken in swift succession will unrevive the corpse."

"Nice," Ari said. "Quoting Harry Craddock before noon."

Neil grinned, and I squashed a little stab of jealousy. I knew the quote, too, but Ari's swift compliment appealed directly to Neil's nerdy tendencies and was awfully sneaky, in my opinion.

"Can your people help serve?" Neil asked her. A couple more Tipple bartenders were lining trays with clear cups.

"All ready," she said.

"Luke, pour a few of those for family dinner, OK?" Neil said. A minute later, our crew and the Tipple bartenders held up shot glasses filled with the Corpse Reviver as Neil toasted. "To Dickens, Craddock, and London gin. Cheers!"

"Cheers!" we echoed and took the shot.

The liqueurs balanced the bite of lemon, and the potent absinthe took it to another level. Good thing the cups were small. "Whew," I said. "That'll pop the pennies off your eyes."

Neil smiled. "That's the idea. All right, everybody. Let's do this."

The whirlwind began. First, we helped Barclay get the punch into the small cups so Ari's crew could take the trays over to the dining room and serve them. When that was done, we started on the classic Corpse Reviver No. 2. Luke and I dropped the big, chunky cubes Alastair's crew had provided into the shakers, shook each batch just enough to get it cold, and poured furiously into fresh cups on the trays that had come back from the other room. With the intensity of a machine, Melody garnished them all with lemon twists.

When those were done, we moved on to chilling and preparing the Resurrectionist—Barclay and Melody did the shaking, and Luke and I garnished the little cocktails with dark red dried hibiscus petals.

By the time we were done, my arms hurt and I had lemon juice spatter all over my cat's-eye glasses. I cleaned them on the apron I wore over my black pants, low-cut pinstripe vest and white blouse, then ditched the apron so I could catch the last few minutes of Neil's talk.

I poured one more Resurrectionist, this time in a pretty coupe glass. I used a silver cocktail pick to stab one end of a lemon twist, then added a whole hibiscus blossom, the kind you buy in syrup, dark red and glistening. I secured the other end of the twist to the pick, rested the garnish atop the cocktail glass, and headed over to the dining room to watch Neil in action.

Chapter Seven

Drinkers packed The Dandy Tipple's grand dining room under the sparkling chandeliers. Sunlight poured in through the tall windows, and what looked like a fake fire flickered in yet another fireplace.

Ari and her crew served the last of the little cups to the people crowded around the tables. I recognized a few of them, including Mark, Alastair, Cray, Mr. Mixy, and Nigel and Lottie. Oleanna Lee was there, too, enjoying a day off from filming her latest movie, and she gave me a little wave.

Neil stood by a table up front stacked with copies of his book, describing the Resurrectionist. I carried the ruby-red cocktail to the front of the room and presented it to him. There was a sigh of appreciation behind me from the cocktailians as he paused and accepted the pretty drink with a smile. I nodded and melted away to the back of the room while he lifted the glass and asked, "How do you like it?"

A roar of approval greeted him, and he took a sip and lifted his eyebrows at its potency before setting the glass down. The guests laughed.

"As I was saying, a resurrectionist was what they called a body snatcher here in the eighteenth and nineteenth centuries, back when doctors had trouble getting corpses for research," Neil told them. "I thought it was a fitting name for a spin on the Corpse Reviver No. 2. Dickens featured a body snatcher in *A Tale of Two*

Cities. And though some lowlifes resorted to murder to supply anatomists with the research subjects they desired, no doubt gin helped kill off a few subjects as well.

"We talked about Dickens a little bit earlier and his fondness for theater. In fact, the gin punch we served is a variation on the Garrick Club Summer Gin Punch, named for a group of patrons who loved the theater as Dickens did. He probably drank there and himself was known to don wild waistcoats and assume the role of 'the compounder,' theatrically making punches at parties. Though he had a fondness for milk punch with rum. But I digress, and I understand there's another session this afternoon re-creating one of these occasions.

"My real point is that Dickens had a love-hate relationship with alcohol. His characters in *Pickwick Papers* spend most of their time drinking in one venue after another, but he was well aware of the terrible toll gin took on the poor of London, especially. Let me read a little bit from his *Sketches by Boz,* which were his descriptions of London life, and in this case, the gin shops. In one passage, he compares them to a plague taking over every business imaginable. But he recognizes their allure. Here's how he describes one."

Neil picked up a piece of paper from the table, held it up and read:

"All is light and brilliancy. The hum of many voices issues from that splendid gin-shop which forms the commencement of the two streets opposite; and the gay building with the fantastically orna-mented parapet, the illuminated clock, the plate-glass windows surrounded by stucco rosettes, and its profusion of gas-lights in richly-gilt burners, is perfectly dazzling when contrasted with the darkness and dirt we have just left." Neil extended his hand to take in the grandeur of The Dandy Tipple. "Sound familiar?"

The crowd tittered, and he continued. "Dickens contrasted this with the slum life of London, where the 'Blue Ruin' could be had for almost nothing, and where toxic, poor-quality gin flowed every-where while the rich drank Holland gin, or genever. At one point in the 1700s, about five million gallons of raw spirits were distilled in London each year, and almost all of it was drunk in London." A small gasp greeted this factoid.

"In his *Sketches,* Dickens lists some of the concoctions patrons could order." Neil consulted his paper again: "'The Cream of the Valley, The Out and Out, The No Mistake, The Good for Mixing, The Real Knock-me-down, The Celebrated Butter Gin, and The Regular Flare-up.' There were plenty of other suggestive nicknames for the stuff, too: crank, diddle drain, flash of lightning, rag water because people ended up in rags once they were addicted to it, jacky, dead white, deadly, shove-in-the-mouth"—here Neil raised an eyebrow and paused for the inevitable giggles—"and my favorite, strip me naked." Now we all laughed as I idly thought about stripping Neil naked.

"I could go on about this all day, but I tell you this because it's important to remember that the refined and wonderful gins we have now came from a pretty dark place. So all I ask is that you respect this elegant and versatile liquor by making wonderful cocktails and sipping them with care. Thank you."

Hearty applause followed, and Alastair strolled to the front of the room. "Thank you, everyone. And thank you to sponsor Mark Fairman of Fairyland Distillery for the excellent Frilly Fairy Gin." Mark stood and bowed. How incestuous this all was, but money talked, I supposed. "Neil will be signing books now," Alastair continued with only the slightest edge to his voice, "but feel free to get a drink at our bar, and the dining room will be open for luncheon in an hour."

How very Alastair. He set up Neil for success and failure at the same time.

The happy crowd began to move, chatting and laughing, and I headed to the front of the room before Neil's public could get to him. "Do you need anything?" I asked.

"No, they have staff processing the book sales, so I just have to look pretty and sign them. Did everything go OK back there?"

"No problems. Did they like the drinks?"

"All of them," he said as the fans started lining up to buy books at the sale table and gathering around to talk to him. He leaned in and said softly, "Wait for me?"

My face warmed. "Will do. See you in a few." I returned his smile, then spun and headed back into the room that held the bar. Customers already stood two deep there, and Ari and her people were busy mixing and shaking. Talk about stamina.

I ventured into the kitchen, thinking about gin's rough past. Sometimes we bartenders, especially mixologists like us who made high-end cocktails, forgot the dark side of alcohol.

Much of the cleanup was finished, but I helped my colleagues pack away Neil's giant bag of bar tools. He'd brought enough for all of us, given we didn't want to check several bags full of sharp knives and mallets on the airplane. Though in my messenger bag, I still had a cocktail knife that had traveled to London in my suitcase. I slung the bag over my shoulder and idly ran my finger over the little orange-slice patch that covered its war wound from New Orleans.

I found the Bohemia Bartenders, sans Neil, gathered near the bar, which was too mobbed for me to consider ordering a drink.

"We're thinking of playing tourist this afternoon," Melody said. "Oh, hey, Oleanna!"

The actress came over to join us. "Ladies and gents!"

"I was just saying we're going to play tourist this afternoon," Melody said, "meet up with Gina and hit a couple of museums."

"And bars," Luke and Barclay said at the same time.

"Want to join us?" Melody asked Oleanna and me.

"I'd love to," she said.

"I do," I said, "but I told Neil I'd wait for him, and I don't know how long he'll be. Why don't you go ahead, and I'll ping you."

They all gave me knowing looks, and Melody covered her mouth. It didn't help. The giggle came out anyway.

"What?" I said.

"You know what," she answered.

I did, but I wasn't going to admit it. "Oh, go on. We'll catch up later, hopefully before the dinner, OK?"

We were all going to a gin-themed dinner at one of the oldest restaurants in the city, as guests, for once, so we could really enjoy it.

"Whatever you say." Melody hugged me and whispered in my ear. "What happens in London stays in London."

I whispered back, "Enjoy your afternoon. Maybe this is the date Luke is longing for."

Melody had the nerve to look confused. How could she be the only one who didn't realize he had a crush on her? Or maybe she thought Luke had a thing for Oleanna.

I laughed and pushed Melody toward the door with the others. "Have fun, y'all."

When they were gone, I peeked into the dining room. There was a long line at the book-signing table. Mark was busy chatting, so I couldn't fall prey to his distractions.

I got to thinking about the vault and its pesky thief. I wanted to take another look at it. Surely no one would care, would they?

I drifted to the end of the bar, and when I thought no one was paying attention, I slipped through the *Staff Only* door. I headed down the short corridor and opened the door to the staircase and began my descent. It was quieter this time. I was alone, and no party music shook the walls. The walls of the staircase amplified the tiniest whispering noises from below, and I shivered. Maybe this wasn't such a great idea.

Just when the darkness seemed impenetrable, I spotted the light switches and turned them on.

A skittering noise from inside the vault drew my attention, and I stepped up to the gate to check it out.

"Ew!"

I could've sworn I saw a rat tail slithering off into the shadows. I'd have to tell Alastair so he could set out traps.

Now I bent over the lock, turning it carefully so it caught the light. It didn't seem any more scratched than before. Through the bars, I surveyed the contents of the vault. It didn't really seem different, though there were a few extra cases of Frilly Fairy Gin that hadn't been there before. Probably from the stash Ben had brought in this morning.

"Huh." Nothing to see here. Plus this place gave me the creeps, and I'd just as soon get out of it.

This time, I turned on the light on my phone before I turned off the wall switches so I could ascend the stairs without colliding with a rat or a bat or something. In a minute, I was up on the main floor and back out in the bar. I slipped into the WC, as it was labeled, did my business, repinned my hair and freshened my lipstick, and then I returned to the bar.

And almost ran into the world's largest mixologist beard.

"Pepper! What a treat to run into me!"

"Mr. Mixy," I said with as much civility as I could manage. Wait, what did he say? A treat to run into *him?* It was never a treat to run into my ex-boyfriend. "How's the TV show going?"

"Fantastic. They're going to film me making a cocktail over by Big Ben later."

"Uh, great."

"We're also going to do a bit with the changing of the guard at Buckingham Palace. I've had a genealogy service looking at my history, and apparently I'm descended from royalty. They just need a little more money to get the actual papers. I might inherit a crown or a castle or something."

"Wow." Mr. Mixy as royalty? If his "genealogy service" was any more sketchy, they'd be selling him London Bridge. "Good luck with that. I've got to go. I'm, uh, meeting someone."

"OK, Pepper. See you at the dinner tonight!"

Oh, fudgesicles. He was going to that too? I waved and ducked out of the front of The Dandy Tipple. I just had to pick somewhere to lie in wait for Neil where Mr. Mixy wouldn't find me again. I looked up and down the block. There were several small businesses.

A glittering jewelry store on one side of the Tipple caught my eye, but then the gift shop on the other side seduced me.

Ten minutes later, I'd bought British flag oven mitts for Aunt Celestine and a miniature British red phone booth for Jorge, along with a rubber royal Corgi toy for Astra, and stuffed them in my bag. Then I stood outside Alastair's bar to wait for Neil.

A steady stream of festival-goers left as I watched the door, and then a couple of familiar faces appeared.

"Nigel! Lottie! Did you have a good time?" I asked as they strolled over to meet me.

"Excellent," Lottie said. "Love the cocktails."

"And I was pleased to get Neil to sign this without having to worry about carrying it home on a plane," Nigel said, holding up a copy of Neil's book.

"Nigel's a mad collector," Lottie added. "You should see how many cocktail books he has. Even a first-edition *Savoy Cocktail Book* signed by Craddock himself."

"No way!" I exclaimed.

"He found it at a jumble sale. Would you believe it?"

"Lucky. I'm very lucky," Nigel said.

"Well, lucky and spendy," she said, and they laughed.

A tiny spark lit in my brain. "Do you collect all kinds of books?"

"Well, not all kinds, or there wouldn't be room in the house," Nigel said. "Cocktail books and signed first editions, mostly. I prefer twentieth-century literature."

"Have you ever talked to Mark about his collection?"

Nigel's pallid face turned slightly pink. "Not in any detail, but I did see he had several fine volumes during a party at his library a while back. I really should ask if he'd be up for selling any of them."

"Great to see you, Pepper," Lottie interrupted. "Off to the chemist's." She angled her eyes at her husband. "I have to lay in a supply of hangover cures for the weekend."

I chuckled at her droll humor and wished them well. And got to wondering about Nigel's habits as they walked away.

"Oh, good, you're still here."

I whirled to find Neil looking dapper and happy.

"Did you sell a lot of books?"

"The bookstore staff who handled the sales did. I'm happily surprised."

"Don't be surprised," I said. "The book is outstanding. And I wish I'd heard more of your talk. I'm fascinated now."

"Really? Well, if I can talk you into it, there's this thing at the Dickens museum, and I have tickets ..."

"Oh, yeah, the one you mentioned? Do we have time for lunch first?"

"Absolutely."

"Where's your bar bag?"

"One of Mark's staff is going to take it back to the house. Anyway, you have yours, so we're prepared for anything." He smirked.

"Smart-ass." But he was right. My bag was full of useful things. And a squeaky rubber Corgi. "OK. Where are we going?"

Chapter Eight

"I love walking in London," I said to Neil as we exited our lunch stop, a fromagerie where we stuffed ourselves with charcuterie and, in a break from the usual cocktails, a nice glass of cabernet.

A kind of electric energy filled the streets. Modern flashy structures of steel and glass alternated with gorgeous old buildings given gravity by brick, stone and history.

"Dickens was obsessed with walking," Neil answered my comment. "He did something like twelve miles a day. His *Sketches* are mostly recounting all the things he discovered as he walked around London."

"And this museum is a place where he used to live?"

"For a couple of years in the 1830s. He moved a lot."

"And how do you know all this about Dickens?" I was continually astounded by Neil knowing just about everything.

"I've read a couple of biographies. Mostly to prepare for my talk," he admitted with a grin.

We rounded the corner and found ourselves amid a stretch of tall row houses that all looked pretty much the same, except for the shade of their bricks—white, gray, yellow or brown—with black iron fences in front and an arched window over each door. A dozen chatty people milled about on the sidewalk in front of one of them. The clothes, snazzy hats and tattoos all suggested this was mostly the cocktail crowd. Besides, a couple of familiar faces clinched it.

"My dear Kayanne Pepper! Neil!" Cray called out. He wore a tweed blazer, a light-blue sweater that matched his eyes and a white scarf that echoed his hair. He'd been chatting with Ari, who'd changed into jeans, a dark blue sweater and a leather jacket.

"So Alastair let you escape?" I asked her as we strolled up to them.

She laughed. "Finally. He knows he gets to abuse us all again this evening, so someone else is covering this afternoon to give us recovery time. I wanted to experience a bit of the festival myself."

Neil gave the pretty blond mixologist one of his special smiles. "This should be fun."

Oh no he didn't! And why was I jealous? I should know by now that Neil wasn't meant for me. And if I really wanted a little man action, there was always Mark Fairman. Right?

Speaking of whom, Mark strolled up with a man I didn't recognize. At least it was just one guy, a refreshing change from the usual entourage.

"Hello, hello," Mark called. "Have I missed anything?"

"The next demonstration starts in ten. I've already been through the house," Cray drawled. "Rather cramped, but that's why they're doing their little show on the hour all afternoon."

"Splendid." Mark nodded at Cray and smiled at me. "I'd like you all to meet the fellow who's making barrels for a new rum I'm working on—Royce Doucet." He pronounced it "Doo-say," but I knew the name was French because it was familiar somehow. Mark's shorter companion wore a good-looking brown jacket, though it was probably less expensive than Mark's. His light-brown hair was fashionably mussed.

"Nice to meet you all." Royce's gray-green eyes crinkled at the corners as he smiled at all of us and gave a little wave.

We introduced ourselves. "You're American," I said, pointing out the obvious, given his touch-of-Southern accent. "Do I know you? Your name is familiar."

Royce's smile broadened. "Probably because you're from New Orleans, right?"

I raised my eyebrows. *How did he know that?* "I am. Are you?"

"I was raised there, but you're probably thinking of my father. Same name. He's a businessman. Makes the news on occasion."

"Oh, yeah. That must be it." I looked at Royce closely. I could swear I'd met him before, but just where eluded me. "So now you're working for Mark?"

He chuckled. "Not exactly. I've started a cooperage in Kentucky. I own a distillery there too—I mean, doesn't everyone? Anyway, the bourbon business is booming, so I got into the barrel business too. I supply used whiskey barrels to Mark so he can age his rum in them. He was telling me about your client at Cocktailia—the whiskey distiller from Florida?"

"Dash Reynolds and Bohemia Distillery," Neil said.

"That's the one," Royce said. "Maybe we can talk later. I might have need of your services."

I wondered if he knew the whole story about Cocktailia—and whether he wanted more than mixology from us. I supposed we had Mark and Alastair's mysteries to solve first. I'd just as soon retire from crime-solving and drink more cocktails.

"It's almost time," Ari said after glancing at her phone. "Shall we?"

"After you." Neil smiled, stepped forward and opened the teal-green door for her, and all that cheese in my belly did a flip-flop.

"You read much Dickens?" Royce distracted me as we followed Neil and Ari through the door, with Cray and Mark behind us.

"Not really. *Oliver Twist* in school, and I saw an endless play of *Nicholas Nickleby* once. And pretty much all the *Christmas Carol* movies. I mean, who doesn't love those?"

"I'm pretty much in the same boat. But *A Tale of Two Cities* was fun. Really cinematic."

"Thanks. I'll check it out." I'd been trying to remedy my lack of higher education by reading books that were good for me at least once a month, along with my regular diet of romance and mystery. I had a degree from culinary school, but there wasn't much English lit involved, except for the time one of my teachers had us create a tea inspired by *Alice's Adventures in Wonderland*. She didn't love my tea-based whiskey cocktail, but my classmates thought it was fabulous.

We crowded into the narrow hallway and past a gift shop. A woman at the foot of the wooden staircase checked tickets, and then we clattered up two flights.

"Right this way!" a familiar voice called over the sound of a piano, and we entered a parlor where a couple of men in Victorian garb stood by the old instrument. A woman was playing.

"Ben is such a ham," Ari murmured, and I was surprised to realize the familiar voice actually belonged to Mark's right-hand man. He wasn't easy to recognize in his long coat, vest and bow tie.

Ben smiled at us and waved as the last few people crushed in. "Feel free to move into the study there. Perhaps you might convince Mr. Dickens to stop writing for a moment and come out and make the punch!"

A few people moved through the other doorway. I peered inside this adjoining room, where guests crowded around a writing desk. There, a gentleman with longish hair that fluffed out on the sides and a beard that might interest Mr. Mixy looked up from his scribbling and called out. "What, are our guests here already? You should have told me!"

As if he hadn't heard us all stomping into the room like a herd of elephants.

"Ah yes, here is our compounder, the irrepressible Mr. Dickens!" Ben called out. These historical refugees were more cheerful than a barfly at opening time.

And Mr. Dickens *was* irrepressible, with his colorful waistcoat, yellow gloves and flashing eyes. He entered the parlor and introduced himself, talked about this house, cheered on his "wife" playing the piano, and apologized that the children were all abed.

Which seemed unlikely at two in the afternoon, but we went with it.

A woman dressed as a maid brought in a serving cart with a cast-iron pot, lemons, oranges, sugar, a teapot and a couple of bottles. While talking a mile a minute and quoting himself—er, Dickens—the actor playing the author muddled lemon peels and sugar in the bottom of the pot. He added rum and cognac, lit a spoon of the liquor on fire and stirred it into the mix, setting the whole thing ablaze to the gasps of all. It was then I noticed a nervous-looking museum employee standing nearby with a fire extinguisher.

Fortunately, Mr. Dickens put a lid on the pot and put out the fire. Then he removed the lemon peels, squeezed lemon juice into the pot and emptied the teapot into the punch. With the help of the maid and Dickens's friends, including Ben, he dished up the punch into small glasses and hand-grated nutmeg over each one before handing them out to the crowd.

The pleasing scent of gently burnt citrus tickled my nose first, then gave the cocktail a depth I hadn't expected. "Nice."

"I like it," Neil said. "But where's the gin?"

I laughed. "I wondered the same thing."

"Ben promised there would be gin," Ari assured us.

"And I understand you folk are in London for a gin festival, though I do not understand why you wish to celebrate the Blue Ruin when you can find it in every other shop," the faux Dickens said, giving us a mischievous look. "But just for you, I have my hot gin punch as well."

The maid, who'd stepped out, reappeared with another cart and another pot, though this one was already filled to the brim. She used a ladle to fill more glasses with the gin punch, which the small crowd eagerly scooped up.

Mark grabbed two and brought me one. "Cheers," he said, clinking his glass to mine.

"Cheers." I took a sip. It was like a distant cousin of the rum punch, with more spices—cinnamon, nutmeg and cloves, I was pretty sure. "Tastes like Christmas."

"So it does. They're using my gin, you know."

"Because you're a sponsor?"

"Because it's the best." One side of his mouth quirked up. "And because I'm a sponsor."

I laughed. "It's excellent, as always."

"Almost as good as I am." He winked. Before I could groan at his flirting, he lowered his voice and asked, "And what do you and Mr. Rockaway have for me on my vanishing books?"

"I—uh—nothing yet," I stammered. "I want to take a look at the library again. And maybe you can tell us who your bookseller friend is? I'd like to stop by and ask him some questions."

Mark tilted his head. "All right. William Buttersby." He gave me the address, and I entered it in my phone.

The faux Mr. Dickens not so subtly told us to get out by suggesting he expected more guests within the quarter-hour.

"Let me leave you with these words from my own *Tale of Two Cities,* and you may understand my fondness for selective swizzling." He cleared his throat and continued: "'Those were drinking days, and most men drank hard. So very great is the improvement Time has brought about in such habits, that a moderate statement of the quantity of wine and punch which one man would swallow in the course of a night, without any detriment to his reputation as a perfect gentleman, would seem, in these days, a ridiculous exaggeration.'" Mr. Dickens bowed, and we clapped and laughed in appreciation. "Thank you, ladies and gentlemen."

The rest of the cast joined the bows, and we funneled out the way we'd come in. Ben came along, too, and our group gathered on the sidewalk.

"Too bad we can't see the rest of the house, with all the groups coming in," I said. "I'm kind of intrigued by Dickens now."

"He's fascinating," Ben said, completely at ease in his Victorian wear and probably warmer than the rest of us, as the air had acquired a biting chill.

"And when are they going to let you play Dickens?" Ari asked him.

"Never." Ben grinned. "They don't think I look enough like him."

Ari laughed out loud, drawing a few funny looks and a smile from Neil.

"I didn't realize Dickens drank as much as he wrote," I said.

"Maybe a little too much," Cray said.

"I've read that," Neil agreed. "He carried a bottle with him on his travels, and his friends kept him lubricated. Plus he had a hell of a cellar."

"So he had good taste in liquor," Ben said. "So what? He was a great writer. And not just that. He was a real reformer, too. He was always trying to help the poor of London."

"You're such a groupie," Ari teased. "He was also an arsehole."

"Come now," Cray chided. "That's a bit strong, isn't it?"

She shook her head. "I should say not. Look at how he treated his wife."

Ben glowered at her. "You don't know. You weren't there."

"I've heard things," Ari said. I got the feeling maybe they'd had this conversation before.

"What did he do to his wife?" I asked.

Ari shrugged. "Separated from her after declaring publicly in the newspapers that they were over in the cruelest terms. Tried to get her committed to an insane asylum while he had an affair with someone else."

"That last bit is hearsay," Ben said.

"It's in the letters," she countered.

"Not in any of *his* letters that we know about," Ben huffed. "We lack context. Someday everyone will know the whole story. He was a great and compassionate man."

"I hear the museum just acquired a new stash of his letters at a very pretty price," Mark interrupted—trying to defuse the argument, I guessed.

"How much?" Neil asked.

"A few million pounds." Mark shrugged at my shocked expression. "I wouldn't mind 'collecting' a few of his letters at that rate."

Royce looked at him in confusion. "How can there be 'new' Dickens letters?"

"He loved the stage and public speaking and being adored by his public, but he was very private in some ways," Mark said. "He burned all the letters he had connected to his wife, and others ended up in friends' hands."

"And the curator says the museum might have a lead on a new stash of letters. Imagine that." Ben glanced at Ari, who just shook her head.

"I'd rather not," she replied as they exchanged a prickly glare.

I turned to Ben. "Do you do this kind of thing at the museum a lot?"

Ben broke his staring contest with Ari, and his face eased into a smile. "Whenever I can. I'm an enthusiast and thinking of writing a book, actually, so since I volunteer here, they let me poke around in the archives on occasion. And I'm part of a small troupe of Dickens enthusiasts who do theatricals as the opportunity arises. It pays a few extra quid, and Mark doesn't mind."

Mark's eyes twinkled. "I'm always pleased to see my employees do things that make them happy. Though you'd think with what I pay you, you wouldn't need the cash."

"I do it for the love. And the occasional flutter on the horses." Ben bowed, an appropriate gesture in his Victorian wear, as we laughed.

There was an electronic ping from somewhere, and Ari pulled out her phone and glanced at the screen. "Well, I've got to get back to The Dandy Tipple. I've been summoned," she said wryly.

"By Alastair?" I asked.

"Of course. Since he bought us all phones, he now thinks he

owns us." With her joke, her tone softened, and she nodded at Ben. "Your performance was very good."

"Thanks." His cheeks reddened, and not just from the cold. "See you later?"

"I'm working late. You should all come by." Ari turned her smile upon Neil.

Oh, geez.

"Maybe after the dinner tonight," Neil said.

Oh, puh-leeze!

She walked off, and Mark and Royce said their goodbyes and headed the other direction.

I tapped Neil on the arm, and he wrenched his gaze away from Ari's annoyingly petite caboose. This was Neil. Kind, reserved Neil. He wasn't supposed to be watching anyone's caboose, with the exception of mine. Or that of an actual train.

"Mark gave me the name of his rare-books guy," I said to him as his eyes refocused. "So you can, uh, look for that book you wanted?"

Neil took a moment to grok my implication, probably because he was still dreaming of blondes with English accents, and then he nodded. "Great. Let's go."

"Are you going to a bookstore?" Cray asked. "I'd love to come along, if you don't mind. I'm always on the hunt for old books about rum."

"Um, sure!" I said. I couldn't very well say no. And besides, Cray knew things and might be a good confidant as we tried to track down Mark's elusive book thief.

Chapter Nine

We took the tube because it was faster than walking all the way and I was still kind of jet-lagged. Besides, I didn't think Cray appreciated Neil's punishing pace when it came to walking.

Buttersby Books Ltd. was on a street of four- and five-story businesses in red brick and white stone facades. Buttersby's facade had a little of everything, with brick above, white stone adornments and columns, and dark green trim framing the big display windows flanking the double doors. One window held antique travel posters, maps, books and a couple of globes—it looked like Buttersby's sold prints, too—and the other window was dedicated to Victorian literature, most prominently Dickens, whose portrait stood front and center. I had to smile. It felt as if Dickens was following us around.

A bell tinkled as we entered. The shop was more spacious than I would have expected. While low, open bookcases and tables in the center of the room held many books, quite a few volumes were trapped in tall, glass-fronted bookshelves around the perimeter to protect them from devious browsers. A couple of ladders whose wood matched the oak bookcases stood ready to help the staff reach the highest shelves. In one alcove, four chairs surrounded a rectangular reading table subtly lit by brass lamps.

An assortment of framed prints covered the square support columns, and a staircase labeled "Gallery" led below.

"I don't see anyone," Neil said.

"I'm just going down to look at the prints," Cray said. We'd briefed him on our mission on the way over. "If I see your bookseller, I'll send him up."

As Cray slowly made his way down the stairs, I caught the sound of a door opening and turned to see a man emerge from the back. For such an upscale shop, he dressed down, in a plaid flannel shirt, brown corduroy jacket and slouchy khakis. Even if I hadn't detected the faint aroma of sweet tobacco smoke on him, I recognized the tip of his pipe sticking out of his breast pocket.

He had a figure that suggested he enjoyed doughnuts as much as I did. His unkempt mustache and beard, dark against his pale skin, glinted with strands of gray, as did his short, curly hair. Rectangular black eyeglasses framed his brown eyes.

His eyebrows seemed abbreviated, like a perpetually surprised cartoon character, and they lifted when he spotted us. "Good afternoon and welcome to Buttersby's." Even his English accent seemed relaxed. "May I help you find something?"

"William Buttersby?" I asked.

His eyebrows lifted higher. "That's me. So the mob has finally tracked me down?"

It took me a second before I realized he was joking, and Neil and I laughed uncomfortably.

"Mark Fairman sent us your way," Neil said, approaching the wooden counter as William settled onto a stool behind it. "We know him from the cocktail world."

"Ah," William said. "I'd offer you scotch, but we haven't been properly introduced yet."

Neil grinned. "I'm Neil Rockaway."

"And I'm Pepper Revelle. We're mixologists."

"Well, that sounds impressive." William took off his glasses, grabbed a cleaning cloth from under the counter and buffed the lenses before donning them again. "So you're looking for a book? Or directions to the nearest pub?"

I chuckled. "Neither. We're helping Mark with his little problem."

"That narrows it down. Have the goats got loose in the garden again?"

Goats? Mark had goats? Neil laughed, and again I realized I wasn't in tune with William's sense of humor.

"His book problem," Neil clarified. "He's asked us to see if we can track down the thief. Have you heard any more about his missing illustrated *Ulysses?*"

"Or *The Sword in the Stone?*" I added. "Or any other books that have disappeared?"

"Ah. Therein lies the challenge," said William, sounding more interested now. "It's hard to know what books have gone missing since we haven't done a full inventory yet. But no, I haven't seen *Ulysses* or T.H. White. However, this morning I did get a coy email asking me whether I had any interest in a rare edition of Woolf's *To the Lighthouse* with the original Vanessa Bell dust jacket."

"Is that one of Mark's?" I asked.

"Again, I'm not sure, but I've sent him an email to check. I haven't heard back yet. If books are still vanishing, I hope he's rushed along his inventory or we'll never know what's his."

"We've asked him for a list," I said. "I'll tell him to share it with you."

A small smile crossed William's lips. "Pepper, eh? I've heard of you. He may be more likely to heed your request than mine."

Neil made a funny sound in his throat, then addressed the bookseller. "Did you reply to the person who has *To the Lighthouse?*"

"I did. I asked what he might want for it. He or she quoted me a price a bit under the typical appraised value—enough to tell me they've done their homework and are clever enough to tempt me with a lower price but quite possibly want to unload the goods," William said in a droll tone.

"Did they sign the email?" I asked.

William shifted on his creaky stool. "Only as 'Albert,' which isn't much help, I'm afraid."

Wait a second. Albert? As in Mark's employee? I looked at Neil. He nodded at me, thinking the same thing, obviously. But would Albert be stupid enough to put his real name on an email about a stolen book? Maybe he would if he didn't realize Mark was in touch with William.

"Have you had any other odd offers?" Neil asked the bookseller.

"Well, there was the girl who wanted me to read Shakespeare to her naked in the middle of Hyde Park, but if you're talking about books, mostly I have strange enquiries about what I have to sell, not what I'd like to buy."

I was still trying to get the image of William naked in the park out of my mind when Neil asked, "Did you respond to Albert's price?"

William shook his head. "I'm waiting for Mark to tell me if the book is one of his before I commence negotiations. I understand he's rather busy this week with the gin festival."

I huffed in impatience. "Let me call him and see what he knows."

"That will be a short call," William said, and Neil laughed out loud. *Ouch!* The insult seemed good-natured, but William had a sharp tongue, no doubt about it.

I stepped away, pulled the phone out of my voluminous bag and hit the number. Mark answered on the third ring. "Pepper, darling. What can I do for you?"

"I'm at your bookseller's. He's had a nibble, someone trying to sell a book that might be yours." I didn't mention that the seller might be Albert. "Do you have a copy of *To the Lighthouse?* Or did you have?"

"Hang on. I've been keeping the list in my phone." There was silence for a moment—or to be more accurate, the sound of voices and glasses clinking. Another event or bar, I guessed. Lucky Mark.

"Here it is. Yes, I have a copy, a very nice one with the Bell dust jacket."

"And you *still* have it?"

"Well, I'm not sure exactly. I haven't noticed if it's gone missing. I'll have to check later. See if William can keep the seller interested, all right?"

"Will do."

"I've borrowed a special car for tonight to give us all a ride to the dinner. But I'm always available if you'd like *me* to give you a ride." I could hear Mark's lascivious grin through the phone.

"The shuttle will be great, thanks," I replied.

He chuckled. "All right. Catch you later, darling."

He disconnected. Maybe the "darlings" were a bit much, but in that gruff, deep voice and that accent? Yeah. They made my toes tingle.

I reported back to the guys. "Mark needs to check, but he definitely has or had a book like the one your Albert is selling."

"He's not my Albert," William said. "If he were mine and I found out he was the thief, I'd chop him up into bits so tiny they'd be lucky to find a pronoun among the remains."

That brought the conversation to a halt for a second.

"Sooo ... can you string him along?" I asked. "See if he can come in so you can look at the book, maybe tomorrow, which will give us a chance to check and see if Mark's book is missing?"

William's eyes twinkled. "And you two can lie in wait?"

"Better make it Saturday," Neil said. "I told Mark we'd be available for a distillery tour tomorrow morning, and we have to work the Greenwich garden party in the afternoon."

"I'll do what I can and let you know," William said. "I could do with a bit of intrigue around here. The nearest thing we've had in the past year was when the cat made off with the tea cozy, only we didn't know it was the cat until we found the cozy in the box she's adopted in the storage room. Knitted by my colleague Peter's gran, you know, so we had to find it. Quite the mystery. Peter didn't know what to do with himself. He drank coffee for a week."

"Oi!" came a disgruntled shout from downstairs. Not Cray, who was just coming up with a handful of prints in plastic sleeves.

"Peter has enviably keen hearing," William added.

I chuckled. I liked this guy. "We'll be in touch as soon as we know something." I handed him one of my Nola cards and took one of William's from the holder on the counter.

"Developments?" Cray asked as he presented his purchases to William.

I nodded. "The game is afoot."

"I do love a good Sherlock Holmes mystery," William said as he rang up Cray's prints. One titled "Gin Lane" looked terrifying, featuring a bare-breasted pickled woman losing her baby over a stair railing, a feral man fighting a dog for a bone, and other drunken carnage. "Sir Arthur Conan Doyle will be our next window display," the bookseller added.

"After Dickens?" Neil asked.

"Ha, one point!" William marked something on a note pad to the right of the register.

"What?" I scrunched my forehead.

"I told Peter that Dickens was the only English author Americans recognized and were eager to talk about." William slipped Cray's prints into a heavy paper bag with handles. "He said there are several, so I suggested Dickens was, at the very least, the most recognized author. We've been trying different writers in the window all year and counting how many Americans spot them."

I laughed. "How can you be sure they're Americans?"

"Give me some credit. You colonials talk as if you've just disembarked from the Mars shuttle, and the Canadians always assure me they're *not* Americans." He raised one of his stubby eyebrows to see if his humor was working on us. "Let me know about that Woolf book, won't you? And then we'll set our cunning trap for Saturday."

Chapter Ten

We met up with our fellow Bohemia Bartenders and Oleanna Lee nearby for a drink at a charming speakeasy, train-themed after the London Underground. Then we Floridians called on Mark's taxi service to get us to his place to change for dinner.

I was starting to realize just how far out Mark lived and just how much he was doing for us with all this driving around, even if he wasn't doing the actual driving. This time, Albert did the honors. Albert the book thief? I needed to consider what to ask him before we confronted him.

Instead, I turned to my phone. I texted Jorge to see how our bar Nola was doing and to check on the tropical storm, which was now a borderline hurricane in the Bahamas. *Yikes.* I'd have to check in with Aunt Celestine, too, and make sure she was ready. I hated not being there to help, but I was also secretly glad. Hurricanes still creeped me out.

I got some puppy love from Victoria as I got dressed. She'd acquired a tiny squeaky pig toy from somewhere, a slobbery rubbery pink thing, and I threw it for her around my room as I donned a poufy retro halter dress in a soft teal that complemented my eyes. Her long ears flapped as she bounded about, and of course I had to take a five-minute break just to pet her and rub her belly. I missed Astra, but I knew our Cavapoo was getting lots of love from my aunt.

Finally, I was ready, and I headed downstairs with Victoria at my heels. This time I found the fireplace with no trouble, and the boys were already there, hanging out in the leather chairs. Luke and Barclay had gone with dressy hipster shirts, but instead of their frequent tropical patterns, this time Luke's button-up was in a zany multicolored paisley, and Barclay's was in a black-and-white pattern that could've doubled as Victorian wallpaper. It complemented Gina's simple black-and-white shift dress. The truth was, the guys were both so handsome in their different ways that they could've dressed in garbage bags and looked good, though Luke tended to push the limits when it came to taste.

Melody wore a clingy black dress with sheer batwing sleeves. Where the boys' shirts covered their tattoos, her sleeves allowed hers to peek through—music notes and flowers swirling up her arms. And her breathtakingly short dress showed off her long legs. She'd piled her blond hair high, allowing her dangling silver earrings to accent her long neck.

I had accessorized with a short black bolero jacket to add a bit of modesty to the halter dress and to keep me from freezing, though there was no hiding the girls in all their glory. I'd pinned back my hair on one side with a peacock-feather barrette and donned the dressier pair of my black cat's-eye geek glasses, accented with rhinestones. I also sported deep pink lipstick and black, comfy medium heels just in case more walking was involved tonight. And, of course, I wore my good-luck gator-tooth bracelet, which didn't exactly fit the semiformal look—but I wasn't going anywhere without it.

Neil took me in with an appreciative glance, and he gave me a small smile. Maybe he was reserving a bigger one for Ari tonight? Ugh, why did I think this way? Maybe because he looked delicious in a black suit and a dusky blue shirt beneath, with a long tie—hand-painted, I thought, in splashes of blue and white. No bow tie this time. Just sleek elegance. I bit my lip, and his gaze went there.

I opened my mouth and sucked in a breath, his eyes flared, and then the spell was broken at a "Hello, hello, hello!"

We all looked up to see the arrival of our host, and Victoria bounded over to him. Mark, in a natty blue sharkskin suit with a silky white collared shirt beneath, scooped up the dog and gave her love as he explained that he would treat us to a limo ride tonight.

Maybe this dinner was more formal than I'd thought. I looked down at my dress, then glanced around at my friends. My worry must've been all over my face, because Melody caught my eye and grinned. "You look fabulous, dah-ling," she said, mimicking Mark's accent, and I laughed, feeling more relaxed.

Mrs. Pidgeon materialized to take Victoria to get her supper. She gave me the hairy eyeball as we shuffled out to the curved driveway, where the shiny black limo waited. What, was she trying to protect Mark's virtue? Good luck with that.

From the outside, the limo looked kind of like the passenger vans we'd been riding in already. Waiting by the door to help us up the steps was Albert, who'd changed from his work clothes into something resembling a uniform, complete with hat.

Neil and I exchanged a glance, his cautionary, mine eager. We couldn't waste another opportunity. If Albert was driving, why not warm him up and see if he knew anything about the book thefts? Maybe we'd be able to divine whether he was the Albert who'd signed the email to William Buttersby.

"How are you doing, Albert?" I asked him.

"Fine, fine," he said with a shy smile. "Are you and the puppy getting along, then?"

"Oh, she's a sweetheart," I said as Mark and my friends climbed into the vehicle.

"She loves her toys, that one. She'll run forever up and down the gallery if I throw the ball. My arm gets tired before she does."

The gallery. Where the library was. I opened my mouth to say something and caught Neil glowering in my direction before he disappeared through the door.

"Well, we'd better get along now," Albert said, interrupting whatever thought I might've had. "Let me help you up." He held out a hand, and I reluctantly used it to boost myself onto the steps.

"Thanks."

"Not at all." He closed the door firmly. Frustrated, I turned my attention to the roomy, purple-lit interior.

Wow. This was not like our earlier rides. Long, curvy, tufted black leather benches, filled with our crew, nestled around a bar that our bartenders were already diving into.

"There's a seat next to me!" Melody called out. It also happened to be next to Neil. I narrowed my eyes at her as she snickered.

I sat, and the limo lurched forward. There was no easy way to talk to our driver, I noted. No open window or anything like that, just a wall with a video screen playing an old Bogart movie. The audio was all booming bass and pop music, though. Any conversation with Albert was going to have to wait.

Mark poured shots from a bottle of his distillery's Dragonfly Spiced Rum. The bar was further stocked with Frilly Fairy Gin, Vexatious Vodka, and the Bohemia Distillery whiskeys, since he was business partners with Dash Reynolds now. I wondered what else he had up his sleeve.

"Tonic?" Neil asked Mark.

"Of course. Help yourself," he said, pulling a pretty bottle of tonic water from the mini fridge. The label said Lightning Bug Premium Tonic Water, and ...

I squinted at the small print. "Fairyland? You're doing tonic water now?"

Mark shrugged and grinned. "Might as well hit 'em at every level. We're working on a line of garnishes as well. My family's grocers are coming in handy for distribution."

Neil quirked his mouth, accepted the bottle, and held it up to me. "G&T?"

"Naturally." I smiled. Why not? I didn't get to ride in a limo in London every day of my life.

Neil found a couple of highball glasses and proceeded to mix up our cocktails, garnishing them with lime slices he found already prepared. He held up his glass, and we clinked ours together. "To the rapturous, wild, and ineffable pleasure of drinking at somebody else's expense," he said.

I laughed out loud, as did a few of the others who heard him. "That has to be one of your quotes."

He grinned. "Henry Sambrooke Leigh. More or less a contemporary of Dickens, though obscure in comparison."

"To the Blue Ruin," I said, letting the botanicals tickle my nose before I took a sip. *Ah*. Nothing like a gin and tonic with a superb gin, and the tonic water was lovely, too.

"I'd rather call it something less gloomy," Neil said, a faraway look in his eye. "Nothing funny about the plague of bad gin joints back in the day. Or people who just can't help themselves."

I cocked my head at him. "Penny for your thoughts?"

He blinked and looked up at me. "How about a shilling? Do they still have shillings?"

Mark overheard us. "Good lord, no. Do keep up. Shot?"

I shook my head, content with my G&T and wondering again what Neil wasn't telling me. He'd made references more than once to the topic of overindulgence, for want of a better word. I was sure he didn't have a problem, but I was certain he had a story.

The merriment continued until we reached the restaurant, billed as one of the oldest in London. We poured out of the limo, more relaxed than when we'd gone in, and I was grateful for a hand when I stepped out. Only this time, it was Mark who eased me to the pavement and gave my hand an extra squeeze. I caught his glittering golden eyes and smiled. But Neil was still on my mind.

As traffic buzzed by, the last purple and orange streaks shot through the deep blue twilight sky. Streetlights glowed, as did lights around the restaurant's windows.

"Thank you, Albert," Mark said to our driver. "Find a place to park this behemoth and relax. I'll ping you when we're ready. Should be at least a couple of hours."

"Yes, sir," Albert said, and then he was off. Alas. Maybe I'd catch him later.

The restaurant's butter-yellow facade featured two large windows with gold lettering advertising salmon, hare, meat pies and puddings, among other things.

"Where vegetarians fear to tread," Barclay remarked.

"I think we're all still meat-eating savages, am I right?" Luke asked.

Melody stuck out her chin. "Speak for yourself. I'm not a savage."

"That's not what I heard," Luke said, and she swatted his arm as Gina and I giggled. Melody *could* be a bit of a maneater. I was pretty sure Luke would be happy to be next in line as shark food, if she'd only notice his existence.

"All right, my friends, let's go," said Mark, pink of cheek after his numerous aperitifs in the car. "Just to be clear, you all are my special guests tonight. Enjoy yourselves!"

And in we went.

Chapter Eleven

I t felt really weird to be at an event at a cocktail convention and not actually making the drinks. This gin festival was more low-key than Cocktailia or Hookahakaha, though, and I had a feeling Mark funding our trip was about more than our great drinks. Not to say his largesse had anything to do with me, but his mystery had to be part of it. And we'd be working our butts off at events Friday and Saturday, so I didn't feel so bad about relaxing and enjoying tonight.

But oh my, this swank restaurant was a far cry from a normal night out for we Bohemians. Framed prints covered the walls, interspersed with animal skulls of various sizes sporting antlers. I had no idea so many animals had antlers.

Dark wood trim complemented the creamy walls, from the arched doorways to the crown molding, with plenty of gold accents. Burgundy upholstered chairs and rugs added to the opulent look. We passed through a room with a magnificent vaulted ceiling of backlit stained glass, in white and gold painted with theatrical masks and lyres.

A tuxedoed gentleman showed us to an irregularly shaped room with lots more art and antlers, where all the white-clad tables seemed to be filled with familiar faces and boisterous chatter—the domain of the cocktailians. We greeted Cray and bon vivants Lottie and Nigel, who'd already found a table with Royce Doucet, Mark's Kentucky cooper. There were a few other familiar faces, and we said hello and chatted for a few minutes. Another tuxedoed fellow wandered the room with a tray of martinis, each gleaming with dew and garnished with two fat olives.

I helped myself and took a sip as our group, including Mark, settled at a table near Cray's. I inhaled deeply of the cocktail's juniper notes and took a second sip. "Mmm. Another wonderful gin. But not yours, Mark's, unless I'm wrong?"

"You have a clever mouth," Mark said impishly. "And you are correct. I had to share tonight's fun with another sponsor."

There were a couple of seats left at our table, so when I spotted Oleanna coming through the door, I stood and enthusiastically waved her over. "Sit with us!"

And then internally I said, *Whoa, no.*

Not because Mark had beamed, leapt to his feet and pulled out a chair for Oleanna next to him (I was across from him, and Neil was on my right) but because Mr. Mixy had come in right behind Oleanna and took my enthusiasm exactly the wrong way.

My ex's furry face lit up as he hurried over to take the other empty chair, which happened to be at my left. "Pepper! You can't get enough of me, can you?"

I heard Melody and Oleanna murmur and caught Barclay and Luke exchanging conspiratorial glances. The boys had gotten Mr. Mixy, real name Stephan Sully, intolerably drunk once before, to my extreme inconvenience, and I did not want them getting any ideas. Not that Mr. Mixy needed any help acting like an ass.

I sighed and took a deep draft of my martini. "No TV crew tonight?"

"I was told they weren't allowed," Mr. Mixy said with a pout.

"Here you go!" Luke called out, reaching over the table and putting a fresh martini into Mr. Mixy's eager hand. Barclay gathered a few more from the wandering enabler with the tray before he could disappear. He gave one to Oleanna, too.

"Thanks, man!" Mixy said, slurping with gusto, bringing back so many memories, none of them good. Why, oh why had I ever fallen for this guy? I knew the answer, of course. I'd been young and naive, and he hadn't blossomed into his full traitorous idiocy yet. I'd had plenty of years to nurse my anger. But I thought we'd reached detente back in Bohemia Beach when he'd visited the film festival. He shouldn't get under my skin so deep, so fast.

I took another sip of my drink, then sucked an olive off the pick and chewed. I needed to eat something with all this alcohol, and it appeared the restaurant was in no hurry to feed us. I was almost desperate enough to break into the stash of black jelly beans in my bag when I felt a hand on my knee under the table.

I was about to freak out when I realized it was Neil giving me a gentle squeeze, warm even through all my layers of fabric. I turned to look at him, and his smile told me he knew what I was going through. So there was that, at least. And his hand felt really nice until he took it away.

I blew out a breath and pulled the second olive off the pick with my teeth as Mr. Mixy finished his drink and took another from Barclay and Luke. I shot them a dirty look.

"These are delicious! Do they have any with vodka?" Mr. Mixy asked as anyone within earshot gave him a withering look. *Don't ask for vodka at a gin festival.* And among the cocktailians, it's probably best not to ask for vodka at all.

"So how did your Big Ben shoot go?" I asked him.

"Fantastic! I mean, a couple of bobbies or whatever they're called frisked me when they thought I might be a terrorist, but we showed our filming permits and got it all straightened out. We managed to catch the chimes bonging and everything while I made the drink."

I gratefully spied trays of some kind of appetizer coming out. Oysters with accoutrements on a bed of ice. I wasn't that keen on raw oysters—I know, I know, heresy for anyone from New Orleans —but I was desperate and scooped up a lumpy, cold shell from one of the trays that were left on our table.

"Oh, I remember what you're like after oysters," Mr. Mixy said in a lascivious tone and way too loudly.

"Nauseous?" I murmured after slurping down the thing. It was actually pretty tasty. I might have to reevaluate my feelings about raw oysters.

I looked around at the sound of my snickering friends. Neil had acquired a pained look. And Mark looked right at me and licked his lips.

"Oysters, eh?" he said. "I never knew this about you, Pepper."

"I don't like oysters," I said. "I mean, not raw ones, usually. Except these. Don't get any ideas."

Now the snickers became full-out laughs. I rolled my eyes and refrained from grabbing another one as Mr. Mixy said, "That's not what I remember!"

"Yeah, because you're probably remembering one of the other women you slept with at the time," I snapped.

The table got really quiet for a second, and then Mixy roared with laughter. "Oh, Pepper, you're such a kidder!"

The others slowly resumed their conversation, but I saw one or two looks of pity. Ugh. This wasn't going well. I eagerly took an amber cocktail that came around on another tray and glanced at the menus on our table to see it was a type of fizz with gin, lemon juice, vanilla bean simple syrup and root beer.

"I see your series premieres next month," Neil said to Mr. Mixy, perhaps in a chivalrous attempt to divert attention from me.

"Yeah, it's going great! The Bohemia episode looks really good." He waved both hands in surrender at my glare. "Don't worry. You aren't in the show, except in the background."

Well, that was something. "I guess they'll have to pay you royalty rates, literally, when your family tree comes through," I joked.

"You bet!" he said. "I just talked to my researcher on the phone today. He said he's finding amazing things in my background. I might be related to King Arthur!"

I was pretty sure King Arthur wasn't on any family tree websites. "What about modern royalty? Are you cousins with William and Harry or what?"

"He's working on that. I had to shoot him another three thousand dollars, but he said he might know by the end of the weekend! He might even have it for me tomorrow. "

I almost choked on my fizzy drink. "Three thousand dollars? I thought you were in debt?"

"Oh, I'm doing fine, and my book advance will take care of that. Plus just wait till my book hits the charts. I'll be able to pay the twenty thousand for full documentation. Cheap at the price if it means I get to be a duke or something."

Wait. Book advance?

Now it was Neil's turn to cough into his drink. I realized he was choking back a laugh. I happened to know sales of Neil's *Cutting-Edge Classics*, while nice, weren't enough to keep Mr. Mixy's royal genealogist on retainer.

More to the point, what kind of book was Mr. Mixy writing?

"Cocktail book?" Neil eked out.

"It's really novel, though not a novel." Mr. Mixy laughed at his own joke while finishing his second martini and grabbing one of the root-beer fizzes from a passing tray. "I'm juxtaposing memoirs of my meteoric rise through the cocktail world with recipes. Pepper, you're going to love the chapter about our time in Bohemia!"

I looked at him blankly as my mind scrambled to unhear what he'd just said. Then I took another sip for courage. "I—you—"

"So who is this genealogist? Some sort of professor? Professional researcher?" Neil asked as my sputtering stuttered.

"Um, I mean, he has a website. He has all kinds of degrees and a private DNA lab." Mr. Mixy took another big sip of his drink and slurped another oyster.

"Seems legit," Barclay said from the other side of Neil, his tone as dry as one of those martinis. Next to him, Gina giggled and elbowed him.

"He says he's found other people descended from the rich and famous," Mr. Mixy enthused. "And royalty is his specialty."

I bet it was his specialty. Paid better than finding out you were descended from the lord of the chamber pot. Mr. Mixy glowed, from the drinks or from his pending ascendance to the throne, I wasn't sure.

I breathed a sigh of relief as trays of goat-cheese tarts came out and a server came around and took our entree orders, but the relief was only temporary. Mr. Mixy was writing a book? And I was in it? No good could come of this.

I ordered the chicken, leek and mushroom pie because all pie was good, whether sweet or savory. And as Mark and a couple of other conference sponsors stood and gave brief speeches welcoming us to the VIP dinner, I imagined Mr. Mixy learning he was royalty—during the French Revolution. Unfortunately, I was pretty sure he'd keep talking even after the guillotine separated him from his head.

Chapter Twelve

I drank a little too much at the dinner, mostly in an attempt to blot out the blathering of Mr. Mixy. The hearty, heavy food absorbed a lot of the alcohol, but all in all, it was a good thing I wasn't driving.

Albert was, and he seemed cheerful and pleasant when he picked us up. Maybe because he was making thousands of dollars in sales of antique books when no one was looking? Probably not tonight, anyway. I overheard him tell Mark he'd been shooting darts at a pub and had limited himself to two beers in the first hour, so he was fine to drive. Especially since the dinner took three hours.

Three hours of trying not to listen to Mr. Mixy. I wanted to scalp him with a cheese grater, starting with his beard. Fortunately, for dessert, he'd wandered off to bug Nigel and Lottie once he overheard Nigel talking about his collection of signed cocktail books. Trying to get an early sale, I supposed.

Over dessert—I had the sticky toffee pudding and stole a bite of Somerset brie off Neil's cheese plate—Neil and I quietly told Mark what we'd learned from William Buttersby. Mark looked really worried about "Albert" selling the book and whether the correspondent was his trusted employee, but then again, Mark hadn't confirmed his edition was missing yet.

I would've dozed off in the limo on the way home if Mark hadn't queued up karaoke on the big screen. It was a boisterous ride and a lot of fun. Besides, I was happy we weren't headed to The

Dandy Tipple, where Ari lay in wait with beautiful cocktails for Neil.

Who knew Mark could do Frank Sinatra? And Melody, who in her past life had been one singing-waiter restaurant away from making it on Broadway, totally rescued me when I got in over my squiffy head with "Maybe This Time" from *Cabaret*. We belted out the impromptu duet to enthusiastic applause.

The most memorable moment was probably when we all exhorted Neil to sing something, and he finally caved and chose "Take Me Home, Country Roads." Clever choice for a shy guy, really, because none of us could resist singing along. Still, I got to hear a little of his voice, and it was kind of nice, subtle and smoky, about an octave below John Denver's. I'd buy a ticket for a private concert from Neil anytime.

Oh, yeah. Did I mention that gin tended to pique my libido? But fatigue won out over my wicked designs on Neil. Or Mark. Or whoever was convenient. I slipped into my nightshirt as soon as I got back to my room and crashed in the royal bed, Victoria curled up next to me.

The thing about zonking after a happy night of drinking was that I tended to sleep like the dead and then wake up like an electrified zombie after only a couple of hours. And that's just what I did, wondering where in the heck I was and who this cute little puppy was sleeping next to me, until it all came rushing back.

My brain was too wired to go back to sleep. I tried to check the National Hurricane Center site on my phone to see what was going on with the storm, but the wifi kept going in and out. Besides, I was thirsty, my water bottle was empty, and Mark had warned me the tap water was only so-so. And the water wasn't cold enough for me, anyway. So I slipped on a pair of yoga pants under my nightshirt, slid into the sneakers I'd traveled in, and headed for the stairs, Victoria trotting at my heels. I didn't bother with my eyeglasses since I was in jammies mode.

I found my way downstairs, but I wasn't so sure where the

kitchen was. I figured it had to be near the dining room, and I thought I remembered where that was.

I angled down a promising hallway lit by dim sconces and halted at a surprising sound. Were those voices? It was, what, two in the morning? Who would be up and about at this hour?

Victoria had stopped too and looked up at me expectantly. I scooped her up so her nails wouldn't click on the wooden floor and crept forward. It sounded like a man and a woman arguing, though I couldn't quite make out everything they were saying. The accents probably didn't help. It wasn't like they were declaiming Shakespeare on the stage at The Globe.

At least I could be certain they weren't from our group.

"He's onto us," came the female voice. "He's going to put two and two together soon enough."

"Arr, we're sly and quiet. I just want this over with. The lack of sleep is killing me."

Who were they?

Victoria really wanted to know. She must have sensed my tension because she chose that moment to bark.

"Damn Dionysus," I uttered, not helping matters.

The jig was up. I set the dog down just as a female voice hissed, "Who's there?" Victoria set off running and turned the corner. I followed.

"It's just me. Pepper. I wanted a glass of water," I said as I rounded the corner and found Mrs. Pidgeon facing off with Albert. He scooped up an enthusiastic Victoria after she jumped up against his legs.

"A glass of water? Here?" Mrs. Pidgeon said, flustered and annoyed but in high dudgeon at the sight of me.

Albert took a step back from her and nodded over his shoulder. "There's a fridge in the billiard room that's usually stocked. I'll get you a bottle, all right, miss?"

"Pepper," I said. "Just call me Pepper. And that would be great."

No ice, but it would be cold. He set down Victoria and vanished into a room off the corridor.

Mrs. Pidgeon gave me the evil eye and ignored Victoria sniffing her practical black shoes. "Do you need directions back to your room?"

"No, I'm fine! Just fine." Albert appeared with the bottle, and I took it. "Thanks. I'll just be heading back that way then."

"Mind that you do," she said, her voice colder than the water bottle.

Puzzled, I turned and headed back the way I'd come, Victoria joining me, happy for her wee-hours adventure. Speaking of wee ... I explored till I came to the conservatory, wandered through its dim paths for a few minutes and sniffed the loamy air, drinking my water while Victoria watered a few plants. I found a recycling bin for my water bottle, then exited and continued my stroll through the house.

I wasn't sleepy now, especially after catching Mrs. Pidgeon and Albert in their odd chat. What were they arguing about at two in the morning? What did she mean by "He's onto us"? It didn't sound good. Neil and I would have to find some way to keep an eye on them.

The library. Maybe they were headed for the library. If I could just figure out where the library was.

After a little more wandering, I got going in a direction I recognized and ended up in the long gallery of portraits and other art. It was as dim as the hallways, with just a couple of sconces acting as night lights. Victoria dashed off into the shadows and came back with her miniature tennis ball.

"You're so darn cute," I said, taking it and hurling it down the length of the room. She dashed off again, and as I approached the library door, she reappeared, hopped up on one of the benches in the center of the gallery, lay down and began gnawing on the ball. Good. I didn't want her in danger, just in case someone really was here.

I stood outside the door for a moment, digging into my fuzzy brain for the code Mark had given us. Once I had it, I reached down and tapped the numbered pad that Mark had hidden with his body the first time we went into this place.

And just as I heard the click of the lock, I heard something else. Something inside.

Chapter Thirteen

ook thieves? Is that what I was looking at here? Or to be
more specific, hearing?

Nerves tingled through my body, and my stomach did a
somersault. What the hell was I doing? But if the thief was in the
library, I had to catch them if I could. And if it was Mrs. Pidgeon
and Albert, they weren't that scary. At least Albert wasn't that
scary.

Another thump sounded through the door. *Crap*. It was now or
never.

I took a deep breath and pushed the door open.

And saw ... no one.

Were they hiding? Or had no one been here at all?

One small lamp on a central table offered the only illumination,
but that meant there were still dark corners. I peeked around the
door first to see if anyone hid there. I looked up to make sure no
ninjas dangled from the balcony that wrapped from the left wall
around to this one. Then, leaving the door open, I gingerly stepped
inside.

I nearly jumped out of my skin when Victoria started barking.
Was someone in the gallery? I ran back out the door and saw no
one, but Victoria had torn off into the darkness.

"Victoria? Victoria!" I called out. I didn't want to lose Mark's
dog, but I also wanted to clear the library. Then again, what if
Victoria was chasing the thief?

If there had been a thief. The library was empty. So what was that noise?

The barking got louder, and Victoria reappeared, sprinting down the length of the gallery and jumping up at me and barking some more.

"What is it, girl?" I knew she couldn't tell me, exactly, and part of me was relieved I didn't have to chase after her—and whoever she might have been chasing. I swallowed. I had to go back into the library, just to be sure there weren't any clues. Or a person hiding behind the sofa.

I petted the dog, calming her a bit, then turned and reentered the library, looking again behind the door in case the thief, if there was a thief, had repositioned. Victoria followed, jumping up onto the same chair Neil had sat in the first night. She lay there panting, her paws hanging over the front, her tongue hanging out and her eyes bright as she watched me walk slowly through the room.

I looked behind and around the minimal furniture, the fireplace. I glanced up at the camera there. It should've caught something. We could look at the footage later.

Then I started paying attention to the books. I made a cautious circuit of the large room, scanning the bookcases, examining the windows while I was at it. Then I eyed the spiral staircase. I was going to have to go all Professor Henry Higgins and get up there.

Humming "The Rain in Spain" for courage—and noting that in Hartford, Hereford, et cetera, hurricanes hardly ever happened, so I might consider moving to one of those places in the future—I climbed the skinny spiral staircase to the balcony above.

I had no idea where Mark kept his most valuable books, so I just looked for anything unusual. I walked softly to where the narrow balcony ended at the wall with the windows, then turned around and eased back, taking in the shelves of old books bound in leather and cloth. Beautiful books.

Everything seemed in order along this wall, though something odd caught my eye. One of the books was upside down. *How weird.*

I looked closely. The topsy-turvy novel, *Our Mutual Friend*, was in a section of old Dickens editions. I snorted. Dickens's ghost was looking over my shoulder. I was sure of it.

Then my eye spied something out of place on the perpendicular leg of the balcony, the one that hovered above the door. I quickened my pace and turned the corner to see a mess of books on the floor, some in a wobbly vertical pile, others in disarray. "Oh!"

Victoria jumped up to her feet on the chair and barked once.

"Quiet, girl. It's OK. I've found something." I sifted through the books, noting the authors: Waugh. Lessing. Du Maurier. Wodehouse. Amis. Highsmith. Orwell. Tolkien. Some of the editions were very fine. Could these be the titles the thief had targeted?

Victoria let out a bark and dashed toward the door. A noise ... footsteps. Someone was entering the library!

I froze for a moment, then lunged forward to spy on them. In doing so, I bumped the teetering pile of books, and they crashed against the railing. A fat edition of *The Hobbit* fell right through.

"Ooof!" came the cry of the intruder. A figure emerged and squinted up at me while rubbing his head in pain.

"Mark?"

"Pepper?"

"Um, yeah." I cringed a little. "I thought you were the thief!"

"Why would you think that?" He gave his head a shake, then ran a hand through his hair, further tousling it. Wild hair looked good on him.

"Sorry about that."

"Good thing I have a hard head." He smiled wryly. "I thought I heard Victoria, and then I checked the security system, and the cameras showed the lights on in here and someone moving about. You, I take it?"

"But there was someone in here before me! Look, your books are all over the place. Is this where the Virginia Woolf would be?"

"Hang on a moment," he said, scooping up the Tolkien. He stopped to give Victoria a scratch behind the ears and a treat from the pocket of his robe (my heart melted a little at the idea he always carried treats for her), then he headed for the spiral staircase.

He wore a plaid robe, though it flapped open slightly as he climbed the stairs, and I saw he had nothing but boxers and a white T-shirt on beneath. I flashed back to that time I saw him emerging from the swimming pool in Fort Lauderdale like James Bond out of the sea. It was a crime to hide those legs, even if they looked awfully nice in pants.

He made his way to me, and we knelt next to the pile of books. He stacked them as we went through the titles, then we both stood and he scanned several shelves along the wall.

"I haven't seen *To the Lighthouse*—is it there?" I asked.

He shifted to the next column of shelves and looked. "I'll be damned. It's gone."

"But we don't even know if it was stolen tonight or previously."

"I expect previously. Let me see if I can tell if something else is missing." He pulled his phone from a robe pocket and scanned what must've been his inventory, then looked at the shelves again. "Bloody hell. They nicked my first edition of *Casino Royale*."

Speaking of James Bond. "Ian Fleming?"

"Not exactly literature, but it's damned valuable. Worth over a hundred thousand pounds."

I whistled. "We'll have to tell William."

"He'll be so annoyed with me."

"Why?"

"He doesn't like stolen books out in the wild. It makes his life more complicated. And this isn't going to be very pleasant for me, either. He's going to have to tell his fellow bookworms to look out for these, and I'm sure my name will come into it sooner or later."

"Maybe not," I said. "Is he indiscreet?"

"No, but I'm sure his friends know I'm a particular customer and friend of his. Oh well. Can't be helped. We need to stop this thief on the back end if we can't stop 'em on the front end. What made you come in here?"

I explained how I'd wanted a glass of water, ran into Mrs. Pidgeon and Albert acting odd—to which Mark's forehead creased—then came to the gallery and heard a noise. I left out Victoria peeing on the horticulture.

"So you heard a noise—"

"Two noises," I said.

"And yet no one was in here?"

I shrugged. "Unless they were invisible. But you didn't leave the books like this, did you?"

He shook his head. "I don't understand it." Then he looked at me more closely, scanning me up and down. "Are those your jim-jams?"

"My what?" I looked down at myself. "Oh. My jammies. Pajamas. Um, sort of. Nightshirt. Yoga pants. I didn't think I'd be running into anyone."

His voice got deeper, more growly. "I like you like this, Pepper. So different without your glasses. And you're adorable in your ... jammies."

Victoria barked again. Talk about timing. We both looked over the balcony and saw her under the spiral staircase, scratching at the floor. She looked up at us and barked, more frenzied this time.

Mark and I exchanged a glance. Then we abandoned the books and sped around the balcony toward the stairs.

I followed him down, and we crouched to see what Victoria was all excited about. She scratched at the wooden floor just under the first couple of steps, behind the staircase.

As Mark squinted, I reached down and touched what looked like a crack. But it wasn't a crack. It was the edge of something. I pushed against it, and the edge of a square panel popped up. The wooden panel easily slid across the floor under the pressure of my hand.

"What the devil?" Mark exclaimed as we peered into a dark hole ... and another set of spiral stairs.

I turned my shocked gaze toward him. "I thought you said you looked for secret entrances?"

Mark shrugged. "I was probably drinking."

"Where does it go?"

"No idea. Shall we find out?"

Chapter Fourteen

"Let me turn on the torch," Mark said, tapping his phone and activating the light. "I'll go first."

As broad of shoulder as he was, the hole was a tight fit. But he sat on the edge and shimmied his way in. "It's not bad once you're in here," he said. "Come on. I'll shine you down."

"What about Victoria?" The dog who'd been so excited to uncover the passage now hung back from the secret staircase. "We can't leave her here. Come on, girl," I called to her.

I swear she shook her head at me.

"Blast," Mark said. "Grab her and hand her to me."

I stood and took a few steps toward Victoria. She jumped back, then ran around the library, creating a game I had no desire to play. Finally she hopped up on her favorite chair, wagging her feathery tail, and I was able to nab her.

"Silly girl," I told her, scratching behind her ears. She tensed up, her tail winding in a circle when I lowered her into the hole in the floor, but she settled down when Mark grasped her and put her under his arm.

"You're next," he said.

I wasn't as big as Mark, but I wasn't skinny, either. That said, this was one time when being short and generally small of frame was to my advantage. I slid into the trap door with minor bumps to my butt, thankful I wasn't wearing one of my poufy dresses.

"All right?" Mark asked, turning the light downward. "Can you see?"

"I'm good. Let's go." What I really meant was, *Let's get the hell out of this staircase,* but I wanted to be a good sport. Besides, I was curious. The thief was surely long gone, but I knew we'd stumbled upon their means of entry and exit.

The rough spiral staircase was made of wood, and it was perhaps even narrower than the one that spiraled up to the library's balcony. This one spun down through a square, chimney-like space. Niches in the walls—made of stone and mortar around three sides of the stairs—caught my eye.

"Mark, are those bottles?"

"What?" He'd been focused on looking down, but he took a moment to turn around and saw what I saw: dusty bottles in some of the niches. "Good God!" He juggled the dog and his phone in an attempt to grab one of the bottles, and the phone slipped out of his hand and clattered down the steps. "Damn it!"

I would've laughed if it hadn't gotten so freakin' dark in here. "Look at the bottles later. We have a little light from above, and your phone is down there. We'll be OK."

"Wherever 'down there' is. All right. Stay close. I'll catch you if you fall."

While the idea of falling into Mark Fairman was mildly tempting, this didn't seem like the best way to go about it. My eyes slowly adjusted to the dim light, and I trod carefully behind him, catching a whiff of his manly scent as he went. Victoria gave off a little whimper, and he whispered soothing words to her that I also took to heart.

It took a couple of minutes of careful descent into the well of darkness before Mark said "ah-ha!" He'd found his phone, and he shone its tiny light up at me, blinding me.

"Ack!"

"Sorry." He turned it back toward the walls.

I blinked, trying to get my night vision back. "Are we there yet?"

He chuckled. "I think so? Come on down."

I made it down the last couple of steps and squeezed next to Mark into a space built for one and a half people, or one person and a dog. Victoria seemed happy to be squeezed between the two of us. I looked up at Mark, fully conscious of how close he was. Was he actually leaning closer to me? Those golden eyes were dark. His lips parted. All my pheromones were exploding like popcorn. With hot butter.

"Um, is there a door or what?" I croaked.

He blinked. Then he smiled. "Let's see, shall we?"

Leave it to me to sabotage my big moment alone with Mark Fairman. Though this wasn't exactly how I'd pictured it.

He turned toward the walls—three of stone, one of wood. Surely the wood wall had to hold an exit. Both of us looked it over, touching it, searching for a latch or something.

"There—what's that?" I asked.

"What, this?" He bent over the circle I'd spotted. "A knot in the wood?"

"Press it."

"Oh, come on." Even cheerful Mark sounded impatient now.

"Please?"

He quirked his mouth at me, then pushed on the knot. And a rectangular section of the paneled wall pushed open on hidden hinges.

"Crikey," he said, stepping out into the dark space beyond.

I followed. And sniffed. "Smells like a wine cellar."

"It *is* a wine cellar!" Mark tapped on his phone, and in a moment, the whole place glowed with up-lighting nestled above row after row of handsome brick alcoves under an arched ceiling. "I had it renovated several months ago, though I don't recall putting in that door."

"Maybe you were drinking again," I teased, turning around. "Look at this. You really didn't know this door was here?"

He set Victoria down, now that he knew the territory. She went off sniffing while we examined the door we'd just passed through.

The cellar side of the door looked like irregular pieces of flat rock stacked together, very pretty, and when he closed it, the rocks fit seamlessly into a wall made of the same stuff, making the door invisible. On the door were three short, staggered shelves, each sporting an empty, unlabeled wine bottle that was lit from within. Accent lighting.

"I just thought this rock wall was a whim of my decorator," he said. "I didn't realize it concealed a door."

"Well, how do you open it?"

"Why?" Mark grinned. "Do you want to go back in there?"

I shook my head with a smile. "No, but it would be nice to know how the thief is getting in and out."

We looked and looked and couldn't find any kind of handle or button. I stared at the bottle lights. Could they be more than decor?

I gently grasped the neck of the left-hand bottle. Mark raised an eyebrow. Man, he had a dirty mind. That's probably one reason I liked him. I wiggled the bottle and found that it pulled toward me at an angle and stayed there.

"What's that about?" Mark asked. He reached out and pulled the rightmost bottle down.

"*Put the candle back,*" I said in my best Gene Wilder impression.

He laughed out loud. "*Young Frankenstein.* One of my favorites. Just don't get trapped in the doorway." He reached and pulled the second bottle. Nothing happened.

"Maybe it's like a combination lock. You have to do it in a certain order."

"Try one-two-three."

I set the bottles upright, then tried them from left to right. "No dice."

"Well, there can't be that many combinations."

"I think you're on the right track," I said. "Keep it simple. Especially if no one even knows this door is here to begin with. Let's try it the other way."

This time he reset the bottles, then pulled them down from right to left.

A click sounded, and the door popped slightly open, just enough so he could grab the edge and pull it wide.

"Bingo!" I exclaimed. Victoria came running back at the sound, sat and watched us expectantly.

"Well, that was fun," Mark said, "but it doesn't get us any closer to knowing who did this, does it?"

"We know it's someone with access to the estate who knows the estate. But I suppose we knew that before, since they've been getting into the library all this time. Maybe one of your friends who's been to parties here? Or one of the resident staff?"

"Or maybe someone who did the renovations down here?" Mark speculated. "I'll ask Mrs. Pidgeon to go through the records, get the names of the contractors."

A dark thought occurred to me. "Are you sure you want to do that? What if she—"

"Highly unlikely," Mark said. "Not with what I pay her. Or any of the staff, really. But I'll be discreet. I won't let on why I want to see the records. I'll ask for names of all the contractors who've done all my renovations. How's that?"

"Sounds good." I yawned. "Let's walk and talk. I'm exhausted, and tomorrow's going to be a long day."

"Oh, Pepper," Mark said, closing the secret door and guiding me down the rows toward what I presumed was a more conventional exit. "I finally get you in my wine cellar, and all you want to do is sleep."

I laughed. "It's, like, three in the morning!"

"Three thirty," he said. "Another time, perhaps. I have some lovely Châteauneuf-du-Pape that is best drunk among the bins. And down that way, I have a perfect tasting room." He gestured off to our left, where indeed there was a sitting area with comfy modern furniture, a low coffee table and one of those faux fireplaces, dark, of course.

"Fancy."

"One thing you need to know about me, Pepper, is that I am anything but *fancy.*" He'd stopped and turned to me. "I mean, you could just lounge here all day in your *jammies* and I'd be delighted."

I answered his grin, then sucked in a breath when he took a step forward until our bodies were almost touching. He leaned in, slipped a hand around the back of my neck and pressed a lingering, warm kiss to my cheek. Followed by one below my ear that set my pulse racing. I put a hand on his chest—warm and hard through his T-shirt under the robe—and he watched me as heat sizzled through my body all the way out to my fingers and my toes. We locked eyes for a full minute, I think, as I breathed him in and tingled. He'd put the ball into my court. What was stopping me? Besides fatigue and my less than glamorous nightwear?

Finally, almost involuntarily, I gave him the tiniest push, and he stepped back. He let out a little sigh with a half-smile, turned and led me around a corner to a conventional staircase that went straight up to a closed door that opened with zero shenanigans. We popped through into a pantry and then into the cavernous kitchen. With the dog, we strolled through the house until we reached the main staircase to the east wing.

"Go to bed," he said. "Take Victoria. I'm going to go secure the library. We'll chat tomorrow."

"All right." I struggled not to touch my warm cheek, where his kiss still burned. "Good night, Mark."

"Good night, darling Pepper." He winked.

Pshew. I wasn't sure if I'd gotten away unscathed or missed the opportunity of a lifetime, but I was going to bed alone.

Even Victoria seemed tired as we got up to our floor and headed down the hall to my room. I halted just shy of it. In the shadows, a figure leaned against the wall, a figure who unfolded himself and stepped forward into the golden light of a sconce.

"Where have you been?" Neil asked.

Chapter Fifteen

I 'd never been good with men who liked to control me in any way, but I didn't think that was what this was.

This was Neil, and I realized he wasn't angry. He looked worried sick.

"Are you OK?" he asked softly. "I heard something earlier, came out of my room and saw your door was ajar. I hope you don't mind, but I peeked inside, and you weren't there. And you weren't answering your phone—probably because you left it on the night-stand—and you were gone forever. Are you OK?" he asked again.

I looked around. "Not out here," I whispered. "Come in so we don't wake everyone up."

He looked skeptical, but he glanced both ways and followed me into my room. I closed the door.

"Don't worry. I'm way too tired to ravish you," I said, giving Neil the side-eye. I couldn't tell if he was amused or disappointed. I observed his very nice jammies, with top and bottoms that actually matched, dark blue with white pinstripes. No, not jammies. Pajamas. So very Neil.

Victoria didn't mess around. She used the steps at the foot of the big bed and ran right up, did a few circles to make a nest in the soft bedding, curled up and zonked. I kicked off my sneakers and joined her, lying on my side and leaning on my elbow so I could see Neil. I was tired of standing.

"Sit down," I commanded, pointing to the edge of the bed.

His creased brow betrayed his uncertainty, but he sat sideways on the edge of the bed so he could face me. His voice was resigned. "You were with Mark."

I quirked my mouth at him. *There's no way he's jealous. Is he?* "Not by design. Does this look like the costume of a seductress to you?" My nightshirt and yoga pants were dusty from our encounter with the hidden staircase. I needed to change those before I went to sleep.

"You look good to me," Neil said.

"Oh, Neil. You haven't even seen my real lingerie game." Despite our brief, unfulfilled encounter in New Orleans. I could tell he was thinking back to that moment, too, and I enjoyed the way he squirmed slightly.

And then I took pity on him and told him the whole story: the quest for water, Mrs. Pidgeon and Albert, the library, the stolen books, the secret stairs, and the wine cellar, which I emphasized was an extremely small part of the journey. I might have left out one or two details.

"And then Mark went off to lock up the library, and I came up here," I concluded.

Victoria let out a ripping snore that made us both laugh.

Neil sighed and rubbed his forehead. "So maybe we got this thief on camera?"

"We know what to look for. We'll check out the footage in the morning, I guess. Mark and I just wanted to go to bed. I mean, I wanted to go to bed. To sleep. Argh!" I dropped my head into the pillow. I couldn't say anything right!

But I lifted my head when I heard Neil chuckling. He'd moved a little closer. He ran a hand over my hair, taking away what I feared might be a bit of cobweb. "It's OK, Pepper. I was just worried about you. And maybe—other things."

"Oh, Neil." I lay back against the pillow and yawned again. "It's so late to worry about anything."

"You're right. I hope it's not too late." He sat there for another minute, just watching me. I got caught up in his eyes. Then he stood and turned to face me once again. "I'll see you in the morning."

He walked to the door and vanished through it, closing it softly behind him.

I didn't have a lot of time to think about what he meant before I drifted into unconsciousness, dust and all.

I HEARD the bustle in the hallway of my friends heading down to breakfast. The promise of eggs and bacon (and scones? I hoped there were scones—and clotted cream) did more than my alarm to get me out of bed. Just as I'd rolled out of the comfy bliss of the mattress, wondering if this bed would fit in my duplex, a soft knock came at the door.

I answered it in my dusty jammies. "I'm here to take the dog on her constitutional, miss," said Albert.

"Oh, sure." Victoria dashed past me and jumped up on Albert. He cooed to her, slipped a harness on her and led her away. He sure was perky this morning considering he was conspiring in the middle of the night with Mrs. Pidgeon.

I closed the door and mentally went through my checklist of what lay ahead today: first, a tour of Mark's distillery, on the premises. That meant I could change before we left to work the garden party this afternoon at Greenwich. So after my shower and rinsing out my jammies and hanging them to dry on a towel rack, I donned jeans, a white scoop-neck T-shirt and a form-fitting black vest, along with my plain black nerd glasses, comfy chunky black shoes, cute cocktail earrings and my good-luck bracelet. I pinned my damp hair up to deal with later.

Of course, the other thing on the agenda would be dealing with whatever fallout there was from the Jammies Incident.

Fortunately, I ran into Luke first among our crowd. We chatted on the way down to the dining room, and he was the first to "Woohoo!" when we came upon Barclay and Gina sharing a passionate kiss next to the buffet.

"Suck it," Barclay said as they popped apart, Gina's face turning pink. But they both smiled.

"Speaking of, no sucking face in the dining room," said Melody, coming in behind us, dressed as casually as I was.

I thought they'd have all eaten by now. "Where were you?"

"Since I can't do my morning beach run, I took a walk in the garden. You're going to love it." Melody had a short commute to the beach—and the Bohemia Beach hotel bar where she worked— since she rented a cool apartment above a pool house at a swanky property on the barrier island.

"Where's Neil?" Luke asked. For some reason, everyone looked at me.

"How would I know?"

"You were the last one to see him last night, weren't you?" Melody asked.

My eyes bugged out. What did she know? "Meaning what?"

"I saw the poor man in the hallway," Melody said. "I peeked out of my room when I heard a noise. He was staking out your door. So if you didn't see him, the question is, were you in your room and ignoring him ... or were you somewhere else?" She raised an eyebrow.

She enjoyed interrogating me a little too much. And since a couple of Mark's staff were moving in and out with food for the buffet, I didn't want to get into a long explanation of what I'd been up to. So I went for pure ignorance.

"I have no idea what you're talking about."

"You have something you want to tell us, Pepper?" Luke asked.

"I already said—"

"Good morning, Bohemians," came a deep, gruff, delicious English accent behind me. "Please, help yourself. Cook's breakfast is top-notch. And you want to fuel up for the Fairyland tour."

I slowly turned, and Mark met my look with a broad grin. "Did you sleep well last night, Pepper?"

I swear, every single one of my colleagues had a coughing fit at the same time.

I nodded at Mark, trying unsuccessfully to put our moment in the wine cellar out of my mind. "Eventually. After I got my *drink of water.*" I spun and glared at each and every one of the bartenders.

Where was Neil, anyway?

We dove into the buffet, with Mark telling us just what constituted a full English breakfast. I loaded my plate with fried eggs, thick bacon, sausages, beans, fried mushrooms, grilled tomatoes, and I even found a scone and clotted cream. More of a tea item, apparently, but the stomach wants what the stomach wants.

By the time I sat at the long table with my meal and a hot cup of coffee, Neil strolled into the room wearing jeans and a T-shirt advertising his bar, The Junction Box. He and Mark exchanged a friendly nod, as if the Jammies Incident had not occurred. And really, what had occurred? Not much, except a certain amount of sexual frustration.

Neil filled his plate and sat across from me. He glanced at me, then at Mark, who sat to my left. Our host was preoccupied with discussing rums with Barclay, which was fine by me.

"I don't feel like I'm contributing enough to this trip," Gina piped up. She sat across from Barclay and next to Neil. "I feel like a fifth wheel. Or sixth wheel."

"I have plenty for you to do today if you want to help," Neil said.

"Really? I don't know anything about bartending except for what I see you guys do."

"I need about three hundred flower garnishes assembled."

"Oh, good. I'm crafty. I can do that!" Gina said. I expected she could do just about anything; she was a software engineer at the space center.

"Well," Melody said from the other side of me, "it just so happens I brought a costume for you, too."

"Costume?" Luke asked from next to her. "I thought we got to choose our own outfits for this thing?"

"You know Neil loves us to coordinate," I said. "Though I thought we were just going to dress like it's summer. Even though it's September."

"Melody told me she had an idea," Neil said, "so I told her to run with it. I hope you all don't mind."

Oh, boy. I had faith that she knew what I looked good in, but the boys?

"So what were you up to this morning?" I asked Neil.

"Using the amazing kitchen here to batch our vanilla simple syrup for the Corsage cocktail. Barclay made the cucumber juice."

"Oh!" Now I felt really bad that Neil had stayed up half the night waiting for me to reappear. "You should've said something. I could have helped."

"I figured you needed your sleep." The smallest hint of irony laced his tone, but it was enough to make Melody snap her eyes to me.

I just shook my head, trying to tell her with my eyebrows to shut the hell up. She gave me a look that said *I want details later!* and went back to her eggs.

As breakfast wound down, Mark asked if Neil and I could join him in his office for a few minutes before the tour. "The billiards room is open if the rest of you want to play. Oh, Ben, good!" Mark's assistant had popped into the room. "Can you show them the billiards room while I have a chat with these two?"

"Sure thing, boss," Ben said, grabbing a piece of toast. "Do you all play?" he asked as Barclay, Gina, Luke and Melody followed him out. But not before Melody shot me another glance. I swear, her glances were louder than some people's shouts.

Neil and I stood along with Mark, and we all looked at one another for an awkward second or two. Finally, Mark spoke.

"I thought we might look at the security footage from last night. I assume you've filled him in?" he said to me, nodding at Neil.

"Yes, Neil knows all about the library and the staircase," I said. *But not your hot lips* was implied.

Mark nodded. "Excellent. Maybe we can finally nail this prat."

Chapter Sixteen

Mark's office sported many of the details I was getting used to in his house—carved wood, exotic rugs, precious-looking furniture. But there were book-shelves, too, stuffed with books that appeared to have actually been read. While an antique-looking desk sat in the center of the room, a much more modern setup to the side sported a computer with three monitors, gadgets and a few knickknacks that spoke more of Mark's personality than all this posh stuff. They included a bobble-head of a footballer who seemed to be from the same club I'd met in the pub on my first day in London. Was that Blue Eyes?

"I asked Mrs. Pidgeon for information on all the contractors we've hired in the past two years." Mark sat at the central chair in front of the monitor, indicating we should pull up chairs on either side of him. "I have to admit, Pepper, you have me worried. She seemed quite taken aback, even though I assured her I was simply working on my budget for renovations going forward. She acted as if she had something to hide. I just don't understand it."

"Why did you want the contractor files?" Neil asked.

"Oh, sorry I didn't mention that," I said to him. "We were thinking maybe someone connected with the contractor who put in the secret door might be linked to the thefts, especially since Mark didn't know about the door."

"You didn't notice it during construction?" Neil looked surprised.

Mark shrugged as he moved his computer mouse around, woke his monitors and entered a password. "I have other things to do. I give my staff free hand in most things, and I trust them to carry out my wishes. I prefer to see a project when it's all shiny and done, not when it's a construction site. But I was in on the wine cellar plans, and there was no mention of a door."

"Very strange," Neil said.

"Indeed," Mark agreed. "Anyway, Mrs. Pidgeon said she'd email the contracts to me."

"You don't have them on your computer?" Neil asked.

"Not this one." Mark kept moving his cursor around, then homed in on an icon, double-clicked and sat back while it took its time opening. "There's a business office in the old dairy, associated with the distillery. It's easier to manage contracts and such out of there. I trust Mrs. Pidgeon with organizing my business files. She's not just a housekeeper. She's what you might call an executive assistant."

The program opened on his central monitor. The computer window had several smaller images on it.

Now we were getting somewhere. "Is that the security cameras?"

"Yes, this is the live view," Mark said. "The library is just part of this system. There's a camera on the front door and several around the grounds. I don't have them throughout the house because I don't want the staff to feel like Big Brother is watching. Big Brother only watches the library."

"Orwell would approve," Neil said.

Mark clicked a link from the main page that took him into another window that required a password, which he typed in. "I keep the library camera feeds secured as well, just to keep anyone from casing the joint."

I giggled at his film noir lingo, and both of the guys looked at me. I adopted a sober expression and tried to look intelligent.

A new window popped up showing two camera views. One

displayed the door of the library and most of the room, as seen from the balcony at the window end. The other showed the half of the room that included the windows from a lower angle. The spiral staircase was in both shots.

"Can you go back in time on these?" I asked.

"Yes. It's an entirely cloud-based system that stores six months' worth of video. But I've never seen anyone on the feeds, even when I've noticed something missing," Mark said. "True confessions: I could've missed something. I don't have time to watch every single minute. But still, one would think I would've seen something unusual, especially since we know how they're getting in."

"How are the videos captured and stored?" Neil asked.

"It's a wireless feed that writes to the cloud. Really clever," Mark said. "I don't have to run extra wires through all of those ancient stone walls."

He cued up the full-room shot in its own window and entered the time stamp he wanted to see. "We'll try 1 a.m. and go forward. You got there shortly before I did, Pepper—two thirty or so?"

"Maybe a little before. One a.m. is plenty of time."

Mark set the camera to a slow fast-forward. The feed was a little jerky at times, but the images were clear. And then all of a sudden, I winked into existence in the middle of the room.

"Wait—what?" Mark stopped the feed.

"Go back," Neil said.

Mark grunted and did just that, using a slider to go back in time at a much slower pace. There I was, and then I wasn't. The door was closed up tight, and the room was empty.

"What the hell?" he said.

"Something isn't right." I focused on the display around the video. "Do that again—go forward, then back."

Mark did as I asked.

"There! Look!" I pointed. "The time stamp—it jumped!"

We all leaned in as Mark scrubbed back and forth with the controls. "Damned if you're not right," he said.

"So someone erased the video?" Neil asked.

"Impossible," Mark said. "I'm the only one with the code."

"Anything is hackable. Or so I hear," I said to his dirty look.

Mark went to the other camera feed, and the same thing happened at the same time.

"Let's assume it wasn't hacked." Neil rubbed his beard thoughtfully. "What else could explain the gap in the video?"

"Whoa no." I looked at them, and they looked at me.

"What?" Mark asked, his golden eyes reflecting the light of the monitor.

"Wifi. You said this system transmits video through the house's wifi?"

Mark nodded. "That's right. It all goes to the cloud so we don't have to worry about cards filling up and such."

"I noticed my wifi going in and out on the phone last night when I was trying to look up hurricane information. And the other night, too. Maybe you have flaky wifi."

"I have excellent wifi," Mark said.

"You probably do." Neil pointed to me appearing out of nowhere on the feed. "Maybe it's not flaky. Someone could be turning it off. Someone who knows the system."

"Bloody hell." Mark shook his head. "I suppose it's possible. There's a repeater in the gallery that services the library. Perhaps they're interrupting the signal at the source while they're browsing my books. With a jammer or something. Is that possible?"

"It is," Neil said. "I've read about that."

"This doesn't help us much, does it?" Mark sounded as down as I'd ever heard him. A ping sounded from his computer. "Ah. Email. Perhaps the contracts I asked for."

He opened the window. Neil and I both looked away so we wouldn't be snooping in his mailbox, but we looked back when he said, "Here we go! Mrs. Pidgeon's sent the contractor files."

He dragged them to a folder, then did a search for "wine cellar."

Several files popped up. He opened a couple. They mentioned the same contractor.

"I know this name, and not just because I signed the checks," Mark said. "You know what's really strange? I'd forgotten this until now, but Stout Boy Builders was recommended to me by William Buttersby."

"Buttersby?" Neil asked in surprise.

"Ha!" I said. "Maybe Mr. Buttersby is an expert in more than antique books."

Chapter Seventeen

N eil and I went out to the garden to wait for the start of the distillery tour after our meeting with Mark. We agreed on one thing: We needed to shake up this investigation, such as it was. We only had a few days left in London.

"I feel like we don't have enough suspects. Or maybe we have too many," I said to Neil as we strolled through the rose garden. Through a tall hedge, I could hear the voices of the other bartenders, who'd found a badminton court and were batting the shuttlecock back and forth. I guessed they ditched the billiards in favor of the fantastic weather.

"So who are our suspects?" Neil asked.

"First, anyone who lives here, and that includes all the household staff, including Mrs. Pidgeon and Albert. Second, anyone who has access, which includes a great deal more staff—everyone who works at the distillery, the accountant, the master distiller, and so on. Third, friends of Mark's who may or may not have an accomplice. Nigel also collects twentieth-century literature; did you know?"

"Then I doubt he'd be trying to sell Virginia Woolf."

"Point taken," I said. "But he and Lottie are total spendthrifts. I mean, they may have invisible means of support, but still."

"Anyone else?"

"Someone who works for the contractor who built the secret

door, who knows a way into the house or who may also have an accomplice."

Neil stopped to sniff a deep red rose with almost black undertones labeled *Deep Secret* on a little sign stuck into the ground. "I don't think this is helping."

The delicious rosy scents of all the bushes almost overwhelmed my supernose. "Maybe we need to draw them out. Put it around that we're helping Mark figure out where his books are going. At least that way we'd have the freedom to ask the staff questions. Surely one of them has seen something."

"Is that something he'd want?"

I sighed. "Probably not. But he thought William Buttersby alerting others in the rare-book world might be the end of keeping this under wraps anyway."

"Would Buttersby ping his colleagues if he's collecting the books for himself?"

I stopped to think, touching the velvety petals of a rose of rich crimson dusted with purple speckles. *Precious Time,* the sign said. "Honestly? I have a hard time believing William Buttersby would burn his own bed, as it were. One, he didn't strike me as the type, though I'll admit he befuddled me a little. Two, he's owned that bookstore for a long time. I looked it up. He has a massive reputation."

"OK," Neil said. "Let's see if Mark agrees to let us put the word out, and then we'll spread the word at the garden party. Or maybe even during the tour."

"And he needs to put another camera in the library, hidden this time, that records to a card or something."

"You have the number for the contractor—why not call them now?" he suggested.

"Good idea." I pulled out my phone and pulled up the number for Stout Boy Builders that Mark had given us. I put it on speaker, hit the call button and waited through several *ring-ring, ring-ring* sounds before someone picked up.

"Stout Boy Builders," the woman said in a nice, round accent.

"Hi, there. I'm working with Mark Fairman, who's one of your customers, and we'd like to talk to whoever did the work on his wine cellar project."

"Is there a problem?"

"Oh, no, nothing like that. Well, um, he just has a question about ... how the technology works."

I heard clicking. "Samuel Stout managed that project. He's out of the office, but I can have him call you back."

"That would be great. Is an American number OK?"

"Not a problem. We have contracts all over the world."

Interesting. I gave her my number and ended the call.

Neil looked up. "Do you hear a bell?"

I stopped and listened. A *bong-bong-bong* rang out over the formal gardens. "I think we're being summoned."

A few minutes later, our group, along with Ben and Albert, who'd brought Victoria outside, gathered at the spacious terrace at the back of the house. There I saw the bell attached to a post; Mark said it came from an old ship. Another of his collectibles, I guessed.

From there, we had a spectacular view out toward rectangles of plantings and paths in the formal garden, with lots of flowers, topiaries and a central fountain.

With Victoria merrily trotting at his heels, Mark took us down the terrace steps and off to the side of this geometric layout, leading us along a meandering stone path through shady trees toward the distillery. "I built it in the old dairy. It has a separate drive, of course, but it's much more pleasant to go this way."

He pointed out a sweet little barn with a handful of adorable goats in a pen (Mark really did have goats!); the beehives, whose honey contributed a touch of sweetness to his Frilly Fairy Gin; and a vast herb garden. "That's a tour in itself, but you'd have to get it from our wandering botanist."

"You have a wandering botanist?" I asked.

"Diana Silva. Travels the world foraging and looking for new flavors for me and a few other distillers. But I have her save the best for me. Oh, look, there she is hiding behind the rosemary."

A figure popped up from behind a large, unruly rosemary bush. "Fairman!" she bellowed in a sturdy contralto. "You've got some volunteer *Borago pygmaea* growing under here."

"Is that a good thing?" he called out as Diana walked over to us, clad head to toe in khakis like a safari guide.

She presented a short green stem sporting a tiny blue flower to Mark. "Could be interesting. Enough of it, and you might put someone to sleep." She wore a mischievous expression. "A pretty garnish, anyway."

Diana Silva looked to be in her thirties, wore no makeup, and her short, wavy, dark brown hair complemented her amber skin, enhanced by a glow that suggested lots of time in the sun. Her accent was English with a touch of something else I couldn't identify.

"And who do we have here?" she asked.

Mark introduced us each by name. "They're from Bohemia, in Florida."

"Florida, eh?" she said. "I've done quite a bit of work in the Everglades. Are you anywhere near the Everglades?"

"Not really," Neil said, "but you're never far from a swamp in Florida."

"Capital. I really must visit. Tour then?" She stomped off toward the long building that had come into view.

Neil and I exchanged a smile. Diana was a take-charge kinda gal. I liked her immediately.

We followed in her wake to a long building of mostly pale yellow brick adjoining a large two-story barn of dark gray wood and stone.

"I've invited a few of our friends to join us. Go on in," Mark said, holding open a handsome, heavy, glass-and-wood door, definitely a modern addition, etched with *Fairyland Distillery*. Victoria sat at his feet and looked up at him adoringly as the group went in.

I lingered behind, and when it was clear I wasn't going to enter, he closed the door and watched me expectantly.

I cleared my throat. "Neil and I were thinking we might need to shake things up and let people know we're looking into your book problem to try to bring the thief out. They might make a mistake or make themselves known. As a bonus, we have more freedom to ask questions. What do you think?"

Mark picked up Victoria and scratched under her chin. "I don't love the idea, but I trust you. I'll tell the staff that you and Neil may be asking some questions. I hate to think any of them are involved, but maybe they'll be helpful."

"I know it doesn't feel good to have anyone you know rip you off," I said, "but maybe it's no one you know."

"Be careful, all right? I doubt a book thief has violent tendencies, but one never knows."

"I'll be careful. And Neil will look out for me."

He quirked his mouth. "I'm certain he will." Then he granted me a rueful smile—just enough to activate his dimple and my hormones—tucked Victoria under one arm and opened the door for me.

"Um, thanks." I pushed down my emotional confusion and entered the spacious room. I quickly realized this was a visitors' center—like so many distillers, Mark had stepped up to cash in on the tourist trade. Another glass door on the other side of the space looked out onto a parking lot.

This lobby was beautiful, with a soaring ceiling, lots of rustic wood details, attractive displays of bottles of Fairyland's various liquors, tonic water and merchandise, and a life-size fake cow that had already attracted my colleagues. Neil and I joined them and got Ben to use Neil's phone to take a picture of all of us with the bovine. We were in a former dairy, after all.

Alastair was here, and he tried to corner Mark by the cash register, but Mark waved him off so he could chat with Ben. Albert reappeared and whisked away Victoria.

Across the room, Royce Doucet and Nigel and Lottie Dashwood browsed a bookcase full of cocktail books. I went over to say hi.

"Hey, how's it going? Did you survive the dinner OK?" I asked.

"Let's just say I was grateful for tea this morning," Nigel said in a sleepy voice.

"And beans on toast," Lottie added. She laughed when I made a face.

"We had beans with our breakfast, too. I just never thought to put them on toast," I explained.

"I expect you had a proper fry-up at Mark's," she said in good humor.

"Delicious," I agreed, seeing an opportunity to start the gossip engine. "And interesting breakfast conversation. Turns out someone's been stealing some very nice books out of Mark's library. It's such a shame. But we have a lead on who it might be."

Nigel's bloodshot eyes widened. "Wha— I— What sort of books?"

"I think some of the kind you collect," I said. "Twentieth-century literature?"

"Really?" He'd gone even more pale, if that was possible.

"Are you all right, sweetie? Let's get you some water," Lottie said, leading him off to a glass-doored fridge full of water bottles.

Huh. That was a heck of a reaction.

Royce, looking amused, watched them leave. "I loved the dinner," he said. "It gave me ideas for events our distillery has planned later this fall. Though that guy Mr. Mixy was ... interesting."

I rolled my eyes. "Trust me when I say you should avoid him at all costs."

Royce looked at me sideways and winced.

"Oh, no," I said. "What did you do?"

"I told him he could bring his TV crew to Kentucky to film our launch of a very special bourbon. Should I not have done that?"

I looked at him with pity, and then I burst out laughing. "Better you than me!"

"But I was hoping you all might come work that event for me," Royce said. "Neil seemed excited about it."

"Oh!" *So that's the gig Royce talked about earlier.* But Royce seemed nice enough, and I wasn't going to let Mr. Mixy get in the way of a cool job. "Well, I've always wanted to visit the Bourbon Trail."

Now it was his turn to laugh at my obvious attempt at diplomacy. "I see where you'll be especially helpful in handling this Mixy guy. You know him well?"

"Oh, Royce." I put a hand on his shoulder. "It's a long story for another day. Just don't date him, OK?"

"He's not my type," he said with a grin. "But between us, it's unfortunate your friend Barclay isn't available."

Ah. Interesting. But Barclay's beauty was a flame few moths could resist. "It wouldn't work out anyway," I joked. "Barclay's a rum guy."

Royce snorted just as Mark called us over to the center of the room. Cray had joined us, too, and he waved at me as we gathered around our host.

"As you can see, we've added a visitor center to our distillery," Mark said, "but this tour is exclusive to our little group. I thought you might enjoy seeing the operation that produces our award-winning gin, spiced rum, vodka, and—oh, you know the rest. Just pretend you're impressed, all right?"

We all laughed, and then we were off. Diana Silva described the unusual botanicals Fairyland used and let us sniff wonderful herbs and flowers, many of which I'd tasted in the Frilly Fairy gin—the obvious juniper and the popular coriander and angelica root, and more surprising notes, like sea buckthorn and water mint. The master distiller talked about the addition of fresh botanical flavors to the gin through both steeping and vapor infusion, followed by blending. We were introduced to a gorgeous copper still named June and walked through racks of rum barrels aging in an outbuilding.

After we watched bottling in progress, we got to sample a couple of expressions of the Frilly Fairy Gin—along with a special aged edition of the Dragonfly Spiced Rum, which also had a touch of Diana's expertise—in a handsome tasting room that evoked The Dandy Tipple without being as extravagant.

"Happy?" Mark asked us after we'd tasted everything, to our hearty affirmations. "One thing you didn't see today was an additional neutral spirit distilling operation we've opened outside the city. We provide this base spirit to other distilleries for generous compensation. We have more rum aging there as well. Yes, Cray, I'll give you a tour later." We chuckled as Cray threw up his hands as if he hadn't lobbied for such a thing.

"All right then," Mark added. "I know you're a bunch of lushes and are well-stocked with my liquor already, but if you want anything special, let me know, and I'll be glad to send you home with a bottle. Sandwiches are laid out in the cafe. Please help yourselves. And to my special guests: I'll have a mini bus ready in an hour to take you to the garden party."

We thanked Mark for his seemingly limitless generosity, found the cafe he talked about—another nod to the tourists—and scarfed delicious sandwiches and fruit from the buffet, along with (mercifully) nonalcoholic beverages.

As I was sitting at a tiny cast-iron table with Neil, where I told him I'd already started spreading the word about Mark's books, I overheard Alastair talking quietly to Mark over by the food.

"I just don't understand it," Alastair told him, "but when I stopped by the Tipple this morning and checked on our deliveries, I discovered bottles of my good stuff were missing. And not the watered-down stuff they'd hit before—entire, unopened bottles. Someone stole from my vaults again last night."

Chapter Eighteen

W hat? More thievery? I thought Alastair's problems were over. But I didn't have time to ask him about it because we had to get ready for the garden party at Greenwich Park.

When we got back to the house and upstairs to the hallway outside our rooms, Melody told us to hang on and came back a moment later with a stack of flat packages wrapped in brown paper.

"Shirts for the boys—please wear khaki or coordinating pants if you have them—and dresses for us," she said as she handed them out. "Gina, I hope you don't mind, but I brought one for you just in case you want to join us."

"Sounds like fun," she said, though she eyed her package with suspicion.

"OK, let's meet downstairs in thirty minutes," Neil said. "We don't have that far to go, but we have a lot of prep."

With that, we disappeared into our rooms. Victoria was already in mine, and she wagged her feathery tail and gave me kisses when I picked her up and gave her some love.

Fifteen minutes later, I looked at myself in the mirror in the dress, reserved judgment, and sat up against the pillows on the bed to make a video call home. Victoria hopped up and got in my lap as my phone rang through.

"Pepper! I've been worried about you," Aunt Celestine said when she answered. It was obvious she sat poolside in our shared jungle of a backyard. She'd piled her curly red hair, accented with strands of silver, on top of her head and wore one of her flowing hippie cover-ups.

"Are you kidding? I'm worried about *you*," I said. "What's the latest? Are you all boarded up for the hurricane?"

"I don't think it's going to be a hurricane, sweetheart. Probably just a strong tropical storm. But we installed those automatic shutters last year, so I just have to push a few buttons and hide plants in the garage if it comes to that. It'll be fine."

By "we" she meant "I," because she was the one who paid most of the upkeep on our duplex—basically two adjoining houses on either side of a wall—and rented my half to me at a super nice price. She'd retired at forty from an engineer job at NASA. Now she enjoyed the single life, managed her investments and wrote best-selling science books about natural healing and herbs, many of which she grew in our backyard.

"OK, if you say you're ready, I believe you." Some of my worry over the storm melted away just at hearing her voice. And it was a sunny morning there now. "How's Astra?"

At that, our adorable Cavapoo jumped up onto my aunt's lap and sniffed, her nose huge in the phone's camera. I laughed.

Victoria barked excitedly.

"Pepper?" Aunt Celestine looked more closely at her screen. "Whose dog is that? Did you get another dog?"

"Um, no." In the background, I heard a soft growl. Was Astra jealous? "She's a loaner from our host. I mean, she belongs to Mark, and she's just hanging out with me." Why did I sound like a cheating spouse?

"Mark, eh?" Aunt Celestine said, mischief in her tone. She'd heard a little about the legendarily hot distiller.

Astra's low rumble escalated to an anxious bark as she took in the dog on the other side of the ocean. *Bark, bark, bark!*

Victoria answered with her own stream of high-pitched barks.

"Quiet, now!" I exhorted both of them. "Everything is OK! You're basically cousins, you know!"

I could barely hear Aunt Celestine say, "You've got some explaining to do!" before she dissolved into laughter. "We'll talk later. Take care, OK? I love you."

"Love you!" I called through all the barking as the dogs both got their faces up into the phone cameras. Then I ended the call and turned to Victoria, who looked at me breathlessly, panting with a big dog smile. "I can't tell if you liked her or wanted to bite her head off. Maybe you'll get to meet her someday."

Yeah, like how? Not a lot of dogs made the trans-Atlantic voyage. And it was hard to imagine bringing Astra here for a visit— or something more permanent.

I entertained the idea for ten seconds. Mrs. Fairman?

I chuckled and shook my head. Who was I kidding?

Our crew was amusingly quiet on the ride over to Greenwich Park. I thought I knew why, but I wasn't going to say anything.

It wasn't until we were setting up our tools at our canopy tent— among several others pitched on the vast, green, sloping lawn that overlooked the National Maritime Museum, the River Thames and the spectacular London skyline—that Luke spoke up.

"Why do I feel like one of the children in *The Sound of Music* after Julie Andrews turns the drapes into playclothes?" he said.

"I didn't know you were into musical theater, Luke," Melody said.

At that, we all started giggling. Because Luke was a hundred percent right. We women made out OK—we wore dresses in white with green floral designs, each slightly different and only slightly resembling wallpaper. They were flattering enough. But the guys' shirts made it look as if they should be yodeling their way through Salzburg.

"At least they aren't lederhosen," Neil said, and then we were all laughing out loud as we set up the ingredients we'd brought with us.

"This might not have been one of our better ideas," Barclay said, "but you have to admit we're memorable."

Luke snorted. "I'll never live this down." But when he saw the doubt in Melody's eyes, he added brightly, "Still, we look very, um, garden-y."

"Oh, I almost forgot the hats!" Melody cried out, reaching into a box that had been packed with our things. The guys cringed until she brought out boaters that made the shirts look less like curtains and more like something they'd wear punting in Oxford. In a movie.

"Slightly better?" Barclay asked, putting his on.

Gina nodded, though she couldn't stop her smile. "I say, old chap, much better," she intoned in a fake English accent, and we dissolved into laughter again.

Fortunately, we girls didn't have to wear the hats, though they were kind of cute. Neil looked adorable in his. Maybe he carried it off because he did attend Oxford, however briefly.

We didn't have a lot of time to worry about looking like the Von Trapp Family Singers. Hundreds of people were expected at today's ticketed, gin-themed garden party, and several bars and restaurants had set up tents offering cocktails and food under the bright blue sky. Several feet away, Alastair, Ari and other bartenders busily prepped drinks in a tent representing The Dandy Tipple.

We had a couple of cocktails on the menu—a Corsage with gin, orange liqueur, grapefruit juice, the vanilla simple syrup Neil had made this morning, and topped with a lavender soda. For that, Gina set to work on the multicolored floral garnishes, and very pretty they were in the pale golden cocktail, which we served in lowball glasses.

We also had a bright green cucumber drink called the Duke of Cuke, a bit less sweet, with gin (obviously), Chartreuse, lime juice, simple syrup, cucumber juice, and a cucumber and mint garnish served in a highball glass. I was happy to see we weren't contributing to the plastic problem and equally happy the glasses would be collected and taken away for someone else to wash.

Barclay squeezed the limes fresh for Neil to shake and pour for the Corsage. I mixed the Cuke, and Luke did the shaking and pouring. Melody and Gina garnished everything.

The crowd had gotten into the spirit, and many looked as if they'd walked off the pages of a 1920s novel in their garden-party attire. So we felt a little less conspicuous in our drapery garments, at least until William Buttersby came by in pretty much the same outfit he'd worn at the bookstore. Puffing on his pipe, he looked us over.

"Do you take requests?" the bookseller asked. For a second we looked at one another, wondering what cocktail he wanted. "I'd love to hear 'The Lonely Goatherd.'"

We all cracked up again, except Melody, who looked a bit sheepish. I gave her a thumbs-up, and she smiled. It was all in good fun.

"No, but we can hook you up with a great drink," Neil said.

"Done." William picked up a green cocktail, took a sip and said "Aaaahhh."

I wasn't exactly sure what else to say to him. He could be a suspect in Mark's book thefts, given he recommended the contractor who installed the secret door. Or he could be our only means of catching the thief. I decided to go with our original plan of trying to entrap the seller of *To the Lighthouse*.

"Mark says his Virginia Woolf is definitely missing," I told him quietly. "Can we arrange for the seller to come to your shop tomorrow morning?"

"Already done. I had a feeling," William said, making excellent progress on his cocktail. "If you come by before ten, that's when I expect our suspect. We'll hide you somewhere. Are you sure you want to do this?"

"Absolutely!" Maybe this trap would work out after all. "Neil and I will be there." I looked to Neil for confirmation, and he nodded.

"Excellent," William said. "Same goes for the cocktail." He tipped the glass at us with appreciation and wandered off humming "Edelweiss."

I looked at Neil. "I just don't see it. Do you?"

"Time will tell," he said. "I hope." He looked around. "I can't believe we're serving cocktails on the Prime Meridian."

"What?"

"Up there is the Royal Observatory." He pointed up the hill. "Home of zero longitude. Isn't that cool?"

"Really cool," I said wistfully. "I feel like I need to come back to London as a tourist."

"Maybe someday. And if we accomplish our mission, we might have Monday off before we go home." He smiled and shook up another drink.

Nigel and Lottie dropped by. He looked much recovered from earlier, though maybe that was because he was in his cups again. He took a Corsage and pronounced it delightful.

"Wonderful day, don't you think?" Lottie asked.

"I thought it was supposed to rain all the time here?" Luke said.

"Oh, just you wait till tomorrow," Nigel said. "We'll be paying the piper for all this sunshine when the cold front oozes through."

Great. Well, we'd been lucky so far, and I had to see London in the rain if I wanted the authentic experience.

They wandered off. Cray stopped by. Oleanna came through with a few fellow actors, followed by drunken celebrity-stalkers, and gave us an embarrassed shrug at all the attention. Finally, our traffic slowed considerably as the drinkers moved to the food tents.

"Mind if I go talk to Alastair for a minute?" I asked Neil.

"Go ahead. If he lets you," he said with humor.

I rolled my eyes. "I'm not sure if you heard him this morning, but he said someone broke into his vaults again last night. I want to ask him about it."

"We've got this," Neil said with confidence, and I headed over to The Dandy Tipple, nomad edition.

"Alastair, Ari, how's it going?" I asked.

"If I have to squeeze one more lime, I quit," Ari joked. A couple more employees in the back of their tent guffawed.

"You can't quit!" Alastair looked horrified. Probably because she did way more work than he did.

She laughed. "You should be safe. I think we have enough lime juice to get us through."

"So ... I overheard you and Mark this morning," I said to Alastair. I wasn't sure how much he'd told Ari and the others about his little theft problem.

Alastair gave me one of his haughty expressions, but it quickly transformed into understanding. "Oh, yes. Let's talk about that later, all right?"

"OK."

Ari looked between us, puzzled. I had to say something. Then I remembered my mission to beat the drum about Mark's book problem. "It seems some of Mark's nice collectible books are disappearing. He can't figure it out."

Ari's brow creased, and her ice-blue eyes looked troubled. "What kind of books? Old ones?"

"Relatively old. Twentieth-century literature, mostly. Mark asked Neil and I to look into it. We have some leads."

"Strange." She shrugged. "Want to try one of our cocktails?"

The change of subject startled me, but they did look good, especially a pink one with muddled strawberries. "Maybe just a taste of that one?"

She smiled and handed over a cocktail that had already been mixed.

I let the cool, gently sweet drink wash over my tongue. "Mmm." I sniffed and took another sip. "Lemon ... and basil, right?"

"Right," she said. "Gives a hint of savory to the sweetness."

"I love it," I said. "Well, I'd better get back to my peeps. See you later."

I left with the cocktail and spotted Nigel Dashwood talking with William Buttersby. They disappeared around the other side of a meat-pie tent, so I sidled up close to them but out of sight, wondering what they could be talking about.

The only words I heard were "Virginia Woolf" before they moved away, and I almost dropped the drink.

I turned around and rushed the cocktail back to Neil, and he had a sip. "Really good. And pretty. Learn anything?"

"Not exactly. No one seemed interested in talking. But I just overheard William and Nigel talking about Virginia Woolf."

"You're kidding. Did they mention the missing book?"

I shrugged. "It's all I could hear without getting right out in the open and following them."

"Could be a coincidence," Neil said, but he sounded worried.

"We just have to play this thing out. And pin down Alastair and Ari later. Maybe tonight we can hit the Tipple. We're not working, are we? I've lost track."

He chuckled. "No. We'll have our hands full cleaning this up. I thought we might take the rest of the day off. Are you available?"

"Me?" I looked around at the others, who were talking about what other movie casts they might've dressed up as.

Neil shrugged. "Might be a good way to see if anyone approaches us. We can stop at Mark's, check in to see if he's learned anything, drop off our stuff, then head into the city. Wrap up the evening at The Dandy Tipple."

With Ari?

No, Pepper. With you.

I tried to tell myself that, anyway.

Chapter Nineteen

Once our group had broken down our garden-party bar, packed up, taken the shuttle back to Mark's and changed out of our "Do-Re-Mi" clothes, it was time for some fun. I went with a comfy outfit for our jaunt—loose black pants, a pale blue-green knit top the color of my eyes, the usual bracelet, cocktail shaker earrings and comfy boots, along with a black wool blazer. I left my hair loose; my scalp needed a rest after I'd pinned up my locks during our gig this afternoon. It was getting long. Might be time for a haircut.

Mark begged off to attend to business but said he'd try to meet us later at The Dandy Tipple. Albert and Ben flipped a coin to see who would take our crew into the heart of the city, and Albert ended up driving us again in the unglamorous shuttle, which had bus-style seating.

Neil looked yummy in jeans, a crisp, open-collar white shirt and a dark gray sport jacket. No tie, for once. "I'm going to pick Albert's brain," I whispered to him as we got underway.

"Don't hurt him," Neil joked, and I punched him gently in the arm before moving up front, hearing a chortle in my wake.

"Hey, Albert. Do you like to read?" I asked our driver after sitting in the seat behind him. "I'm looking for a good novel about London to read while I'm here. Any era."

"Oh, I'm not much of a fiction reader," he said as he navigated heavy traffic. "I like my World War II history. I could recommend a good book about Winston Churchill, if ye like?"

"Not really what I'm looking for. You mean you don't like novels at all? Like—" Oh, what could I pick that wasn't so obvious but was still in Mark's collection? *"The Lord of the Rings?"*

"Oh, I like the films very much."

Not the response I wanted. "What about James Bond?"

"I like those films, too. Sean Connery's tops, if you ask me."

I barely restrained my eye roll. Also, put me on the record as being a willing Bond Girl for Daniel Craig. "Ever read anything by Virginia Woolf?"

"Woolf." He seemed to ponder for a moment. "Any relation to Tom Wolfe?"

"No. At least I don't think so."

"You might talk to Ben. He'll have a recommendation for ye. Always reading. Carries around a book all the time."

"OK. I'll do that. Thanks."

"Sure thing, miss."

I headed back to my seat next to Neil. "I don't think he's our guy."

"What do you mean?"

"He has no idea who Virginia Woolf is."

"Maybe he's faking."

"Let's just say I think we need to keep our appointment at Buttersby Books tomorrow."

Meanwhile, the bartenders argued over which cocktail bar to hit first while Gina looked on in amusement.

"If we go to all of these," I said of the list Barclay had started on his phone, "I won't get to do my touristy stuff. And I definitely want to go to Westminster Abbey."

"How about we compromise?" Neil suggested, pointing to a name on the list. "This hotel bar is supposed to be fantastic. It's near the Abbey. We can get a drink, then we can split up and do our own thing."

Albert dropped us off in front of a swank old hotel. Maybe starting a long walk through the city with a cocktail in my belly wasn't the best idea, but it was a beautiful classic gin cocktail. The bow-tied bartender served the Clover Club—a lovely pink with raspberries on a silver pick resting across the egg-white foam on top—in a graceful coupe glass. The art-deco decor didn't hurt, and the hotel lobby's massive chandelier was nothing less than stunning, made of crystal drops that together formed a huge suspended sphere.

While my happy friends made plans to hit their next spot, Neil looked at me. "Shall we go look at the dead poets?"

I grinned. "Absolutely."

Westminster Abbey hosted grand royal weddings, but I wanted to see it for its graves. Specifically, all the famous writers and other folks buried or memorialized there. And I wasn't disappointed. I talked Neil into saving the Poets' Corner for last, after we'd had our eyeballs stuffed with glorious architecture, mysterious tombs, exquisite carvings, brilliant stained glass, and enough statues to populate a small town.

"I can't believe all the famous people who are buried here," I said as we gazed at carved names and effigies.

"Or memorialized. It's not all bodies."

"But Chaucer is buried here. Spenser. Isaac Newton—talk about gravity."

Neil chuckled. "No bartenders, though."

"Oh my gosh. Look who it is." While sculpted figures looked down on us from elaborate niches in the walls, practically under our feet was a black stone etched with the name and crucial dates for Charles Dickens.

Neil bent over the big rectangle set in the floor. "I would say he's been watching us, but it's clear he's been here for some time."

"Not a bad place to end up."

"It was totally against his wishes. His family got talked into it. At least that's what I read."

I looked at Neil in surprise. "What was he hiding from?"

"I think he just didn't like the fuss. But he put a lot of energy into protecting the identity of his mistress, so that might have been part of it. He wanted to appear as the upstanding example of Victorian morality that the English thought him to be."

I shook my head. "I wonder how many other secrets are buried with him."

"You'd think a man who wrote so many words wouldn't have any, but time obscures a lot." Neil gently elbowed me. "Want to walk? I'd like to see Big Ben."

"As long as Mr. Mixy isn't still there," I said to Neil's laugh. "Oh, and I want to ride the Eye. Can we? Can we?"

"You read my mind. We might hit it right at twilight."

As we turned to go, a sudden movement caught my eye. I twisted around, but nothing was there.

Ghosts? I shivered and leaned a little into Neil. He slipped an arm around my shoulders as we headed for the exit, but let it fall once we got outside.

It was a short walk past Big Ben to the Westminster Bridge. We paused there to watch boats on the Thames and hear the chiming of the clock tower over Parliament. Throngs of tourists wielding selfie sticks seemed oblivious to anything but themselves.

And again I thought I saw an unusual movement in the crowd—not the stroll of a casual tourist but a furtive dash and concealment. Definitely concealment, because I couldn't find the figure again. I was pretty sure they wore a dark hoodie, though, and were shadowing us.

"Neil?"

"Yeah?" He looked so content leaning on the stone railing, gazing out over the river.

"I think someone might be following us."

"Really?" He casually stood, turned and leaned back against the rail, looking around. "If it's anyone really dangerous, the cops will be all over them. They've had terror attacks here."

"Not a happy thought."

"Come on. Let's go to the Eye. And we'll keep our eyes peeled."

"I suppose they can't get to us up there." I looked beyond the bridge and down the other bank of the river to where the towering Ferris wheel spun slowly against the sky. The clouds eased from white into lavender and pink as we headed that way.

"Oh, crap, look at the line." I squinted as we got closer and took in the crowd.

"That's where my extreme thoughtfulness comes in," Neil said. "I got us Fast Track tickets."

"You did? What does that mean?"

"We enter the fast lane, of course." He answered my grin, and I hugged him. Then realized I probably shouldn't have and disentangled myself, my face hot.

He was still smiling as he led me through the access point. Soon we strolled onto an enclosed pod—and we moved fast, as it never stopped on its slow glide past the platform. The curved walls were all windows, like something out of a science-fiction movie. The pod was maybe two or three times the size of the Angry Orange, my small car at home. About twenty other tourists joined us, but it was roomy enough. I rushed to the far side to get the best view over the river.

Neil slipped up behind me, and as the car slowly moved forward and then up, the city of London spread out before us. The bridge lights were just coming on. Headlights streamed in the dark rivers of the streets. The Thames glistened, dark green with a sheen of pink borrowed from the sky.

"Oh, look!" I pointed. The clock face of Big Ben had just lit up, glowing golden, with green and red lights accenting the tower. Amid the historic buildings, skyscrapers shone. And on the many cranes over the skyline, red lights blinked. I looked back and below us at the next car rising like a giant egg. And sucked in a breath.

"What is it?" Neil put a hand on my shoulder and looked out.

"You're going to think I'm crazy."

"I already think you're crazy."

I laughed. "Shut up. I think that the person of interest might be in the next car."

"Shut up," he whispered in good humor, but he scanned the pod, too. A shadowy figure in a dark hoodie stood by the windows, looking up at us, but when they spotted our interest, they whirled and moved to the other side of the car.

"Who is that?"

"No idea."

"Well, if this isn't the dumbest, slowest chase ever," I said. "We're going to be on this thing, what?"

"Thirty minutes. No use worrying."

"Thirty minutes. And you're right. Thirty minutes of magic. I'm not going to let them ruin it for us."

"Even if we are imagining things," he said. I whirled to face him, and he shrugged at my surprised expression. "You have to admit, it seems a little unlikely that someone is following us around London."

"Not if we're getting close to something we're not supposed to get close to."

"Like this?" He stepped closer to me.

I looked up at him, at his blue-gray eyes in the soft twilight. I'd thought he was joking, but now I wasn't so sure. "Are you not supposed to ... get close?" *Did the temperature just spike in here?*

"Not if you and Mark have reached some kind of understanding."

I chuckled. "Does my life look like a Jane Austen novel to you? There's no 'understanding.'"

"That's good. Because it's been driving me insane watching you with him." He reached up and casually shifted my messenger bag so it was slung behind my back.

And then he stepped closer still, slipped a warm hand behind my neck and another around my waist, pressed into me and slanted his mouth over mine.

Omigod. My lips burned and parted under his heat. *Neil is kissing me!* And this was a really good kiss, way different from our hormone-driven moments in New Orleans. I wasn't saying hormones weren't involved here, too, but there was a lot of water under the bridge, and I didn't mean the Thames.

I slid my arms around his waist, melting into him.

When he released me, I stepped back, a little dizzy, and looked around. *Where am I again? Oh, yeah.* Our car had made considerable progress toward the sky, and all of London was laid out before us. I looked up at Neil, who almost seemed taken aback, like he hadn't planned it either.

"Wow," I breathed.

"That's a good reaction." He pushed his fingers through my mussed hair, and the corner of his mouth hitched up in a shy little smile.

I tried to catch my breath. "Is this a one-time thing? Because I thought you were going to hook up with Ari or something." I slapped a hand over my mouth.

He chuckled and stepped back, turning me toward the window and draping an arm around my shoulder. "Now you *are* imagining things. And you think too much."

Nothing like the thinker in our group telling me I thought too much. But I had a lot to think about. For now, I just enjoyed Neil's arm around me and basked in the panoramic view of the city. We watched the twilight deepen, London's lights like a carpet of stars as our pod crested its arc and began the slow descent.

Some kind of kids' group in matching green T-shirts filled the car in front of ours, and they waved at us, grinning. I waved back, and I could practically hear their giggles as they turned to each other, chattering.

"We are probably not what they expected to see on their field trip," I joked. "Maybe we should see what our other friend is up to."

"No. I don't want to think about all that for the next ten minutes. How often does a moment like this come along?"

Ten minutes. Would that be the end of it? A romantic moment in the sky above London, and then we'd go back to our carefully distant lives? We probably had to keep it professional while we were here.

Geez, listen to me. Keep it professional—ha! How long have you wanted this? But his mixed signals up till now still had me confused. Maybe that kiss had been a spontaneous outburst, nothing more. I bet people kissed spontaneously all the time in the Eye. This view was pure aphrodisiac.

So I took a deep breath, watched the world spin below us and enjoyed the moment. Mostly.

OK, maybe I did think too much. But I had time to figure this out, whatever "this" was. I'd waited this long. I didn't need to rush it.

"Let's hurry," Neil suddenly said, releasing me and practically pushing me off the car as we spun in slow motion past the platform again. "Let's see if we can lose them."

Chapter Twenty

"Let's take a detour through the park," Neil suggested. "Maybe it will throw off our shadow."

But his notion hurt us more than helped when we ran into a large crowd. Shoulder to shoulder, people blocked our way as they watched a busker do the limbo under a pole that sat about a foot off the ground. While loud rap music played, he performed in the glow cast by a bright lantern that flashed multiple colors. The island of brilliance in the darkness just made it harder to see as we pushed our way through the audience. I hugged my bag tight and endured multiple bumps as I tried to look in all directions at once, then breathed a huge sigh of relief when we escaped.

We spun back toward the Thames and hurried along the South Bank of the river.

"Well, that sucked," I said.

"Sorry about that. Are you all right?"

"I think so. Just a little cold." I took a deep breath and willed the tension to leave my neck and shoulders as we walked. The wind had picked up. I stuck my hands in my blazer pockets to warm them.

And froze.

Neil took a second to realize I'd stopped. He halted and spun around, a worried look on his face. "Pepper?" He reached me in three long strides, grabbed my shoulders and looked into my eyes. "What is it?"

I pulled my hand from my pocket, holding the piece of paper I'd found there. "Something's in my pocket," I whispered.

He took a second to process what I said. "Something you didn't put there?"

I nodded, then forced myself to look down at the folded paper in my hand. "Guess I should open it, huh?"

"Maybe it's just an ad for something?" Neil suggested. "Or something you forgot."

I looked around to make sure no one scary lurked nearby, then unfolded the paper. It was maybe five by eight inches and not much to look at, though one edge was ragged as if it had been torn from a notebook.

Its words, written in block letters in plain blue ink, chilled me even more than the biting breeze.

You'd make a lovely corpse.
Death is as cheap as darkness.
Walk away and live.

I started shaking, and Neil snatched the paper from my hand, scanning it. Then he looked around, wrapped an arm around me and pulled me along. "I think you're right. About being followed."

"I know."

"I don't see anyone around us now. Do you?"

His arm around me calmed me, and I focused on his warmth and the fact that nothing had really happened to me. Just a little death threat, that's all. I looked around, too. "I don't think so. Maybe they delivered the message there in the crowd and let us be."

"I suppose the good news is that they could've harmed us. Instead they warned us."

I looked at him askance. "That's the good news?"

Neil's eyebrows peaked in the middle. "I'm trying here."

Suddenly, I laughed. "You make me feel better. I mean, in spite of someone wanting to kill me."

"They probably want to kill me, too," Neil said dryly.

I smiled. And looked around some more. Maybe we were in the clear—for now. "We'll have to be careful."

"Very."

My stomach grumbled. "Do you think we can grab something to eat and hide from Jack the Ripper, too?"

Neil seemed to relax a little. "Let's hope it's not Jack the Ripper, and yeah, I think we can. Just keep your eyes open."

"I'm never closing my eyes again."

He snorted. "Here, let's grab a burger."

"Not very English," I managed to joke, but we grabbed thick burgers from a stall and ate as we walked. There was a lot of dripping.

"Messy," I said, awkwardly wiping my mouth with a napkin.

"But good."

The food made me feel better. Our shadow had made a threat, but they hadn't made good on it. And what did they mean, anyway? "So I guess someone thinks we're a problem?"

"I guess so. Maybe we should stop asking about Mark's books."

"What kind of book thief is a killer? I don't think we should stop."

"Pepper." Neil's tone was grim. "I don't want anything to happen to you."

"And I don't want anything to happen to you. But I feel for Mark. Not just the thefts and the money, but that book he got from his dad? He needs that back. It means something."

Neil shook his head. But he didn't outright object. "We'll talk to him."

"OK. Maybe tonight. Are we heading to The Tipple?"

"I want to make another stop first. Make sure we've lost our tail."

"Oooh, you sound so Nick Charles when you talk like that." I loved the *Thin Man* movies.

He snorted. "I'm not going to be a 'thin man' if I eat any more of these burgers."

We finished them, tossed the wrappers in a waste bin and crossed Waterloo Bridge, where it would've been really hard for any lurkers to hide, then turned left. My optimism snuck back into my soul. We were OK. I had friends who would help me. And we were in wonderful, magical London.

"The Strand!" I said. "Sounds so grand. Gawd, I'm such a tourist."

"Enjoy it. We're about to get a treat."

When we came upon the Savoy Hotel, my awe was complete. This was where Harry Craddock made his reputation in the 1920s, at the American Bar.

But Neil steered us toward the Savoy's Beaufort Bar, an exquisite art-deco room in black and gold and accents of soft warm light, filled with happy chatter and live piano music. And there was nowhere for a hoodied figure to hide.

"Both bars are wonderful, but there's something about this room that makes me think I'm F. Scott Fitzgerald," he said to my chuckle.

There were many people here who were glamorous or wealthy or both. I figured we could get by on our cocktail IQs. We settled at the bar, where a clean-cut mixologist in a dark vest and white shirt handed us a menu.

"A little more vodka than I remember," Neil murmured as he scanned it.

"Scandalous. I think we have to order something with gin, don't you?"

"Or champagne." He gestured to the big golden bowl on the bar, frosty with condensation, that held five bottles.

My eyes bugged out at the prices. "It's going to cost you to get drunk here."

"This is one occasion where I don't mind dipping into my reserves," Neil said. "One for the road. My treat."

Oh, yeah. Neil did have reserves. His grandfather, a wily old treasure hunter, had helped set up Neil in his bar, paid for his school and more. This familial fund gave Neil an edge that I didn't have, so I gratefully accepted his offer and ordered a Hanky Panky. "Signature drink of the female bartender who trained Craddock, if I remember right," I explained.

"Nice!" Neil loved a good factoid. "Ada Coleman, wasn't it?"

"Smarty pants."

"And you, sir?" the bartender asked.

Neil cited a cocktail I'd never heard of.

"What's that?" I asked when the mixologist stepped away to work his magic.

"You didn't see it on the menu? Good. I'll make you guess."

When the drinks arrived, graceful in elegant stemware, I tried Neil's first. "Gin, obviously. I saw him add the champagne. A tad bitter ... is that rhubarb?"

"Bravo." He took it back and took a sip. "Not a starter cocktail, that's for sure."

I sipped my Hanky Panky, which had just the right balance of bitter and friendly gin botanicals. "I could get used to this."

"Mmm. Sometimes I have dreams about the walls here."

"What?" I looked at him funny.

"Oh, you don't know the story? Craddock buried cocktail time capsules of some of the most popular drinks in the walls here— shakers with a martini, a Manhattan and so on. No one's found them yet."

"Talk about an aged cocktail."

Our idyll soon ended, and I left on a cloud, and on Neil's arm.

He dipped further into his reserves and grabbed us a sleek black cab to get to The Dandy Tipple, as I confessed to creeping fatigue, enhanced by the stress of the note. He had to be exhausted, too, given he slept even less than I did and got up to do cocktail prep this morning.

I startled awake on his shoulder as the cab wrenched to a stop. The Hanky Panky had relaxed me a little too much, but the catnap refreshed me just enough to want another drink. Neil paid with a card, and we climbed out onto the sidewalk.

We paused outside The Dandy Tipple. Its windows glowed, and rock music leaked out through the doors. The adjacent souvenir shop where I'd bought my trinkets was mostly dark, but at the jewelry store on the other side of the bar, spotlights glowed on gleaming bracelets, rings and necklaces behind thick glass window displays embedded in the walls. There was a picture window, too, showing a subtly lit interior that looked bulletproof. A very posh jewelers, as the Brits might say.

Inside the old gin palace, The Dandy Tipple buzzed with the buzzed—gin festival folks as well as random revelers. Alastair and Ari worked the bar, and the Bohemia Bartenders and Cray gathered around a couple of tables pushed together. I was among my people again. Everything was going to be all right.

We called out greetings, and Neil and I headed to the bar.

"Hey, Alastair," I said. "How about a classic gin and tonic?"

He pushed his floppy blond hair off his forehead. "My G&Ts are always classic. But I'm going to have Ari make it."

She dimpled. "No problem." Then she turned her pretty gaze to Neil. "And what can I get you?" Implied was "gin ... and me?"

Or maybe I was a tad bit paranoid.

"A G&T sounds fine to me." He leaned against the bar.

"All right. It'll take a few minutes." She nodded over at the Bohemia Bartenders. "I'm still working on your crew's latest round."

"I like watching you," Neil said.

My head snapped around to look at him.

And then Mark came in the door.

"Hello, hello!" There were more happy greetings—Mark was

winning a lot of friends this weekend—before he approached us. "How was your ramble? See anything interesting?"

"Westminster Abbey and other cool stuff." I didn't want to mention the London Eye because I didn't want to betray what had happened between Neil and me. Though I did want to tell Mark about our tail and the note and ask about Alastair's cellar without anyone else hearing. "Excuse me a moment?" I said to Neil.

He nodded, his eyes darkening as I gestured to Mark to join me at the end of the bar. I pointed at Alastair and crooked my finger at him as well.

In a moment, we'd gathered there, Mark and I on one side, Alastair on the other.

Alastair didn't look happy. "Do you want another cocktail already?"

"Very funny. I want to know about your latest vault break-in."

"So do I," Mark said. "It slipped my mind with everything else going on."

"Oh, that." Alastair dropped the attitude, and his forehead creased. "I got here early this morning to make sure we were stocked for all the gin fiends this weekend and found the vault gate lock undone."

"You'd never found it that way before?" I asked.

"No."

"Maybe you caught someone by surprise," Mark said.

"Maybe, though there's only one stairway in and out of there. I suppose someone could have heard me coming in, hid, then slipped out when I wasn't looking. But that again points to staff. I just don't see it."

"Somebody could've just forgotten to lock it," I noted. "But aren't you the only one with a key?"

"Clearly not. I suppose someone copied it or reverse-engineered the lock."

"No chance you left it open?" I asked.

Alastair glowered. "Of course not."

Mark raised an eyebrow at him, a subtle warning to play nice. "You said this morning that bottles were missing?"

Alastair nodded. "A handful of very nice bottles. The kind of thing that goes for a pretty penny online."

"No clues?" I asked.

"You're welcome to look." He pulled a key ring from his pocket, popped one off and handed it to me. "I'm busy." Then he moved back down the bar to take care of a new customer—*whoa, no.* Mr. Mixy!

"And how are you doing, Ms. Revelle?" Mark's tone was warm and flirty, and he looked yummy in a chocolate-brown sweater. He still prompted a giddy reaction in me, but I had an equal and opposite force pulling me away from him now.

"Very well, Mr. Fairman. I have more to tell you, but do you mind if we look at the vault first? I'd like to grab Neil."

"Don't trust me in cellars, eh?"

I couldn't help a smile. "I just want Neil's input, that's all." I turned and gestured to Neil. He saw me—probably because he'd been staring—and moved down the bar. "We're going to check out the vault and see if we can get any ideas about Alastair's bottle thief. You game?"

"Sure." Neil's tone was cool. "Ari said our drinks will be a couple more minutes anyway."

In a minute, we were behind the *Staff Only* door and headed down the stone steps. The dank smell rose up to meet us. Mark hit the light switches at the bottom, and I handed him the key, figuring that as part-owner, he was more familiar with the lock—now secured—than I was.

"What I'm worried about is that it almost has to be one of the bar staff," Mark said, unhooking the lock and opening the cellar gate. "I hate to see this happen."

I wandered through, noticing gaps on the shelves where I'd seen the finer liquor bottles last time we were in here. "I think you're right. This isn't casual sipping of the good stuff or a wayward customer. They've escalated to theft."

"And theft is about one of two things," Neil said. "Money—or possession. Were the missing bottles all that collectible?"

Mark contemplated the half-empty top-tier shelf. "From what I recall, no. But pricey and drinkable. My guess is they're going to sell what they stole."

"So now we scour sites online? Message boards? That kind of thing?" I asked.

"By the time the bottles get there," Neil said, "they'll probably have passed through multiple hands."

"Maybe. Mark?"

"Yes, darling Pepper?"

I caught Neil's scowl and winced before I asked my question. "Do you think the same thief who's ripping off The Dandy Tipple has something to do with your books?"

Mark looked over at me, his eyes wide. "Well, that would complicate things."

"Or make it simpler," Neil said. "If it's someone who needs money, who has access to both your estate and the bar, we could narrow down the suspects a lot."

"Unless it's some kind of uber-collector like you, Mark," I teased.

"Ha ha." His smile was a little sad. "What a depressing thought, to think it really is someone I know."

I wandered deeper under the stone arches that supported the space, into the shadows. And heard a squeak. "Ew!"

"What?" both men said at once.

"I—I think it might've been a rat."

Mark shook his head. "I told Alastair to set traps. I don't know where they're coming in."

"Must be a hole somewhere. Maybe where they used to load in the gin barrels?" Neil wandered toward me, and I relaxed. I didn't actually see the rat, and it was probably more afraid of me than I was of it.

"The old load-in point is along the street wall," Mark said. "It's all been blocked in, but there may be gaps. We'll check it out."

Neil had come up beside me. "What's down there?"

He pointed to an especially dark shadow in one of the deeper recesses of the cellar, at the back of the alcove with all the old junk I'd seen last time. We both advanced to look closer.

I squinted, rummaged in my messenger bag till I found a small flashlight—brighter than anything my phone could provide—and turned it on. "Does that look—"

"Like someone's been digging?" Neil asked.

Chapter Twenty-One

"**D**igging?" Mark asked in alarm.

The junk in the recess in The Dandy Tipple's vaults was piled in such a way that it obscured the irregular hole in the stone wall. In fact, stones didn't comprise the wall back here. Bricks did. Some of the bricks sitting in the hole looked loose, and several bricks lay about, as if someone had been in the middle of putting them back to conceal the gap when they were interrupted. The wall was several bricks thick, so busting through it must've been a big job.

Mark came up behind us. "What the hell?"

He and Neil stepped up and pulled more of the loose bricks away. The hole extended maybe eight feet beyond the thick brick barrier into a small space with brick walls.

"Are those more holes in the walls?" I asked.

"Niches, I think. Secret storage?" Mark surmised.

The space had a handful of niches on either side, lined in old brick. They were empty.

"If anything was stored in here, it's gone now," Neil said as we peered inside.

I shined my light beyond to the far wall, where a shovel and pickaxe lay on the floor. It appeared someone had tried to make a dent in the bricks there but hadn't gotten very far.

"Mark," I said. "What's beyond that wall?"

He looked at it closely, then sucked in a breath. "I do believe it's the jewelers."

"Holy hell," Neil said.

"Holy heist movie, Batman," I added.

Neil looked at me. "I think you're mixing your movie metaphors."

"So the stolen bottles are incidental to a larger plot?" Mark asked.

"Or stolen by someone else?" I asked.

"This is crazy," Neil said. "If the digger, whoever they are, ultimately wants to break into the jewelry store, I doubt they're also raiding your library."

I stepped back so the guys could retreat and have space to stand up straight. "Plus, these kinds of thefts don't really work, do they? I mean, except on TV."

"I know a little about alarm systems, given my collections," Mark said. "Vibration sensors would be de rigueur for high-end jewelry displays like they have next door. Digital locks are common. A burglar would have to have all that figured out before digging their way in. You can't just dig through a wall and steal all the jewels without triggering alarms."

"They've obviously been working on this for a while to get through that thick wall," I said. "They're determined. Maybe they have it all figured out. I don't think this secret room was a casual discovery."

"Bloody hell," Mark said. "We're going to need much better locks until we figure this out, and Alastair's going to have to control access a lot more tightly."

"Maybe you shouldn't do that just yet," I said. "Now that we know someone's digging down here, maybe we let them continue. Set a trap?"

"If it's the book thief, we might catch them tomorrow at William Buttersby's shop," Neil reminded me.

"I'll give you a day before I unleash the knights and secure the portcullis," Mark said dryly, "but I can't afford to let someone get into my neighbor's shop. I'll need to get some professional security in here. Rats indeed."

I wasn't offended, exactly. We hadn't made much progress. But all of Mark's professional security hadn't stopped his library thief. In fact, the thief had used the high-tech hidden door to access and steal the books.

"That sounds fair," Neil said. "We're not going to be in London much longer anyway. But we'll do our best."

"I appreciate your help," Mark said. "And now that I know the weaknesses in the library, I'm sure I can put a halt to those thefts as well."

Mark secured the lock, and we returned to the bar. He gave Alastair the key and had a quiet word with him—I'd never seen Alastair's eyebrows lift that high—and Neil and I returned to Ari's station.

She reached down below and brought up the highball glasses, glistening with condensation. "I kept them in the fridge for you. Getting a tour?"

"Oh, Mark's talking to Alastair about storing some of his surplus wine in the vaults," Neil said casually. "He wanted us to take a look at it." He took a sip and smiled. "Delicious. Thanks."

Oh, my. I never knew Neil was such a glib liar. But he wasn't lying about the cocktail. Ari's gin and tonic was perfect.

I thanked her, and we headed over to join the crowd. Another table had been added so we could spread out. And everyone turned and shouted greetings as Ben arrived with Nigel and Lottie.

"Your driver is finally here," Mark remarked loud enough for all to hear.

"We're in no hurry!" Melody said, grinning at Ben. She always had an eye for cute guys. Especially cute guys with accents.

"Am I really late?" Ben looked concerned. "Nigel and Lottie called and asked if I was driving, so I gave them a lift."

"Which we very much appreciate," Lottie said as they took a

seat amid the bartenders and next to Cray. She was bright and energetic and snappily dressed, as was her wont. Nigel looked a bit
sleepier than usual.

Ben hung his jacket over a chair next to Melody, beamed a
sunny smile at her, and took a seat. Luke, on her other side,
narrowed his eyes at the newcomer.

"You're not too late," Mark said. "Fortunately, these lushes have
only just gotten started."

"Ari!" Ben called out to her. "Driver's special!"

She nodded, obviously familiar with his request, and in a few
minutes, a server brought him a club soda with lime and took more
orders.

I walked over and said hello to the drinkers at the far end of the
table. "I'm almost surprised to see you here after this afternoon's
indulgence," I said to Lottie and Nigel.

"Oh, we're professionals," Nigel said, and I laughed.

"Of course he can say that," she said. "He took a nap while I
went shopping."

"We all cope in our own way." He ordered a Corpse Reviver No.
2 from a passing server.

Interesting. Lottie was out and about earlier. Or maybe Nigel
was, too, and she didn't know it, since she thought he was napping.
Did either of them own a hoodie? It didn't seem like their usual
fashion, but one didn't dress up to go stalking.

Neil and I took chairs next to each other at the other end of the
table, leaving the only empty chair between Ben and Mr. Mixy. So
that's where Mark sat.

Which left me next to Mr. Mixy. Again. What had I done to
deserve this?

*Universe, don't answer that question. I'm trying to be a good girl. I'm
much better than I used to be, anyway.*

"Pepper, I have news," Mr. Mixy confided.

I took a sip of my drink. "You've found a sponsor for your beard?"

"I'm in talks with Bristlebutt's Beard Oil about that. But no, something else."

Now I had an image in my mind that might never be erased. "You're going home?" That would be good news for me, anyway.

"Not yet." He paused for drama. "The evidence is in. I am, for sure and true, *royalty!*" His hazel eyes shone brightly, and he took a brisk sip of his red cocktail that left disturbing vampiric droplets on his facial hair.

My gin and tonic, on top of the Savoy cocktail and the nice warm feeling of having Neil next to me, mellowed me out, so I played along. "What kind of royalty?" Maybe he had an ancestor who was king of one of those fake countries where all the princes come from in Hallmark movies.

Mr. Mixy looked around as if he were trying to keep a secret, but he didn't lower his voice. He loved attention too much. *"English* royalty, of course. My genealogist is confirming it with a rush DNA test and thinks he can get me the paperwork by tomorrow night. I just sent him twenty-five hundred for the rush job."

I blinked and gulped another sip. "And then what? Do they name a battleship after you?"

"Maybe a pub," Neil interjected.

Mr. Mixy shook his head. "My guy says there's an ancestral castle or something that my line is heir to. I mean, I doubt they'll work me right into the rotation on royal appearances, but I feel sure I can get a cut of the treasury, maybe a crown jewel or two."

Neil made snuffling noises next to me.

"Did I hear you say you're royalty?" Mark interjected with a face so serious, he had to be joking.

"That's what my guy tells me," Mr. Mixy said.

"And who is this guy?" Ben asked.

Mr. Mixy, realizing he had the audience he sought, relaxed into his new role as royal scion and warmed to his topic. "His company is called Bespoke Genealogy."

I tried not to laugh. Of course it was bespoke. It had to be made up.

"I've heard of them!" Ben said. "They have a great reputation. In fact, some members of my family had them do some work. Fascinating results. We're not royalty, of course."

I sat upright. Dear God. Could Mr. Mixy actually be royalty?

"Aren't they great?" Mr. Mixy exclaimed. "I can't wait to get the final results."

"Well done, mate," Ben said.

Mark and Neil exchanged a look. I closed my eyes and drained my G&T. Mr. Mixy would be, what? Sir Mix-a-Lot was already taken. The Duke of Mixy? *And don't forget, he's writing a book.*

I put down my empty glass. "I need another drink. Do they do French 75s here?"

Neil looked amused. "I'll get you one." He headed for the bar.

"Oh, Mark. I almost forgot." I used my head to indicate he should sit in Neil's chair, and Mark came over wearing a delighted expression. I whispered in his ear. "Somebody was following Neil and me tonight. I'm thinking our chatter about finding the book thief has someone worried. I—I found a threatening note in my pocket."

His flirty expression immediately darkened. "What happened?"

"Just a poetic little death threat," I murmured as our whispered back-and-forth continued.

"That's not good. You don't have to do this, you know."

"They've pissed me off, so I think I do."

"I do admire you," he whispered in my ear, "but I worry about you, too. They might be more than a book thief. You'd best watch yourselves. Did they look familiar?"

I returned, "Not really. I couldn't even tell if it was a man or a woman. Kind of an average build, wearing a big, dark hooded sweatshirt."

"Be careful, darling Pepper," he whispered into my ear. And

then I felt him pause there and sniff my neck. "What a lovely shampoo."

The sound of a throat clearing had us both jumping and looking up. Neil stood there holding my drink, his eyes flashing lightning.

Chapter Twenty-Two

I felt guilty all of a sudden, with Mark sniffing my neck and Neil looming over me like the Count of Monte Cristo on a bender. I hadn't done anything wrong. I was the sniffee. And could I help it if Mark's voice went straight to my girly parts?

"Excuse me," Mark said, getting up and returning to his seat—no, not his seat, but the chair on the other side of Ben, who'd moved a spot closer to Mr. Mixy. The two chatted happily about genealogy, oblivious to our little drama.

Neil settled into his chair and set the French 75 down without a word.

So I put a hand on his knee—his eyebrows lifted—and leaned in to whisper in his ear. "I told Mark about the tail. I didn't want anyone else to hear."

Now Neil bent close to whisper in my ear. But he didn't whisper. He just pressed a little kiss on my neck right there.

I sucked in a gasp as he sat up nonchalantly and sipped his gin and tonic. I looked around to see if anyone had noticed.

The only person looking at us, miraculously, was Cray at the other end of the table. His pale blue eyes twinkled, and he lifted a glass.

I began to realize that if Neil and I really got together, *everybody* was going to be up in our business.

I sipped my cocktail. *Ah.* It brought me right back to New Orleans: lemon, gin, champagne.

"If you need a few bucks to pay for the genealogy research," Ben was telling Mr. Mixy, "I've got an in at the racetrack."

"Horses?" Mr. Mixy said.

"I'm quite a follower of the races. Let me know if I can help you out with a tip."

"Excellent!"

"I thought you lost the last time you bet," came Ari's voice over my shoulder. She pulled up a chair, and I slid over. *Ha, now she's next to Mr. Mixy.*

Ben looked startled. "Oh, Ari. You spooked me. I win more than I lose."

"Everyone loses sometime," Mr. Mixy said.

"On a break?" Neil asked her. She nodded. "Think Alastair will have a cow if I go back there and make you a drink?"

"Oh, I'd like to see him have a cow." She smiled broadly, and Neil left the table.

It wasn't like Neil to toy with me. Was he toying with me? Or just being the gallant guy he was?

After we chatted for a few minutes about the festival, I turned to Ari. "How'd you end up working here?" *Know thine enemy. Er, frenemy.*

"Oh, the usual way. I studied literature at university."

I laughed along with everyone else nearby. "So of course you ended up at a bar where Dickens drank."

She lifted one shoulder, then smiled as Neil appeared with a cocktail in hand. He handed it to her. "Tuxedo No. 2."

I could sniff out the absinthe rinse in the classic Craddock gin drink from here.

"Thank you," she said to Neil, then slowly moved her gaze around to Ben as she spoke. "The Dickens connection is just a bonus, though I don't know if I like the idea of being connected to Dickens."

"Not this again," Ben said. "He was a great guy."

"Not to his wife."

"He never divorced her," Ben answered. "He supported her even though ... you know."

"And ordered their children not to live with her," Ari said. "At least I had the privilege of divorcing my cheating spouse."

"Oooh, I'm sorry to hear about that," I said, genuinely sympathetic. I'd only had the cheating boyfriend many years ago, who happened to be sitting right next to me looking like a fountain of hair, but I knew the feeling. "It seems like you know a lot about Dickens."

"Educational hazard when you study English literature," she said. "The more I learned, the less I liked him. He was such a hypocrite. Posing as this Victorian paragon of virtue when he'd tucked his mistress out of sight and pretended she was like a daughter to him. Kind of disgusting, actually."

"Don't be that way," Ben said. "He was just a man, take him for all in all."

"Shakespeare. Don't get me started on him," Ari said to more laughs.

"So Dickens had a mistress, left his wife, but stayed married?" I asked.

"Some of his writer friends had mistresses too, according to the biography I read," Neil said, "but they didn't make a big deal about keeping their affairs a secret."

"That's right," Ari said. "He would've loved a divorce, but it didn't fit his image, and he was obsessed with Nelly. Hid her away in France for some time, then in England. Got her pregnant."

"A couple of his children said the baby died," Ben murmured into his club soda.

"How horribly sad." I looked at the bubbles in my French 75, thinking back to things I'd overheard my parents talking about when I was a kid, learning my mother had had a baby before me—before marriage and her dive into religion—and gave up the infant.

Ari sipped her cocktail and shot a sultry glance of appreciation at Neil. "Did you know Dickens was in a terrible train wreck coming back from France with Nelly? She was injured, and he pretended not to know her to protect his secret."

"I can't imagine doing anything so ... duplicitous," Neil said.

"Quite so," Ari said.

"Can't you?" Ben lifted an eyebrow at her.

"Happiness lies in truth," Ari replied to him, then her expression relaxed as she warmed to her topic. "Of course, back then, women were judged more harshly than they are now. Marginally, anyway."

I had to chuckle at that. It was funny because it was true.

Ari smiled. "Nelly was in an impossible position, much worse than Dickens ever was, and she probably couldn't imagine telling the truth, especially when she was connected to such a revered man. People wanted to believe he was great and pure; they would have crucified her. So after he died, she pretended to everyone she was just a child when she knew him, that the affair never happened. Even the children she had with the man she married later didn't know about the true nature of the relationship until she died. And I have to respect her desire to keep it quiet, especially as critics over the years have accused her of all kinds of things while leaving Dickens blameless."

"You have to admit," Ben said, "she's only famous because Dickens took an interest in her."

"The fate of most women of her time," Ari answered. "He took her out of her theatrical career and hid her away. Even if she wasn't a great actress, she was well-read. She wrote verse and drama. She looked over his manuscripts and gave him feedback. She wasn't just his love muffin. She deserves more credit and consideration."

I shook my head. "Amazing. Are there any letters between Dickens and Nelly in that stash the Dickens Museum just acquired?"

"Oh, no," Ben said. "It's assumed that any such letters were

burned, though there were hints of their existence in other corre-
spondence."

Mark snorted and took a pull from his cocktail. "They'd be
worth a bloody fortune. I would think once word gets out about
how much the museum paid for the latest collection, they'll magically appear if they exist."

"Don't you think they would have by now?" Ben asked. "I'd love
to research them for my book, but I'm sure they've been destroyed.
So what are you guys making for the Eltham Palace party tomorrow? I can't wait."

BY THE TIME Ben drove us back to Mark's mansion, I was too tired
to think and tipsy, too. I dragged myself to the kitchen to grab a
bottle of water and had a start when I interrupted Mrs. Pidgeon
and Albert deep in conversation. Albert hurried off and out a side
door with a guilty look.

Mrs. Pidgeon glared at me as I rummaged through the big
fridges, probably to make sure I didn't steal the silver.

"Have you discovered anything about Mr. Fairman's book
thief?" she asked me as I finally hit upon a stash of beverages in the
third fridge.

I stood up straight with a Perrier in my hand and let the door
close. "What? I mean, we're making progress." I'd forgotten that
Mark said she knew everything. But just in case, I wasn't going to
tell her a thing.

She walked closer, almost gliding in those sensible shoes, and
invaded my personal space. When she spoke, her voice was colder
than that mint chocolate chip ice cream I'd spotted in one of the
fridges and planned to liberate later.

"Mr. Fairman is doing perfectly fine without you. So do not feel
obligated to help him. Your interference is ... *undesirable*."

And then she turned and went the same way as Albert.

What the—?

I resisted the ice cream. I already had a chill, thanks to Mrs. Pidgeon's ominous message. She made me feel like a real femme fatale.

By the time I got upstairs, most of my friends were in their rooms, but Neil waited by my bedroom door.

"You OK?" he asked.

"Just ran into Mrs. Pidgeon. I'm not quite sure, but I think she was warning me off."

Neil's eyebrows lifted. "Warning you off what?"

"That's the question, isn't it?" I opened my water and took a long sip, then leaned against the doorjamb, facing him.

He leaned opposite me, facing me like a mirror, a smile playing about his mouth. There was still a sense of caution between us. But that attraction was there, too.

"I really enjoyed today," he whispered.

I smiled at him as heat rushed to my face. It wasn't like me to be bashful, but something new was happening here.

"So did I," I whispered back.

He didn't try to kiss me. But he did give me a look that suggested he was thinking about it, a long look that sent a hot thrill through me. He reached out and took my free hand and lightly caressed my fingers with his thumb, shooting sparks over my skin.

"I'll see you tomorrow," he murmured. He gave my hand a brief squeeze, and then he went off to bed.

I guessed he was taking it slow. And maybe that was a good idea because I was still kind of in shock at his sudden interest, or renewal of interest. When I first met Neil in New Orleans, I was pretty sure he felt the same heat I did. There were serious sparks, even if we never got around to the fire.

Then, as he seemed to cool, I spent a couple of months trying to talk myself out of wanting him.

I hadn't really succeeded. And it seemed the rules of the game had changed again.

With Victoria nestled by my side, I spent the night—in my freshly washed and pressed Nightcap nightshirt, which I'd found neatly folded on the bed—having strange dreams. In the most vivid one, Mark and Neil drank wine in Mark's tasting area in his wine cellar, oblivious to anything but their intense conversation while a parade of people tiptoed past, all headed for the secret staircase—Nigel, Lottie, Ben, Albert, Mrs. Pidgeon, Cray, Ari, Alastair, Royce Doucet, Oleanna Lee, and Mr. Mixy with an entire TV crew, followed by a corps of contractors doing the conga. William Buttersby followed, deep in conversation with Charles Dickens, trailed by Sherlock Holmes in his deerstalker hat. Creeping after them came a figure in a dark hoodie who stopped and turned and looked right at me, chilling me to the bone. The figure reached up to pull down the hood of the sweatshirt and—

A banging on the door startled me out of sleep, and Victoria jumped to her feet, barking.

"Fudgesicles," I said. OK, that wasn't what I really said, but my campaign to curb my cursing had come a long way, at least in my own mind.

I rolled out of bed and opened the door. It was Albert.

"Here for the dog, miss," he said, looking everywhere but at me. Oh, yeah. My nightshirt didn't come down very far, I wasn't wearing yoga pants, and I hadn't really thought it through when I opened the door. Victoria ran out to him, fortunately abbreviating our conversation, and I mumbled a thanks and closed the door.

I needed action clothes. I'd be doing a lot of running around before changing for the party tonight. I went with a little black jumper—not a sweater, which is what the Brits called a jumper, but a high-waisted shortish black skirt with simple suspender straps over a gray knit top with three-quarter sleeves that had a little flounce on the ends. The neckline was modest, but the outfit still accented my assets. With black tights, the comfy short boots again, and accessories, I was ready to go—after a full English breakfast, of course.

This morning, Neil and I had a shot at catching the book thief. Or was it the booze thief—or maybe a jewel thief?

I hoped we'd soon find out in the lair of William Buttersby, bookseller.

Chapter Twenty-Three

U nder scudding gray clouds, and while the rest of the bartenders made ginger syrup and squeezed oranges and lemons in the kitchen for our event later, we rolled out from Mark's mansion in a compact car I'd never seen before. Ben, our driver, was his usual cheerful self, even though Mark had asked him to show up early on a Saturday to drive us into the city. He wore a light blue sweater that matched his eyes, and his blond hair looked more tangled than usual. It had been a late night for all of us.

"What is this car anyway?" I asked from the back seat as Ben zipped nimbly through traffic. I'd opted to sit in the back with my big bag while Neil sat up front on the left. It was still weird for me to see the driver on the right.

"Vauxhall Astra," Ben said. "It's mine. I thought it'd be better than the mini bus, since it's just us. Do you like it?"

"It's nice, but I really love the name. My dog at home is named Astra."

"How sweet! Is she as adorable as Victoria?"

"Well, it would be disloyal of me to say otherwise," I hedged, and the guys laughed.

"Mark loves that dog to pieces," Ben said. "It's a mark of his regard that he's lent her to you for the weekend."

Neil made a grumbly sound in his throat. "How'd you come to work for Mark?"

"Oh, I met him when he gave a talk at my business school, and I asked him if I could apply for a job. We hit it off, and I came in as an assistant at the distillery, but soon he had me doing all sorts of things."

"That must mean you're good," I said.

"Of course I'm good!" Ben grinned at me in the rearview mirror.

"I assume you know by now that we're looking into some books missing from his library," I said.

"They were talking about it in the kitchen this morning."

Ah, so the gossip had spread faster than hot butter on a scone. Maybe that would help. "Have you heard anything or seen anything unusual around the house?" I asked.

He appeared to think for a minute as he worked his way around a parked delivery truck. "I can't think of anything. Though ... Nigel Dashwood is quite a collector. He came by late one night not long ago to have a drink with Mark, and they met in the library."

Now this was interesting. Especially because Nigel didn't mention visiting the library outside of that party Mark had a while back.

"How did he—how do guests usually come into the house?" Neil asked. "The front door?"

Good question.

"Usually, but Nigel's a good friend, so he came in via the staff door around the side of the house. It's usually open."

What? Why did Mark not mention this? "Uh, is that such a good idea?" I asked.

"It's just easier to keep it unlocked, though I noticed Mark tightened access with a new lock a couple of months ago. But we all know the key code."

So Mark did address the security concern. Sort of.

"Who do you mean by 'we'?" Neil asked.

"You know. The staff. The occasional vendor or delivery person. It's not really a concern. Someone is almost always in that part of the house. A stranger couldn't just barrel in, and besides, they'd almost certainly get lost on the way to the library if they didn't know their way around."

Yes, but we were talking about someone who probably did know their way around. And they'd be going to the wine cellar, not the library, though we hadn't included that tidbit in our gossip, and neither had Mark.

"They'd have to have a front-gate code, too, wouldn't they?" Neil pointed out.

"If visitors buzz the intercom, Mrs. Pidgeon can open the gate with an app on her phone. But pretty much anyone who does work in the house has the gate code, too," Ben said. "I've mentioned it to Mark as a vulnerability, but he doesn't want everyone to have to buzz Mrs. Pidgeon, and he hasn't wanted to hire security."

"So the gate is not all that secure right now." An idea struck me. "That's not all. Someone could get in from the distillery side. There wasn't any kind of locked gate over there."

"They'd have to walk in," Neil said. "But you're right. I'm starting to think Mark's security has more holes than a Hawthorne strainer."

"If you think of anything that can help us," I said to Ben, "let us know, OK?"

"No problem," Ben said. "So where am I dropping you in town?"

Neil and I exchanged glances before I spoke. "Uh, Old Bond Street, I think. I wanted to do some shopping."

"Jammy," Ben said (leaving me thinking again about jammies, but I was pretty sure that wasn't what he meant). "A bit dear for me, but maybe someday I'll be minted enough to shop there."

"I just like window shopping," I said, hoping I sounded convincing. It didn't seem like a good idea to tell Ben or anyone about our planned stakeout this morning. He might pass it on, and that wouldn't help us at all.

A few minutes later, he pulled up in front of Tiffany & Co. "Here you go."

"Thanks." I went to grab my bag off the floor and saw something soft and dark that had blended into the carpet. I picked it up. A hoodie. "Hey, there's a sweatshirt back here." I sounded a lot calmer than I felt.

"Oh, yes. Nigel and Lottie left that in the mini bus last night when I gave them a ride to the Tipple. I thought I might see them today, so I brought it along."

"That was nice of you." Inside, I screamed, *It's a black hoodie!*

"All part of the service," Ben said puckishly. "Will you need a ride back later?"

"I don't think so." Neil opened his door to get out.

"Happy to help if you do. Just ring Mark and he'll dispatch one of us. Cheers."

We bade him goodbye and exited the car, and then he was off, zooming into traffic.

"He had a black hoodie in his car," I said in disbelief.

"I have a black hoodie in my car," Neil said.

I laughed. "Yeah, but it's not in London, and you weren't stalking yourself yesterday."

"He said it was Nigel's. That's interesting."

"Or Lottie's. Ugh." I looked around at the posh shops that surrounded us, wondering if Mark shopped here. "These people are all so nice. I can't believe they're bad guys."

"We can't make any conclusions yet," Neil said. "Still, that was good thinking, having him drop us here. Just in case."

"It's not that far of a walk, and I think we'll still get there before ten."

"If we hurry." Neil set off at a brisk pace toward Buttersby Books that I had to hustle to match.

"So do you think Nigel is worth watching?"

"There have been a lot of little bells ringing around Nigel. He's a collector. He's seen the library. He's a friend and probably knows the gate code. He's visited Mark by the staff entrance and could've seen someone use their door code to get in. And there's the hoodie, though that's hardly conclusive."

"Nigel seemed taken aback when I mentioned the book thefts to him. Plus he and William were talking about Virginia Woolf."

"We'll ask William about that when we get to Buttersby's," Neil said.

Once we reached the bookseller's street, we took a good look around to see if we could spot anyone surveilling the place and then headed in at nine forty-five.

"Nothing like cutting it close," William Buttersby said from behind his counter.

"Any action yet?" Neil asked.

"I had a customer inquire after a nineteenth-century book we roundly know to be cursed, and Peter got a terrible paper cut trying to look up where we'd stashed it, but otherwise—"

"Oi!" came Peter's voice, presumably, from downstairs.

"It's been quiet," William said.

"So where should we hide?" I asked.

The bell at the door rang, and we all looked around to see who was there.

"Good morning!" the visitor said with a broad smile. "Fancy seeing you here."

Chapter Twenty-Four

My first reaction was to say to myself a word I was trying to say less frequently in public. Well, several words.

My second reaction was, *What if this isn't the person we're waiting for?*

But it was. It had to be.

"And a good morning to you, Nigel," William called out after shooting us a scalding glance. It was too late to hide from Nigel. And it would look weird to duck out now.

"What are you two doing here?" a cheerful Nigel asked us. He wore a sharp tan blazer over a white shirt and jeans and seemed energetic, not his usual mellow self. Sober, in other words.

I thought fast. "I wanted to see if they had any Craddock first editions. You mentioning it made me curious."

"You're always welcome to come over and see my collection anytime," Nigel offered.

"And the working poor can find a facsimile edition of the Craddock for very reasonable prices," William quipped.

Gee, thanks.

"And what brings you to Mr. Buttersby's establishment?" Neil asked in a friendly tone.

"Well, it's rather interesting," Nigel said. "When you told me some of Mark's books were missing, of course my first thought was to my own collection. If someone were nicking rare twentieth-century editions, might they be after mine as well? And then the most curious thing happened."

We all stared at him. Finally, Neil asked, "What?"

"I got an email."

"An email," William deadpanned.

"Yes. From someone who asked me if I might be interested in purchasing a rare edition of Virginia Woolf."

"Oh, yes," William said. "You told me you wanted to ask me about Virginia Woolf yesterday at the garden party."

Nigel nodded. "And you said to stop by anytime and you could look up what I wanted to know. Well, I'm here."

I looked nervously toward the door. Was the conversation I'd overheard between them yesterday completely innocent? What if Nigel wasn't the person we were waiting for?

What if that person walked in right now?

"Did they say what rare edition they wanted to sell you?" Neil asked.

"*To the Lighthouse*, with the Vanessa Bell dust jacket, 1927 first edition," Nigel said.

"Damn," I said.

"Quite so. A rare find indeed. And the price was more than reasonable."

William wore a blank expression. He could've played poker with that face. Probably a good talent for a man who bought and sold rare books for a living. "Did this seller have a name?"

"Albert. No last name. I found it all rather odd, which is why I wanted to speak with you. Do you think it wise to pursue?"

"I do not," William said flatly.

Nigel sighed. "That's what I thought you'd say. It's stolen, isn't it?"

"Probably," William answered. And we all got pretty quiet. I personally didn't think we should tell Nigel we were lying in wait for the thief because there was still a chance that *he* was the guy, that he'd realized we weren't there to look for *The Savoy Cocktail Book,* and that his questions were all just a performance.

But Nigel seemed sincere enough. "Well, that's unfortunate, but that's why I came to you. Is it from Mark's collection?"

"We're not sure," William said, then looked at us.

Nigel looked at all of us looking at one another. "Then you must let me help you. What if we set up this Albert fellow, lured him in by telling him we'd like to buy his book?"

"That's a clever idea," Neil said. *Wow.* Neil really was a good liar. Or pretender. Or whatever you called what he was doing now, playing as if setting a trap wasn't exactly the reason we were here. Did Nigel know we not only knew about the book but knew he might know and therefore didn't want to let on that he knew?

Ouch.

"Let me think on it further," William said to Nigel. "And please take care of your collection. Are you looking for anything else today?"

"No, I'm afraid not. I've been a bit splurgy this month already, and Lottie will have my head if I come home with another gilded first edition. See you all at the party tonight?"

Neil and I assured Nigel we would be making cocktails, and he headed out into the cloudy morning.

"Should we hide now?" I asked William.

"I've no idea," he said. "But it's not quite ten. Go on downstairs and meet Peter, and I'll text him to tell you to come up if anyone interesting comes in."

With no better plan at hand, Neil and I scurried downstairs, where Peter, a fortyish wisp of a man with long brown hair clinging desperately to a receding hairline, was hanging pictures. He brandished a hammer in one hand, his thumb wrapped in a chunky white bandage. That must've been some paper cut.

We wandered through the print gallery for thirty minutes till Peter began shooting us annoyed looks.

"Do you hear anything?" I finally asked him.

"I hear everything," he grumbled.

"I mean, anyone besides William upstairs? A customer?"

"None. Except you two and your clicky shoes."

I didn't think that was fair. I had rubber-soled boots, even if they did have a small, chunky and perfectly reasonable heel. And Neil moved like a freakin' ninja.

"Might as well go up," Neil said, and we did. "Is our 'Albert' a no-show?" he asked William.

"I guess that depends on your working theory," he replied. "But I believe we've been made, one way or another. You're not going to catch your thief today."

We might not catch our thief here, but I wasn't going to rule out today. Not when time was running out.

NEIL and I scanned the street as we exited the bookstore, but if anyone else lay in wait, they hid out of sight.

We went over everything as we wandered in no particular direction. It was clear "Albert" got cold feet, figured out we were onto him, or hid in plain sight in the form of Nigel Dashwood. Or William had orchestrated the whole thing, but we both had our doubts about that.

We still had no idea if the digging at Alastair's was connected to the book thefts, but it all just seemed too coincidental. And what if someone really was trying to pull off a jewel heist by digging through the walls under The Dandy Tipple?

We approached a lovely classical structure of three arches, which my map app told me was Marble Arch, on the edge of Hyde Park. We headed into the park and walked along a wide, paved path.

"This will be glorious when fall really arrives," I said as we strolled among pretty trees bordering wide-open green spaces.

"You can see hints already, plus there's a chill in the air. It feels like rain."

"Kind of refreshing after Florida's tropical stew." *Oh, great. Now we're talking about the weather.* "What do you think of Nigel?"

Neil cocked his head in a half-shrug. "He's fun. Interesting. Enjoys his cocktails immensely. What I might call a perfect customer."

I snorted. "You know what I mean. Is he our thief?"

"I seriously doubt it. Have you heard from Stout Boy Builders?"

I dug my phone out of my bag and checked it again for any call from the contractor who'd built the secret door to the staircase. "No response. Maybe Mark should call them." I texted Mark to tell him our bookstore stakeout had come to nothing and we hadn't heard anything from Stout Boy.

Mark texted back immediately. "Samuel Stout left me voice mail. Wondered who in hell you were LOL. Will be at party tonight. We can talk with him then."

I held up the screen to Neil ... just when a new message popped up and a cloud moved over Neil's face. I turned the screen back to me.

"Be careful, darling Pepper," Mark had written.

"Darling?" Neil said, only the word wasn't directed at me. It was more like a question.

"He always says that. I think it's an English thing."

"Right." I couldn't read his expression, but it wasn't altogether happy. "Looks like we have most of the day free. Want to do something fun?"

"I can't."

Now Neil really looked disappointed.

"I mean, what I'm doing should be fun, but I promised I'd meet the girls for a shopping jaunt in Notting Hill," I explained. "We want to see the market."

He relaxed his shoulders and released a resigned sigh. "Well, I guess I have to respect the sanctity of the girls-only outing."

"Yes, you do." I grinned.

"And this explains why Barclay messaged me to meet the guys for day-drinking at cocktail bars near the British Museum. Though I think I might visit the museum first. It's been a while, and I want to see the Egyptian collection again."

"Opposite direction, I think?"

"I'm afraid so. How about I walk you to the nearest tube station and we can go our separate ways?"

That sounded a little ominous but also nice. "OK."

We wended through the park, detouring to take in the Italian Gardens—a formal area of carved stone and water basins with fountains and a lovely structure at one end.

"I think this was a gift from Prince Albert to Queen Victoria," Neil said as we paused to look.

A few drops of rain fell on us, and I wondered if I'd have to get my collapsible umbrella out of my bag. But the gray weather didn't make this place any less romantic. "All I can say is that Albert knew what he was doing."

Another Albert.

Neil slipped an arm around my shoulders, and we just stood there for a few minutes, taking in the bubbling water and the people strolling by. But it was like we had trouble getting into the romantic groove, in spite of this place. Maybe I had too much on my mind. Maybe Neil was worried about Mark's "darlings" or had retreated too far into the friend zone, with the exception of yesterday, when he came running out of it fully engulfed in flames.

Finally, we disengaged, walked toward the Lancaster Gate tube station and paused just outside.

"I think I'm going to walk. It's not that far for me," I told him.

"You sure?"

"It's fine. I'll see you back at the house."

"OK." Neil took both of my hands in his, leaned closer and then, after a moment's hesitation, lightly kissed my lips. A fleeting bolt of electricity lit up my body. Then he whispered in my ear, "Be careful ... darling Pepper."

I pulled away with a laugh and lightly smacked his arm. "Go look at your mummies."

"The Rosetta Stone, at least. Maybe it will help me decipher what's going on." He gave me a little salute and headed into the station.

I started walking toward Portobello Road with the feeling that I was missing something. Something important.

And missing Neil, too.

Chapter Twenty-Five

There's nothing like hanging out with girlfriends to remind you why boys were such a pain in the ass. I mean, anyone who knew me knew I loved men, maybe a little too much, but sometimes you just wanted to get away from them.

And talk about them.

"So tell us about your morning with Neil," Melody said. She, Oleanna, Gina and I had browsed the stalls and stores of the crowded Saturday market in Notting Hill for a couple of hours. Vendors showed off everything and every food imaginable—books, art, porcelain, silver, old cameras and other intriguing antiques, barrels of olives, delicately wrapped perfect figs and other produce, herbs, and pastries sweet and savory that we scarfed first thing for lunch when we arrived. Each of us carried bags full of treasures; I'd snagged a vintage polka-dot silk scarf and a pretty antique mortar and pestle for my aunt and her herb-blending. Clearly we were done shopping and had turned to more serious matters.

"Yes, tell us about Neil," said Oleanna.

"He's Neil," I said cryptically. "We went to see Mark's bookseller to talk to him about his missing books."

"Ooo, a bookseller," Gina said, fortunately diverting the chat away from Neil. I definitely wasn't ready to gossip about the recent twist in our relationship. "Is the bookshop in Notting Hill? Do I feel a Hugh Grant vibe coming on?"

"Love that movie," I said, "but I think if anyone is going to play the Julia Roberts role in this situation, it would be Oleanna."

"What?" she asked. "Why me?"

She just had to look around to answer that question. In spite of her cute little hat and extra-large sunglasses, more than one person did a double-take and whispered after spotting her.

"Maybe because you're a movie star like the character in the movie?" I said quietly to avoid further attention.

"Oh, stop. I'm just like anyone else. And I'm not in the market, really. Though I wanted to ask you—what do you think of Mark?"

"Yeah!" Melody sounded delighted. "Yes, Pepper. Tell Oleanna all about Mark."

I didn't say anything for a minute. "Look. Trailer Happiness is open. We have time for one drink before we have to get ready for the palace party."

They were agreeable enough, but they weren't going to let me off the hook. Once we'd descended into the nearly empty basement lounge with its moody lighting and seventies-meets-tiki decor, taken a table and ordered cocktails, Melody pressed again. "Pepper —you were saying about Mark?"

I shot her a look that promised revenge. "I would say that Mark is really a great guy. Full of bad double entendres, but he's charming. Surprisingly smart. And he's genuinely nice."

"Plus he has that *house*," Gina said.

"And a whole lot more besides," I agreed.

"Planning on spending more time there?" Melody asked with mock innocence.

"No." I turned to Oleanna. "I would say that Mark is very much available. Interested?"

"Well, he is hotter than a ghost pepper on fire. And he makes a gin I like very much."

We all laughed, and I considered what she'd said. Mark and Oleanna were both at a jet-setting social strata that would naturally enhance any connection between them. I kind of liked this idea.

And I didn't think the age difference would matter. Oleanna was in her early forties, older than Mark by about the same amount he was older than me, and she could kick all of our asses. More to the point, I didn't think I minded the thought of Mark pursuing someone else, though his attentions were fun.

Then the beautiful cocktails began to arrive, interrupting my romantic rumination. After we'd all had a taste and shot our photos for posterity and social media, I turned to Melody. "And what is your current man situation?" I asked.

"Oh, I'm always looking. You know that."

"And you've never looked, say, right under your nose?" I lifted my eyebrows at her and sipped my Port Light, with its unusual banana accent.

"What are you talking about?" she asked.

Gina looked at me. "I really don't think she knows."

"What?" Melody asked. We were good friends, but I'd never pointed out Luke's obvious crush. It was almost as if something in her subconscious had generated blinders where Luke was concerned.

I had a feeling that if anything were to happen between them, interference would only hinder the process. This was something that had to grow naturally from the ground up.

"You know what? I'm not going to tell you, for the sake of discretion," I said. "But maybe you should start paying a little more attention."

Melody frowned and sipped her Polynesian Princess. I texted Mark and asked if one of his shuttles could come get us, and our conversation turned to other pleasantries until our ride arrived. Oleanna grabbed a cab and promised to see us later at the finale party at Eltham Palace.

It was time to get ready for the biggest night of the gin festival. And maybe, finally, get some answers.

MARK HAD a simple buffet waiting for us in the dining room so we could all top off before working tonight. I felt a sense of obligation to Mark for everything he'd done for us on this trip, and that sense would be overwhelming if we didn't solve his mystery for him. I had high hopes that his contractor would tell us what we needed to know at the party.

The gin festival party tonight had an art deco theme, given the setting—the remnants of a medieval palace with a huge 1930s addition—but Melody and I had decided flouncy 1930s gowns would just get in the way of making cocktails. So for once, we dressed a lot like the guys. We all wore sharp black pants, but while the guys donned dark vests over their white shirts, we sported white blouses open at the collar, flattering to our curves, and black suspenders. I went with my comfy boots again; Melody had a bit more of a heel, making her extra tall next to me. (Gina wore a red dress since she was technically a guest, not a bartender.)

With up-dos and dangly earrings, plus my geek glasses and bracelet, we were cute enough and ready to work. Especially after I brushed Victoria's dog hair off my trousers.

While the pup was happy to see me, she ran off as soon as she saw Mark, and he scooped her up and gave her lots of attention before all of us—the people, anyway—left in a shuttle with Ben driving.

On the way, I tried texting Aunt Celestine about the storm but got no reply. I tried Jorge, too, to make sure Nola was buttoned down. The hurricane—it was a Cat 1 now—looked like it was on a final bombing run for Bohemia, and the fact they didn't write back made me even more worried.

When we parked and disembarked, Ben pulled umbrellas from his backpack, bigger than the miniature one in my bag. He handed me and Neil one and held another over Melody and Gina under a light rain as dusk settled in. We walked from the passenger van and around the forbidding yet beautiful exterior of Eltham Palace to the grand entrance.

Barclay and Luke did the hard work, maneuvering an overloaded dolly carrying our supplies and getting damp. They didn't seem to mind.

Mark's place wasn't all that far from Eltham Palace, on the southeast side of London. And even though I'd read a little about it, words and pictures couldn't capture just how marvelous the palace was. When I'd heard Henry VIII played here as a child, the last thing I expected upon entering the front entrance of this huge castle, complete with a moat, was a scene right out of Agatha Christie—an art-deco dream.

We were there early enough that I had a moment to stop and gawk at the round entrance hall with its domed skylight above, curving staircases on either side, wood-paneled walls inlaid with scenes and figures, and art-deco furniture.

"If you get set up in time, you can take a quick tour," Mark said, which was enough motivation to get our bar team in gear as he went off to take care of festival business. We headed down a corridor toward the Great Hall.

What a contrast! This vast room looked like a place where medieval kings would have feasts, as indeed it was. A hundred feet up, a gorgeous dark oak roof featured carved arches and beams, reminiscent of a cathedral. Just under the roof, elegant stained-glass windows were set into the stone walls. Farther down and to the floor, drapes lined the walls, to dampen sound or drafts, I wasn't sure. Probably a replacement for tapestries of times gone by.

Now this English Heritage site was open for tours and events, and instead of medieval banquet tables, eclectic temporary bars lined one wall and formed a line down the middle, with food tables against the other wall. A small jazz band warmed up at the end where royalty might have sat.

Neil led the way, talked to an organizer and found our spot, in the middle and near the food. Bonus.

Boxes of fresh apricots and oranges awaited us at the bar we'd been provided, with a long table behind for additional prep. Neil

distributed the bar tools. We quickly set up to make our two cocktails. One was simple enough and evoked the 1930s: the Eddie
Brown from Craddock's *Savoy Cocktail Book,* with gin, Lillet Blanc
and apricot liqueur.

We also planned an orange-themed cocktail, the Orange You
Glad We're Here, in a nod to our Florida roots, with gin, orange
liqueur, orange juice, lemon juice, the ginger syrup our crew had
made this morning, and orange bitters. A little on the sweet side,
but bright and refreshing.

Once initial setup was complete, Neil cleared the rest of us to
do an accelerated tour of the art-deco addition to the palace that a
wealthy family, the Courtaulds, built in the 1930s. All I could think
of during our quick walk-through with Mark and a guide was that I
had to come back and experience it at leisure. Talk about art-deco
heaven. From the glorious round bedroom and onyx-lined bath,
with a tub set in a golden-tiled niche, to the exquisite dining room
with its series of geometric-patterned doors, it was like walking
onto a movie set from another era, a time of streamlined design,
elegant decadence and excellent martinis.

"You should see the gardens," Mark told me as we walked back
to the hall. "They're lit tonight because of the party. When you get
a break later, snag me, and I'll show you around. They filled in part
of the moat to make the garden, and the flowers are glorious. Oh,
have to dash. I'm being flagged by the chair."

"See you later!" But not necessarily on a romantic tour of the
garden. We had a lot of work to do first, so who knew if we'd get a
chance.

I waved at Ari and Alastair, who headed The Dandy Tipple
team at the bar next to ours. She smiled and waved while he barely
lifted his chin in greeting. Still, an improvement for Alastair, I
thought.

I also ran into Mr. Mixy, who was guest-bartending for one of
the London bars. "Pepper!" he called out.

Argh. Against my better judgment, I stopped by his booth,

where everyone else sliced, squeezed and prepped and a camera crew loitered, ready to film him in action whenever he decided to do some actual work.

"Yes, Stephan?" He frowned briefly. He never liked it when I used his real name.

"I've got exciting news. The genealogy guy is supposed to be here tonight and bring me my paperwork. This is really happening!"

"What, exactly?"

"Proof of my royal ancestry!"

"Do you have a title yet?"

"Uh, apparently that's going to come later once I get certified by some royal bureaucrat or other. But it's going to come with a title for sure, plus land and a family inheritance. I can't wait to tell you all about it!"

"Great!" I sounded fake even to myself. "Gotta run!"

I stomped back to our booth. Why did he still get under my skin so badly? Maybe because he kept being rewarded for being a total dumbass while the rest of us had to work so hard to get recognition?

"You OK, Pepper?" Neil asked as I arrived, lagging behind the rest of our group.

"Great!" *Uh-oh.* Now I was using the fake "Great" on Neil, too. "I mean, yeah. Sorry. I just spoke with Mr. Mixy. He is not a mood enhancer."

Neil laughed. "I get it. Maybe you can lose yourself in work."

I smiled at him. "It's not work when it's a pleasure." In fact, that was why Mr. Mixy's successes shouldn't bother me. I actually loved my job. It was its own reward.

And so I got down to business, cutting fine slices of fresh apricot for the Eddie Brown garnish; it was just the end of their season, and they were plump, peachy little fruits. Sticky, though.

Melody and Gina—risking her dress—created pretty double-twist orange-slice garnishes for the other drink. We measured out the ingredients, and the guys stirred, poured and presented the gleaming glasses at the front of the bar until we rotated stations just to keep it interesting.

The jazz band played peppy pre-war tunes, the room filled with revelers—many snazzy in vintage outfits—and our friends began to swing through: Cray, Royce Doucet, Lottie and Nigel, Oleanna Lee.

William Buttersby came by in an ill-fitting suit and surveyed our vests and ties and suspenders as he helped himself to the Eddie Brown cocktail. "Doing musical numbers from *Chicago* this evening?"

I mock-scratched under my eye with my middle finger, and he cackled in delight. "Keep me updated, all right?" he said, then strolled away.

It wasn't as if I had time to solve the book thefts right now. The party was a mad rush, as these things usually were, and then the flow of drinkers slowed as they reached their liquor limits, grabbed food and went outside to look at the gardens in spite of the rain. I guessed Londoners were used to rain.

With the hall nearly empty of visitors, we and the other vendors started our cleanup. But we had one last customer, a suntanned man wearing a simple dark gray suit, stocky, built like he did a lot of physical labor and enjoyed the beers that came afterward. I put him at around fifty, with graying brown hair.

"You the Bohemia Bartenders?" he asked in a gravelly voice as he looked at the sign on the bar that said who we were. "Mr. Fairman texted me and said he'd meet me over here."

"Yes, that's us," Neil said just as Mark came up and grabbed the last cocktail for himself, the orange one.

"Mmm," Mark said, then looked up at our other visitor. "Samuel Stout?"

"Mr. Fairman. Pleased to meet you."

Oh! This was the elusive contractor for the wine cellar renovation—and the secret door.

Chapter Twenty-Six

Mark shook Samuel Stout's hand enthusiastically. "Please, call me Mark. Thank you for meeting me."

"Happy to do it," the contractor said. "It's a great party." *And you're a great customer* was implied.

"If you have a moment, could I ask you a question or two? In the company of my friends Neil and Pepper here?"

Neil looked around at Barclay, who said, "Go ahead. We're good."

Mark set his half-empty glass down, and Neil and I stepped out of the booth and joined Mark and Samuel in the middle of the aisle, within spitting distance of the Bohemia Bartenders and The Dandy Tipple crew.

"Pepper, why don't you go ahead," Mark said.

All eyes turned to me, and I pushed down a little rush of nerves. "Ah, Mr. Stout, what can you tell us about the secret door in the wine cellar?"

Samuel nodded. "You mean about how it works? It has a magnetic combination lock. If you're having trouble with it, I can send someone over to help."

Mark shook his head. "To be honest, that's not it at all. I was wondering how you came to build the door in the first place. Who asked you to do it?"

Samuel's eyebrows lifted. "Didn't you?"

"This is rather embarrassing, but no, I didn't," Mark said.

"Oh. Well, we wouldn't do anything without a plan. Let me think." Samuel swirled his Eddie Thomas cocktail and took a sip. "Very nice, by the way." He nodded at Neil and me. "Oh, yes. Now I remember. Sorry, but I do a lot of work, and I'm not always on site. When we were repairing a wall, part of it collapsed. We found we'd broken into a bricked-up spiral staircase. After we evaluated the structure, your man told us you'd like to have a secret door put in there."

"My man?" Mark asked. "Who?"

"Was it Albert?" I asked, a little too eagerly.

"Oh, Albert! He's been great to work with," Samuel said.

Oh, wow! It was Albert!

"But that's not who it was," Samuel continued, popping my balloon. "Younger fellow. Fair hair. Very enthusiastic. Let me think ... I'm terrible with names."

Neil and I looked at each other and said at the same time, "Ben?"

"Ben?" Mark asked in disbelief.

"Ben! That's it," Samuel said.

Mark shook his head in shock. "I'll be jiggered."

"Are you saying you didn't authorize it?" Samuel asked. "Maybe he meant it as a surprise?"

Mark winced, obviously flashing back to the invoices. "It was a rather costly surprise. Such a surprise that I didn't know about it until Pepper and I found it quite by accident."

"That's odd. I—I'm very sorry." Samuel looked really nervous now, like maybe there was something else he wasn't telling us.

"Did someone on your crew work with Ben closely on this?" Neil asked. A good question, given that one of the construction crew could have been behind the whole thing.

"Other than me and the project manager, no. And the project manager wasn't there every day, either. We delegate, but we have the best people." Samuel turned back to Mark. "I take full responsibility for this, Mr. Fairman. I remember now that the plan was presented to us as fully approved, though we brought in a subcontractor to execute the door, as it's rather technical. I do apologize."

Mark, easygoing as usual, put a hand on the man's shoulder. "No need, no need. It really is a cool addition to the cellar. I just need to keep a better rein on my staff, apparently." He chuckled, but the laugh didn't seem quite authentic. While he pretended everything was OK, it was clear that something was very, very wrong.

The men exchanged a few more words, with Samuel promising to be available at any time should Mark need to discuss the topic further. Then the contractor moved off, meeting a pleasant-looking woman who'd been lingering at the end of the aisle—his wife, I guessed—and leaving the swiftly emptying room.

Mark turned to Neil and me, his expression as grim as I'd ever seen it. "I think I need to talk to Ben."

I flashed back to Ben's remarks about betting on the horses, Ari's comment about him losing. I glanced over at her. She caught my eye and smiled, then returned to work; they were already cleaning up. Maybe she knew more. She seemed to know Ben pretty well.

Did Ben need money that badly? And Ben had access to the vault at The Dandy Tipple, at least occasionally, like when he brought in a delivery. Could he be trying to break into the jewelry store too? Plus he had that hoodie in his car. Maybe he thought we were on to him and followed us, slipping that creepy note into my pocket ... I didn't want to think about it.

"How about I text him?" Mark said.

But at that moment, Ben appeared, turning down our aisle, heading our way with one of his bright smiles, his backpack slung over his shoulder. "Hi. How's it going?" he said as he arrived at our little group.

Maybe it was the looks in our eyes or the fact that we were all dumbstruck for a moment. But when Mark said, "Ben, I have a question for you. What do you know about the secret door in my wine cellar?" Ben stopped dead and his smile vanished.

And he spun and started walking the other way.

"Well, that's not good," Mark said.

"Shouldn't we go after him?" I whispered.

Alastair appeared at our shoulders, along with Ari. "What's up?"

"We have to talk to Ben about the book thefts," Mark said. Taking Mark's cue, we all started moving down the aisle toward Ben's rapidly retreating figure.

"He doesn't seem keen on conversation, does he?" Mark quipped, in surprisingly good humor. Maybe he was just glad we finally had a name.

"This place is like a maze. Maybe we should split up," Neil said quietly.

"I'll help. Let's go!" Ari said, not nearly as quietly, and Ben broke into a dead run.

Seeing him flee was like lighting a spark to a fuse.

"Go!" Mark shouted, and we all just exploded forward—me, Neil, Mark, Alastair and Ari.

Partygoers still wandered the corridors, but we dodged them as best we could. And I had to admit, Mark's spectacular physique wasn't all show—he left us in the dust as he sprinted ahead. But maybe he had more at stake than we did.

We heard a scream and a clatter ahead of us, then a shout, and we barreled into the round entrance hall to find Mark breathing hard and visitors backed up to the walls, surveying the chaos before them—a woman in a flapper dress sitting on the floor, her head-piece askew, rubbing her temple as a tuxedoed man reached to help her up; one of the vendors gathering up the contents of a spilled box while tiptoeing around shattered glass; a staff member scurrying off to find a broom and dustpan, presumably.

"He was going for the door and looking back and ran into these folks and stumbled," Mark told us. "I went to block his way, and he saw me and then ran for the stairs. Right, I think."

"We have to split up," Neil said. "There are multiple exits if you ignore the tourist route. I'll take the right stairs."

Ari started moving. "I'll take the left."

"There's a basement, isn't there? I'll go down, just in case," I said.

"And I suppose I'll head back to the banquet hall? In case he doubles back," Alastair added.

"I'd better wait here in case he tries to do a runner out the front," Mark said. "I don't want to call the police until we're sure, you know? He deserves a chance to explain himself, and I'd like to work this out quietly. He's been a good employee and a friend. I don't want him to do anything foolish. Tell him I just want to talk."

"We'll find him," I said, and then we were off.

I wasn't sure why I'd volunteered to go downstairs. I supposed because Neil and Ari were going up. *Ari!* OK, she and Neil probably wouldn't take time to make out if they were searching for Ben, but who knew? That curvy art-deco bedroom could mesmerize anyone.

Seeking the basement entrance, I spotted a sign that pointed me down a hallway toward the bunker. I had no idea where I was going. The problem was, I knew there was a downstairs, but I hadn't visited it during our tour. There hadn't been time. And now I headed down the steps into what apparently served as a shelter when the Germans dropped bombs on the palace during World War II.

I hit the bottom of the stairs and looked around. No tourists lingered down here, and I couldn't hear any sounds from the ground floor. It was kind of spooky and nothing like the swank digs above. This small space didn't seem all that glamorous, and the most exciting thing at the foot of the stairs was what was labeled as a centralized vacuum-cleaning system.

I turned toward the corridor, dimly lit with a few downlights and curving away from me, echoing the curves of the walls on the floor above. Wooden crates were scattered along the way, for atmosphere, I guessed. Rows of fat and skinny pipes curved along the walls and above my head, the necessary arteries of a house this large.

Now the boots I didn't think were loud seemed deafening on the red-painted concrete floor as I stepped forward.

I advanced slowly. Mark seemed to think all this could be resolved by a chat with Ben, but I didn't know what he was capable of, and I wasn't sure I wanted to find out. Especially after that note. I didn't want to make a lovely corpse. I didn't want to be a corpse at all.

Maybe coming down here by myself wasn't such a great idea. But if this was the only staircase in and out, Ben probably didn't even come this way. I allowed myself to relax a little and picked up my pace.

The nice thing about museums is they tell you what you're looking at. I passed a small photographic darkroom, then entered the playroom that had doubled as a bunker, complete with cots. Then turned and found myself in a magnificent billiards room.

"Wow," I breathed, forgetting for a moment my purpose. But no one was here. Neat brick walls interrupted by segments of stone surrounded the tiled floor. In the center of the room glowed the billiards table. A few balls and a couple of cue sticks rested on its bright green felt. Beyond the table, a wall mural depicted a medieval landscape. A closed door at the center said *Emergency Exit Only*.

There were a couple of niches off the side of the room. I'd take a look and get going. As I stepped forward and poked my head into one of them, I heard a soft sound and turned.

The emergency exit door creaked open.

Chapter Twenty-Seven

The door opened wide, and Ben stepped out.

I didn't know whether to curse or cheer.

He spotted me immediately, then looked over his shoulder and closed the door.

"Don't get in my way, Pepper," he said simply.

"Mark just wants to talk to you." I backed toward the main entrance to the room. Why hadn't Ben gone back and found the emergency exit, wherever it was?

"Mark wants more than that. He wants what I have." He adjusted his backpack, then patted his jacket pocket, almost unconsciously, I thought.

I puzzled over his words as I got between him and the tourist entrance to the billiards room. "What do you have that Mark wants?"

"It's what I *will* have, and I'm this close"—he held up a pinch of air between his index finger and thumb—"and you are not going to get in my way."

I swallowed and tried to look brave. "I am in your way. Let's go upstairs and talk. Mark just wants to talk to you."

"I'm getting out of here."

"Why come down here? Why not just go out the way you came in?"

"Because your dear friend Neil is that way, and he's stronger than you are."

"Hey!" I crossed my arms and tried to look taller. I mean, what Ben said was almost certainly true, because Neil worked out, but *don't diss me.* I'd left my bag back at our booth, so even if I could've dug out my cocktail knife in my defense—

Ben jumped forward, grabbed a pool cue off the table and swung it at my head.

"Ack!" I ducked and stumbled backward through the door, falling to the floor, and the damn gazelle leapt right over me and threw the stick at me for good measure. "Ouch! Come back!" I yelled as I struggled to climb to my feet. My butt hurt, but the cue didn't do much damage. I'd probably have a bruise on my arm later where I tried to block it.

The emergency exit door in the billiards room behind me flew open, this time with Neil plowing through it. "Pepper! Are you all right?"

"Fine." I stood up straight and dusted myself off. "He went that way."

"Let's go." Neil, more decisive than I, broke into a run down the hall.

I took off after him, but Ben had already pounded around the curvy corridor, and I heard him on the stairs.

"Does he have to go out the front entrance hall this way?" Neil asked.

"I doubt it," I said as we reached the staircase by the centralized vacuum and started up. "It looked like there was some kind of access hallway up there. I thought I saw a sign for an elevator."

We arrived at the ground floor, paused to look around and saw Ben sprinting down the empty hall, ignoring the doors at right and left, no one in his way. And then heard the sound of a door banging shut.

"Damn it," Neil said, beating me to it.

"We might still catch him."

"Might as well try." Neil ran, and I followed.

WE STUMBLED out into the night and a hard, cold rain. I, for one, was totally disoriented and wondering if this pursuit was even worth it as the downpour soaked into my clothes. I figured we were doing it for Mark, but Ben didn't seem all that cooperative. Maybe we should just let him go and let the police handle it. He stole a few books. It might not be that bad for him, especially if he hadn't sold any of them yet.

To the echoing sounds of a slinky, dance-beat soundtrack, projections twirled over the brick walls of the palace, catching rain-drops in dazzling glints of color. I caught a glimpse of a gin logo—not Mark's—and lots of flowing graphic art. The show helped light up the surroundings, but not much.

"We should split up again," I said, trying to shield my eyes from the rain. "We're above the moat, and the garden's huge. He could've gone any which way. "

"Not so many ways," Neil replied. He pulled out his phone and sent a quick text. To Mark? He stowed his phone, and we moved to the edge of the escarpment where the castle sat and tried to look over the stone wall. "The moat limits his movements, at least on this side—but it doesn't go around the whole house. Not anymore."

"Then we'd better hurry. He's half a blink from being out of here."

Neil looked torn. "Are you sure you'll be OK?"

"I'm fine. Look. Stairs. Let's assume he went down, since the front entrance is covered."

We headed down the pretty stone stairs, not all that fast thanks to the rain-slicked surface, and popped through an archway in the big retaining wall by the moat. The water next to the wall hemmed us in, with a narrow strip of grass and a gravel path our only route.

The moat didn't look deep, but it was hard to tell in the dark. Even if Ben could wade through it, it would slow him down. I guessed Ben would run to the end of the waterway and simply walk through the gardens and out of the property.

No more debate. This was our last chance.

"I'll go this way. He's more likely to head down the path." Neil took off to the right, and then I realized what he meant. The gravel path only went one way—not the way I was going.

I moved left along the stone wall. It was darker here than above, though some of the party light filtered its way down. I wiped the rain off my glasses, trying to see. And it was hard to hear anything over the deluge and the music.

Chunky segments stuck out from the wall. Buttresses? I wasn't up on my medieval architecture. But behind them would be good hiding spots, and they were hard to see as I crept up to them.

Still, I had to stop creeping and start moving if Ben went this way. I might not catch him, but I could let Mark know which way he went. I picked up my pace, and even through the rain, it was clear I was about to run out of lawn. The strip of green took a sharp bend left ahead of me, around the corner of the retaining wall, and so did the moat.

I heard voices. Not just the party voices, I thought—higher in volume and cadence. An argument? Then a strange, piercing cry stopped me cold. And I *was* cold, chilled to the bone, shivering in the rain and the dark.

I closed my eyes, shook my head. "Let's go, Pepper," I muttered. "Don't be a wimp."

And I trotted around the corner.

Ahead of me was a spectacular, strange sight. Growing out of the moat on the left-hand side was a weeping willow, strangely lit in the dark by party projections as it moved in the wind. Beyond it was the grand stone bridge over the moat with its wide, pointed arches, also strangely flashing and glowing. Ye olde poet Chaucer, who oversaw its construction as part of his day job—a fact I'd gleaned from the tour—never could have foreseen this. The lights reflected in the water, creating a surreal, shifting landscape.

Among those lights, something else caught my eye, a strange, dark shape along the bank of the moat, half-hidden by the trailing branches of the willow tree. A sick feeling clenched my gut. Had Ben hurt someone in his flight?

I wrenched myself forward, running this time, and skidded to a stop just shy of the bridge.

The shape was a person. A body? They lay on their stomach, half bent over the stone that retained the edge of the moat, one arm trailing in the water.

Blond hair. Blood.

Oh, no.

"Neil! Where are you?" I screamed.

Perhaps it was telling that I screamed for Neil first, but my screams soon caught the attention of others. As people looked on from the bridge, trying to figure out what was happening, Neil showed up, followed by Mark, then a police officer with big sideburns who'd been hired to do security for the event.

"Is it—?" Mark asked, his face wet and pale in the weird light.

Ari came running up behind him.

"Oh my God," she cried. "Ben!"

Chapter Twenty-Eight

Ben was dead. The officer with the big sideburns checked his pulse to be sure.

Ben. Our fugitive. Our bright and merry tour guide. He was dead. Was it my fault? I'd chased him around the wall.

Ari, crying, ran off.

"Did he fall and hit his head?" My voice quavered.

The policeman, who'd been calling in reinforcements, shook his head. "Not my department, but I don't think so, miss," he said. "Looks to me as if he was struck." He gestured next to the body, and for the first time, I saw a brick there. Something dark and wet glinted on it. Not rain. I was pretty sure it was blood.

I gasped, and my stomach rolled. I clutched my mouth and staggered away, finding myself under one of the arches of the bridge, where I almost tripped over a pile of loose bricks. That explained where the murder weapon came from.

At least I was out of the rain and could breathe without feeling like I was drowning. I leaned against the stone wall, gulping in cool breaths of air.

When I opened my eyes, I saw a rectangular object lying in the grass, and without even thinking, I bent over and picked it up. A book. Leather-bound, about the size and heft of a nice paperback. The edges zipped up. Maybe not a book, then?

Albert had mentioned Ben always reading a book.

I desperately wanted to open it. I was out of the rain here. But a lot of people were around. Maybe it was wrong, but I wasn't ready to share yet. So I untucked my soaked shirt and stuffed the book down the back of my pants. Take it easy—it ended up between my sensible cotton "I'm at work" undies and my stretchy pants seat but far enough down to give it a little protection in spite of my soaked state.

I'd turn it in eventually, but I had questions.

"Pepper?"

I startled, then realized Neil had found me in the protective shadows of the arch.

He put an arm around me. "You OK?"

"Yes. I found something," I confessed. "I think it's Ben's. A book. A notebook, maybe."

Flashing lights appeared beyond the bridge. The full complement of law enforcement would be here any minute. Neil's face reflected his inner conflict. Of course, he knew we should turn it in. But he was curious, too.

"Look at this!" I heard Mark call behind me, and we hurried over to him next to the wall, back in the rain. The officer was distracted, talking to someone on his mobile phone, giving directions to the crime scene, I thought.

"I found this." Mark had Ben's backpack in his hand.

"What's in it?" I hissed. "Here, come out of the rain." And I led him and Neil back under the arch of the bridge.

Mark looked over his shoulder, then unzipped the backpack and riffled through its contents quickly, hunched over to conceal it from the officer for just one more minute. "A wallet. Brollies."

"He had them for us earlier. Thoughtful," I said of the umbrellas.

"He was," Mark agreed. "Or so I thought. There's a big sealed envelope. And what's this?" He pulled out a cardboard tube perhaps a foot in length, plastic caps on each end.

"Can we take a quick look?" I asked.

"I suppose it won't hurt." Mark plucked off one end while Neil looked on. And pulled out a roll of parchment paper.

"Real quick." I really wanted to see it, and we didn't have much time.

Mark unrolled the parchment.

It looked like some kind of certificate. Colorful images decorated the edges, like an illuminated manuscript, but it was obviously new, with fresh, bright ink and heraldic imagery—crowns, horses, lions and that kind of thing.

"Let it be known," Mark read the fancy calligraphic lettering, "that the bearer of this certificate is hereby to be addressed as Lord Stephan Sully, Marquess of Doodleham ..."

Lord Stephan Sully ... Mr. Mixy?

"What do you have there?" Constable Sideburns had noticed us.

Mark swiftly rolled up the parchment, stuck it in the tube and sealed it, then zipped it up inside the bag and turned. "We found this. I'm pretty sure it's Ben's."

"The victim's? I'll take that." The officer looked ticked off as Mark handed it over. I kept my mouth shut about the book.

More police arrived, and Mark knew one of them, a female detective who said she wanted to talk to all of us—inside.

I couldn't blame her, and frankly, I was relieved. I didn't want to be out here in the cold and the dark and near poor dead Ben.

We three made our way inside. I glimpsed Lottie with her arm around Nigel, on their way out; they had their coats on and looked like they'd seen a ghost. And he was seriously wet.

We headed down to the medieval banquet hall. The only folks still there were Barclay, Gina, Luke and Melody, standing and quietly talking among themselves with our gear all boxed up, and Alastair, who'd pulled up a chair from somewhere and slouched on it, looking cranky.

Our bartenders greeted us with concern, but Alastair just seemed impatient.

"I sent my people home," Alastair said. "Ari was a mess. I understand there's been an accident?"

Mark nodded. "Ben, I'm afraid." He shook his head, ran a hand through his wet hair. "I should have let him go. Let the police find him."

"It's not your fault," I said. "I wonder if it's mine. I told him you just wanted to talk."

"It's not your fault either," Neil said. "Ben was on the run. It was strange. Besides, it didn't look like an accident."

"That's what the cop seemed to think," I said as I eased behind the bar we'd used, crouched and slipped the book out of my pants and into my messenger bag before anyone noticed my strangely square buttocks.

"Someone murdered him?" Gina asked in horror.

I looped my bag cross-body over my head and came out from behind the bar. "Maybe. Probably."

Barclay wrapped Gina in a hug.

"But why?" Mark asked.

"Maybe it really was an accident," Melody suggested.

"Only if a brick spontaneously leapt out of the wall and flew across the grass and hit him in the head," I said.

"Ugh." Luke scowled.

"Sorry. I really am sorry." A tear came to my eye, and I wiped it away. I was about to bring up what we'd found, but the detective came in, her short, brown hair messy and her long raincoat wet.

"Hello again, Ilsa," Mark said.

"Detective Inspector Ibsen to you." She had a glint in her eye as she looked him over. Obviously she knew Mark. Perhaps rather well.

Mark smiled one his charming smiles. "My apologies, Detective Inspector."

He took the lead, briefly explaining that he'd been investigating some missing books from his library, that Ben worked for him, and that when Ben left in a hurry tonight, Mark had asked his friends—us—to look for him. It was a simplified version of what had happened but essentially true. The detective asked me a few questions about finding the body and promised to follow up with Mark. Then she headed out, back to the crime scene, I presumed.

"We need to talk this out—but not here." Mark shot me a significant look.

"I want to get out of these wet clothes," I said. It was a sign of just how serious Mark was that no flirty remark followed.

"Well, I'm going home." Alastair rose and stretched.

"No, you're not," Mark said. "Come to the house. We have to talk—Neil, Pepper, you and me."

"Thank God, because I need to sleep," Melody said. "Maybe after a drink. Sorry, guys."

"No, it's fine," Neil said. "You all need a break. It's been a tough night."

While Alastair drove himself, Mark drove the passenger van— Ben had apparently left the keys in it.

Rain doused us anew as we unloaded at Mark's place. I was desperate for dry clothes.

"Fifteen minutes," Mark said to me and Neil as we all entered his mansion, the boys pushing the dolly with the gear. "We'll meet here."

"What about us?" Barclay said. "Do you need anything?"

"You all take it easy," Neil said. "Stow the stuff in the kitchen first, though."

"What about that drink?" Melody said.

"I'll have Albert show you to the billiard room," Mark said. "Where is Albert? He should be here."

"It's OK," Luke said. "We know where the billiard room is. But I'm going to change first."

They all agreed and scattered.

"I'll wait," Alastair said as if waiting was an intolerable inconvenience. He crashed into one of the four wide leather chairs that encircled a round, low wooden table in front of the big fireplace, which crackled with a pleasant fire.

Mrs. Pidgeon emerged from the shadows and addressed Mark. "Sir? Is something wrong?"

Damn Dionysus. She either had great radar or prior knowledge.

Mark pulled her aside and spoke softly to her. To my shock, she burst into tears. Then she shot me a venomous look that seemed to say, *This is your fault.*

Ugh. Maybe it was my fault. Dejected, I trotted up the stairs after Neil, and we went to our separate rooms. It was overly cool in my royal bedroom, but at least it was dry. I had a hasty, hot shower and pulled on jeans, a T-shirt and a black sweater, along with my sneakers. I gave my hair a two-minute blowout just so it wouldn't be hanging off my head like seaweed. And I donned my dried-off glasses, grabbed my bag and headed back downstairs.

The bag was damp, too, from our brief dash from the van to the house, but at least the canvas had shed a lot of the rain. The book should be OK. And I was *very* eager to look at the book.

Neil already sat in the comfy chair opposite Alastair by the blazing fireplace, and I had to laugh. Victoria sat in the chair between them, her head cocked, staring at Alastair curiously.

"Do you have a special affinity with this creature?" Alastair barked at me in his haughtiest tone. "Will you make it stop staring at me?"

I choked back a giggle. Though I was grateful for something to smile at. "Maybe she likes you."

"I seriously doubt it," Alastair said, and Neil and I both laughed.

Victoria looked up, gave up on Alastair, hopped off her chair and bounded over to me, putting her little paws up against my legs. I picked her up and petted her. I needed some dog love after this wretched night.

But she squirmed to get down, and I realized why. Mark had come, in slouchy khakis and a beat-up butternut sweater that looked like it must be a favorite. He was still yummy, no doubt about it, and Victoria seemed to think so too as she ran to him. He scooped her up, hugged her and petted her. Mark needed some dog love, too, it seemed.

He and I took the remaining chairs, and Mrs. Pidgeon appeared with a tray that she set on the round table between us. She seemed fully composed and didn't even look in my direction. "Will there be anything else, sir?"

"That's all for tonight," Mark said. "Thank you, Mrs. Pidgeon."

She nodded, turned, and disappeared back into the shadows.

"Now that the angel of death has left the room ..." Alastair said.

It shamed me that I'd been thinking almost the same thing.

"Now, now," Mark said. "She was very fond of Ben. And she's a remarkable help to me. Besides, she's brought us hot chocolate and biscuits." He distributed the mugs, and Victoria curled up in his lap.

Alastair sniffed his cocoa skeptically, took a sip, and even he seemed to be pleased as he relaxed back in his chair.

And for good reason. The cocoa was delicious. Mrs. Pidgeon wouldn't have poisoned us, would she? I looked at the mug again, evaluating my risk. *Nah.* She wouldn't kill Mark. I didn't think so, anyway. I snagged a cookie, too.

I took another deep sip. Neil caught my eye and smiled. I nodded back. We were OK. Right?

Mark looked around at us. "All right. Let's figure this out."

Chapter Twenty-Nine

My imagination got away from me for a second here in the cavernous hall with just the fireplace and the dim chandelier for light. I felt a little like one of King Arthur's knights as we sat in our four big leather chairs circling the round coffee table. Not exactly *the* Round Table, but still.

Only we were three bartenders and a distiller, with no swords in sight. Not even those little cocktail swords we stick through cherries. And we didn't have Merlin to magically solve our mystery.

"Let's talk about the parchment first," Mark said. "What do you think it was?"

I swallowed a bite of my cookie. Shortbread. *Mmm.* "I think it was intended for Mr. Mixy." Mark raised his eyebrows. "Stephan Sully is his real name."

"Oh!" Mark said.

"Or maybe I should call him—what was it? The Marquess of Doodleham?" I rolled my eyes.

"There's no Duchy of Doodleham," Mark said with scorn.

Neil wore an amused expression. "It's fake. A fake certificate."

"Right," I said. "Mr. Mixy wouldn't shut up about how his pet genealogist was going to prove he was royalty. And Mr. Mixy paid out thousands of dollars for this so-called proof. Ben even egged him on that night at The Dandy Tipple."

"So Ben was scamming Mr. Mixy," Neil said.

"Could Stephan-Mixy or whatever have killed Ben?" Mark asked. "Angry customer?"

Neil and I looked at each other. "No," we both said.

"Mr. Mixy isn't smart enough to kill someone," I said. "Except maybe by accident."

"Besides, Ben hadn't delivered the goods, it looks like," Neil added.

"Ben obviously needed money," I said. "For what?"

"He liked to talk about horse racing," Mark said. "I thought it was just a hobby. I fear it was more. Perhaps he owed money to his bookmakers."

I nodded. "A reasonable explanation. But it must've been a lot if he was trying to pull off a jewelry heist too. Or maybe he just liked stealing things?"

"If I had to guess, I'd say he was the one digging a tunnel into the jewelry store next door to your bar," Neil said to Alastair.

"And he took my good liquor while he was at it. I'm never getting that back." Alastair frowned and sipped his cocoa. "Surely he's sold it by now."

"We'll have to tell the police all this," Mark said. "When they search his flat, maybe they'll find your bottles and my books."

After all this trouble and Ben's sad end, I hoped they found Mark's precious *The Sword in the Stone*. I turned to him.

"Ben said something odd when I ran into him in the billiards room at Eltham Palace. He said he wouldn't let you have it—something. That he was close to getting something you wanted."

Mark appeared genuinely baffled as he stroked Victoria, who gently snored in his lap. "What? I think the only thing he stole from me was books. Speaking of which—Pepper, do you have his book?"

I nodded, set down my mug and opened my bag, which I'd placed at my feet. I pulled out the weathered, slightly damp brown leather book—perhaps a binder with a book's ridged spine, given the zipper that ran around the other three sides.

I held onto it for a second. "Uh, everyone OK with messing around with evidence?"

"Can we get on with this?" Alastair asked.

Mark lifted an eyebrow, and flirtatiousness crept into his tone. "I'll mess around if you want."

I raised an eyebrow back and pursed my lips. And unzipped the ... notebook. That's what it was. In fact, I had to catch a couple of pieces of paper as they started to slide out. I did a quick thumb-through. Scribbles and drawings covered the pages, and lots of notes were stuffed or glued inside.

"Any pictures of the Holy Grail in there?" Neil asked.

I gave him some side-eye, though I always appreciated a good Indiana Jones joke. "It's a lot to process. And I don't want to pass the papers around because I think we shouldn't get them out of order."

"Good instinct," Mark said.

Even Alastair had leaned forward. "So what does it say?"

"OK, let's see. The first page has a big title written on it." I held it up.

"The Lawless Journal," Mark said. "So he was basking in the criminal life? Why don't I believe any of this?"

I kept flipping through pages until something caught my eye. "There are a bunch of scribblings in here about France, along with a letter. I think it's a photocopy. Looks old. Crap, it's in French too. Who knows French?"

"Not my best topic," Mark said. "I'm *fluente* in Italian. And a bit of Japanese."

"I know a little French," Neil said. Of course he did.

I just knew *un poco* restaurant Spanish. "You read it, then."

A corner of Neil's mouth lifted, and I stood and handed over the letter. He met me halfway. Our fingers touched. There was a spark. Our eyes met, and then we both sat back in our chairs, he with the letter in hand. I held my finger in the book where it had been and waited for him to look over the missive.

"Not so ancient. Dated—I think this says 1863. This seems to be a letter to ... a child. It says Mr. Tringham left you with us and that you are ours now. He said to never say anything about you, but we felt you needed to know because the knowledge might come in handy someday. That Mr. Tringham was a very great man and writer and popular here in France as well as England."

My mouth gaped. "OK, as William Buttersby would say, I'm just a dumb American who can name only one author, but could this letter be about ..."

"Charles Dickens?" Neil cocked his head in a "maybe" expression.

"He had a lot of children, didn't he?" Mark asked.

"But probably only one illegitimate one, thought to have died, and that hasn't been absolutely proven," Alastair said. We all turned to stare at him. "What? I did read literature at Oxford."

Oh. So *that's* what Alastair studied at Oxford while Neil was studying astronomy—before Neil dropped out. And then also ended up as a mixologist. It made a certain sense. Bartenders were all about telling—and hearing—stories.

"And this Mr. Tringham?" I asked.

"Dickens used that name sometimes," Neil said. "I remember reading it in one of his biographies."

"So this letter implies Dickens had an illegitimate baby who survived?" Mark said. "My God, why hasn't this letter surfaced before? It would be worth a fortune—and not just in filthy lucre. To history."

"And if it was worth a fortune and Ben had it, why didn't he just sell it?" Neil asked.

"But this is just a photocopy," I pointed out. "Maybe he didn't have the original."

I took the letter back from Neil. On instinct, I pulled out my phone and snapped a photo of it. Then I folded it and reinserted it where I'd found it and kept turning pages, taking photos as I went. "There's a lot about Dickens in here. Holy crap."

"What else?" Impatience tinged Mark's voice.

"More notes about letters. Ellen Ternan's name is in here a lot," I said.

Neil nodded, excitement in his eyes. "Ellen—Dickens's mistress Nelly. The one Ari was talking about. The one he kept secret for years. The one his friends helped keep quiet. And Nelly kept the secret, too; kept it from her eventual husband, her children. When her son found out, he's thought to have burned any letters she had from Dickens. And Dickens's son Henry probably burned anything from her."

I looked at him funny.

"What? I told you I read a couple of biographies," Neil said.

"A conspiracy of silence. It didn't really work, though, did it?" Mark bit into a cookie, and Victoria lifted her head, so he gave her a piece, too. She munched contentedly, the firelight reflecting in her brown eyes.

"We know about Nelly, but we don't know that much," Neil said.

"OK, so wait a minute." I flipped more pages. "There are notes here about letters. But if there aren't any letters—"

"But maybe there are," Alastair said. "Talk about a fortune."

I shook my head. "But if he just wanted money, he would've sold that first letter. I mean, if he had the original."

Neil caught my gaze. "What if Ben had a more—*personal* connection to Ellen Ternan?"

I looked at him, then down at the book. Then up at him. "You mean the letter—that he obtained the letter from the source? Or, I mean—it was *handed down to him?*"

"He's ... a descendant of Charles Dickens?" Mark frowned. "Or was?"

Alastair sniffed. "You walk through London, you'll trip over a descendant of Dickens."

"But not Dickens and Nelly," I said. "And Ben was on a quest—a quest to find her letters. And tonight, he acted like he was onto something. Maybe he wanted to claim a piece of history. He did Dickens reenactments. He volunteered at the museum."

I'd been flipping pages and taking photos as we talked, not really processing what I saw. I knew I couldn't hang on to this journal, and I wanted to preserve as much as possible so I could look at it at leisure.

Most of the inserts didn't seem important, so I got more selective. Then another piece of paper fell out, old and brittle. It had been folded once, in half. If it was original and important, Ben had cared about the contents more than the value.

I gingerly unfolded it and snapped a photo before reading it.

Neil had caught on to my interest. "What is it?"

"A poem," I said, just as a deep *bing-bong* resounded through the hall, making me jump.

"Who could that be?" Mark said. "And where's Albert?"

Was that the doorbell? It sound like the Hunchback of Notre Dame was pulling a rope somewhere.

I folded the poem quickly and stuffed it into the book. I flipped through more pages, snapping photos, as Mark got up, slipping Victoria off his lap and onto the chair. He walked across the large, echoing space and pulled the big doors open.

"Answering your own door, Mark?" came a cocky English voice that I recognized. I looked around to see D.I. Ibsen. Behind her were two police cars with flashing lights and a couple more officers standing outside.

"Good evening, Detective Inspector. And how may I help you?"

"I think we need to chat a bit more about Mr. Burton and the book thefts. And is there anything else you'd like to tell me? Something you found at the scene?"

Oh, shit. One of the officers was Constable Sideburns, who peered inside with malevolent curiosity as rain dripped off his hat. I looked down at the book. He must have noticed something at the time and didn't know what to make of it, then told her. Maybe my square ass.

Mark seemed to put it together, too. "I had one of my colleagues bring back his book. I thought perhaps his family would like to have it."

"Only after we look at it." She gave him a "you should know better" expression. "And we'd like to talk to you, too. Will you come with us, please?"

"Am I under arrest?"

"Not like it's the first time you've been in handcuffs," she quipped. Mid-sip, I almost spit out my cocoa. "But no. I'd rather discuss this down at the station. On the record."

He looked at us and shrugged, then back to her. "All right. If we must. Pepper? The book?"

By this time, I'd shot as many pictures as I could, but I knew I hadn't gotten everything. Still, I left my phone on the table, zipped up the book and brought it over.

"Thank you," Mark said, taking it.

"Thank you," D.I. Ibsen said, plucking it from his hands. "Let's go."

"Text me!" I said.

Mark just winked.

Mrs. Pidgeon emerged from the shadows with a lightweight rain jacket in her hand for him. Was she psychic? Oh, wait. Ben had said her phone pinged whenever someone pressed the intercom at the gate. She'd let the cops in.

Mark donned his jacket and left with D.I. Ibsen. Mrs. Pidgeon melted away again, and an eerie quiet settled over the hall.

I moved back to the crackling fire, but I didn't sit. Victoria sat up on the chair Mark had vacated, looked up at me and whimpered, so I picked her up. Neil got up, too, and came around the table. We both looked back at Alastair. His head had fallen back, his floppy hair veiled his eyes, and he snored softly.

"Might as well leave him there. He'll be all right," Neil whispered.

About this time, the rest of our crew appeared. Neil put a finger in front of his lips in the "hush" gesture, and they all grinned at Alastair as they quietly moved around us and headed up the stairs, looking relaxed after their drink. I had a flash of envy. But curiosity won out.

"I want to talk about this some more, OK?" I whispered to Neil. "I think you need to see this poem."

Chapter Thirty

We left Alastair snoozing and wandered till we found the drawing room where Mark held the reception the first day. Neil flipped a light switch, and a lamp came on in the middle of the room. We went to the antique-looking couch next to it and sat. It creaked and felt antique, too. Meaning a spring poked me in the same place I'd hidden the book. Victoria curled up on a low ottoman at our feet.

"Did you see anyone else when you were searching around the moat?" Neil asked.

"No. I heard some partygoers but no one close. Though I thought I heard a couple of voices before I rounded the corner and found Ben. Maybe even an argument."

"Could you identify anything about the voices? Male? Female? Accent?"

"It was just sounds in the rain, but loud. Agitated. Though I did see one thing that struck me—when I saw Nigel and Lottie leaving Eltham Palace, he was soaked, and he looked freaked out."

"Or maybe just drunk?" Neil suggested. "And a lot of people were wet who were outside looking at the light show. Anyway, let's look at this poem. You got a picture?"

"I did. It stood out for a couple of reasons. The paper seemed old, like it might be from an original source. The edge was rough, as if it had been ripped out of something. And I noticed that the following pages in Ben's book had what looked like pieces of the poem with notes."

"Interesting. Ben must have thought it was important."

"That's what I thought." I called up the image of the poem on my phone and handed it to him. "Here. Read it out loud. Then I can close my eyes and think."

He smiled. "I think you just like me reading to you."

"Maybe." I chuckled and closed my eyes as he began to read.

You always called me Patient,
yet my impatience was great.
You fueled the train with fire,
yet derailment was our fate.

I took your rose and honey
but could never take your name.
The white violet we left in France
Can never be reclaimed.

I know your Lawless secret
though the world does not know mine.
Words that you would have me burn
ferment and bide their time.

I'll be gone if ever
they escape their palace vault.
My ruin was not quite so blue
as black, a widow's fault.

Always you invented lives,
and now I'll make one, too.
I've time to write a second act
and stave off thoughts of you.

I will make the best of times
and plant under the sun
a garden by the sea where grows
a white chrysanthemum.

In the quiet room, the only sounds when he finished were the
rain tapping on the windows and snuffles from Victoria.

"There's that word again—lawless," I said.

"It's uppercase. Wait. Mind if I use this to search for something?" Neil waved the phone at me.

"Go ahead."

He tapped with his thumbs for a minute. "Here. Ellen Lawless
Ternan. It was part of her name."

"For real? Did she make it up?"

"For real. She was an actress, came from a theatrical family. I
think it was a family name."

"Good name," I said. "This has to be about her, doesn't it? The
narrator cites a Lawless secret. The baby?"

"Or giving up the baby? Could Dickens have given up the baby,
as that letter that Ben had suggests? Did he do it with or without
her permission?"

"Without her permission? What a horrible thought. We'll never
know," I said. "And I have to think *derailment was our fate* alludes to
the train accident Ari talked about."

"Could Nelly have written this?" Neil asked.

"Wouldn't that be amazing? Could be. I wonder where Ben
found it?"

"Maybe in the Dickens museum, maybe in a journal in the
archives, and he just ripped the page out. A scholar would never do
that, but Ben might've."

I looked over his shoulder at the screen. "Go back to the
poem."

Neil hit a few buttons and went back to my photo of the poem.

I took back the phone, zoomed in and scrolled through each line. "A lot of flower references."

"That's a Victorian thing. Flowers were like a language."

"Do you speak that language, too?"

He laughed. "No."

"Let me google it." I searched for some of the references in the poem. "Red rose means love. Not shocking."

He nodded. "And bees were a symbol of hard work, so honey could be associated with that. The financial reward of hard work. He gave her and her family money when they really needed it. And it also connotes sweetness."

"Makes sense. OK, this page says white violets were a symbol of innocence."

"Nothing more innocent than a baby," Neil noted.

"A baby left in France. Wow."

"Exactly. What about the white chrysanthemum?"

I looked further on the web page. "A symbol of truth."

"And in the context of that last stanza, she did live by the sea for a while with her new husband. They ran a school, I think," Neil said. "Plus there's that 'best of times' reference, which makes me think of *A Tale of Two Cities*."

"Haven't read it yet." I flipped back to the poem.

"For shame!" Neil grinned as I pressed my lips together. "Anyway, if you went to this poem thinking about Dickens and Nelly, there's a lot to suggest that's who this is about. And it's in first person. She mentions being a widow."

"And this is funny," I said. "In that same stanza, she writes *my ruin was not quite so blue*—is that a reference to the Blue Ruin? Why would she mention gin?"

"Victorian wordplay?"

"But if you go back up, she says *Words that you would have me burn ferment and bide their time*. Fermentation could mean wine or alcohol. Words fermenting ..."

"I'll be gone if ever they escape their palace vault." Neil looked at me. "Palace ... vault."

"Not a medieval palace." Adrenaline zipped through me. I was awake now. "A gin palace?"

"The *vault* at The Dandy Tipple? Is that where Ben thought she'd hidden the letters?"

"Maybe, before the bar was ever The Dandy Tipple. But why there?" I asked.

"There aren't many gin palaces left," Neil said. "Maybe it's just one of many that Ben investigated. But Dickens was known to frequent that place. She knew about it, surely. And about his love of drink. Kind of ironic if she stashed her letters there."

"Sounds like a stretch. But say that's what happened. Maybe she knew the proprietor, had a co-conspirator. Where would the letters be?" I pictured the vault in my mind, the secret room with its empty niches and no other obvious hiding places, though the vaults did have a lot of dusty corners.

"Even if they were there, maybe they're gone," Neil said. "It looks like Ben did a lot of searching in the vaults, even found the secret room."

"But he told me he was close to getting what he wanted. He hadn't found it yet. Said he was keeping it from Mark. He probably figured out that Mark co-owned the bar. Maybe he thought Mark found the letters and took them home, given what a collector he is." I was on a roll. "So Ben went looking in Mark's library—yes! I found a Dickens book upside down on the shelf. I thought it was odd. It was probably him looking around. Then he saw the rare books as an easy way to make money."

"That makes sense." Neil leaned over to look at the poem again.

My body suddenly woke up to the fact that he was sitting right next to me, warm and solid, and he smelled good, too. I closed my eyes and inhaled as he spoke.

"Always you invented lives, and now I'll make one, too. I've time to

write a second act and stave off thoughts of you. Dickens invented lives not just in his books but for real—his and Nelly's."

I opened my eyes. "And she wrote a second act in her life."

"I read that she even lied about her age when she married her husband," he said. "Made herself younger."

"Wow. She learned to lie from the best, apparently. But for someone who kept her life so secret, why would she leave his letters behind so the truth could be known?"

"Revenge?" Neil asked. "Or maybe she *wanted* her progeny to know when the knowledge could no longer harm her, after she was gone."

"Her later descendants, maybe, but not her own children. She didn't trust them enough to tell them the truth when she was alive."

"So she hid the letters and left clues," Neil mused, "knowing someone would come looking eventually since Dickens was just that famous. But I still don't know why she wanted them revealed."

"Maybe she wanted to clear her name, in a sense. Show the world she wasn't just some Jezebel or doormat. Deep down, she must've known how important these letters were. And she resented Dickens, but maybe she had a twisted pride in being the chosen one. Even she couldn't stave off thoughts of him." I reached over and patted Victoria, who looked up at me as if she'd rather be sleeping. *Let sleeping dogs lie.*

Stave off thoughts of you.

"Oh my God," I said. "Stave. Barrels. A barrel stave."

Neil sat up straight. "There are barrels at the Tipple. Some are original, Alastair said. Do you think Ben looked in the barrels?"

"I don't know. But we should. We should do it right now."

"Why now?"

"Because the police have the book now," I said. "It could become public. The tabloids would have a field day. Treasure hunters will be crawling all over it. Let's look. Let's do it for Mark."

Neil quirked his mouth at me. "Do I really have to do it for Mark?"

I laughed. "He's treated us like royalty, you know."

"Because of you."

"Because of his missing books." I fluttered my eyelashes at him.

He laughed. "Let's do it. But first, we have to wake up Alastair."

Chapter Thirty-One

A lastair was none too happy to be awakened, and he was even less happy to be asked to drive us.

"I don't see how I can drive both of you. And I'd rather not."

"Why not?" I grabbed my bag from where I'd left it in the entrance hall, and Mrs. Pidgeon, of all people, appeared to take Victoria from me. She gave me another grim look but petted the dog with care as she carried the pup away, speaking softly to her. Go figure.

Alastair ran a hand through his floppy hair. "My car is not intended for passengers. It's a collectible."

"We have to get there fast, and I don't want to wait for a cab on a rainy night this far out," Neil said.

"Is this *really* that urgent?" Alastair asked.

"Letters written by Charles Dickens may be sitting in your bar right now," I said. "The whole case is about to go public. And we think we know where to look."

A tug-of-war seemed to possess Alastair's face. I didn't know if he was thinking about fame or money or heading off thieves, but he finally agreed. "Don't say I didn't warn you. Wait on the front step, and I'll bring it round."

Neil and I waited in the doorway instead, putting off our walk into the rain, as Alastair ran off to a side parking area. He returned in a tiny roller skate of a car and beckoned us impatiently through the rain-streaked windows.

"I think it only has two seats," Neil said.

"Oh."

"So ... I guess you're sitting on my lap?"

I looked at him, trying to gauge whether this was something he was OK with. "Uh-huh?"

"Unless you want me to drive, and you can sit on Alastair's lap." Neil grinned.

"No! Let's go. But if you're squished, it's not my fault."

"Oh, do squish me, please," he joked as we ran out. He got in the left side, and I squeezed in on top of him, facing forward. For the record, this wasn't as romantic as one might think. I'm only a year or so out from thirty, and my butt is at least thirty-five, so I preferred having my own seat.

Neil tried to get the belt around both of us, but it didn't work.

"Just buckle yourself in. It's OK," I said, squirming so he could do so. He made weird grunting noises, probably because Mr. Safety didn't like the arrangements.

"What are we riding in?" I asked Alastair as he careened around the gravel circle and down the drive, waited for the gate to slide open, and peeled out onto the wet street. I kept flinching because I still felt like we were on the wrong side of the road.

"It's a classic—2005 Smart Roadster."

"I never knew such a thing existed," I said.

"It's a convertible," Alastair said proudly.

"Great night for it." Neil shifted me as I tried not to crush anything important. "I think I saw it on a list of the worst sports cars ever made."

Alastair shot him a glare. "I can very well leave you on the side of the road right here."

"It's cute!" I figured placating Alastair was better than trying to walk through the rain at night. "Great for parking, I bet."

"Excellent," he said, slightly mollified.

On the way, we filled him in on what we thought the poem might mean. "Not a very good poet, was she?" was his main takeaway.

He proved his car's parkability when he wedged it into a tiny space outside The Dandy Tipple. The bar had closed a little early for the evening, Alastair explained, since most of the staff had been working the Eltham Palace party. Still, it was late for most people, around 1 a.m., and the street was fairly quiet.

"Oh, crap. We should tell Mark where we are," I said as Neil and I un-pretzeled and got out of the car. We ducked under the over-hang at the front door to get out of the rain while I dug my phone out of my bag.

"Well, I'm going in," Alastair said. "After all the fuss, I want to be sure everything's all right. I'll get some lights on."

"We'll be right there," Neil said as Alastair unlocked the door and went inside.

I woke up my phone. "You can go in," I told Neil. "It's all right."

He just shook his head—protective or wanting to know Mark's situation, I wasn't sure.

I texted Mark. "Think we have a lead on D letters. At Dandy Tipple."

We waited around for a minute, but there was no reply.

"He's probably still being interrogated," Neil said in an amused tone.

"Or he went to his house and we crossed in the mail. Or he went home with D.I. Ibsen."

Neil raised his eyebrows. "Always thinking, aren't you?"

"Or drinking."

He smiled. "Let's get in there before Alastair makes the greatest literary discovery of our time all by himself."

I snorted, and we went inside. Dance music pounded through the main bar.

"That Alastair loves to party," I said, and Neil laughed.

Between the tiled floor and the pressed-tin ceiling, the music bounced around the space, especially now that no one was in it. Just a couple of lights were on, reflecting off the crystals in the chandeliers and the etched glass. A ladder leaned against the back bar.

"Where is he?" Neil asked.

"Probably the office. Or maybe he went to look at the vaults." I led the way to the *Staff Only* door. We entered the dim hallway beyond, where the music was more muted. The office door was ajar, and I eased it open. "Alastair?"

"Holy hell." Neil saw him first, lying akimbo behind an overgrown old wooden desk.

"Oh my God. Is he alive?"

Neil stepped forward, leaned down and touched Alastair's neck. Alastair moaned. Neil shook his shoulder. "Wake up."

Alastair moaned again, even batting the air as if to wave him off, and Neil stood up. "I think he's OK, but maybe we'd better call an ambulance."

"Wait," I whispered. "Do you hear something?"

Neil froze. I froze.

Playing counterpart to the bass booming in the other room, a clanking sound echoed through the hallway. But not *from* the hallway.

"I think it's coming from the vaults," I whispered. "Somebody's down there."

"All the more reason to call the cops."

"We will. We can take a peek and then get out real quick. Have you no sense of curiosity?"

"I have a sense that we might be dealing with a killer," Neil said. "You'll find out who it is soon enough when they come out. We can wait outside."

"But we can't leave Alastair, and we shouldn't move him. Call 911 and then we'll go down and look, and then we'll come up here and lock the office door and wait for the cops.'"

"We can lock ourselves in now."

I huffed out an impatient breath. "But then we won't see who it is because we'll be locked behind the door!"

Neil sighed. "All right. And it's 999. I'll call." He picked up the receiver on an old-school button phone on Alastair's desk and called, telling the dispatcher we needed an ambulance and police for a possible intruder.

"They're still clanking," I murmured when he hung up.

"Just a quick look, Pepper. We make sure they can't see us. Then we turn around and run like hell."

I nodded. We could do this.

We gently closed the office door behind us, then crept down the hall toward the stairway door. It was ajar, as I pointed out to Neil, literally pointing in an exaggerated gesture.

He nodded, mouthing "I know!" We eased it open. It creaked briefly, and we froze, but the clanking continued from below.

There was no light on the spiral stone stairs. I was a little bit over spiral staircases at this point, honestly. But light leaked from above and below—not from the bulb at the bottom of the stairs, which was not on, but from deep in the vaults. I could see the dim glow back there once we reached the bottom of the steps. And we silently agreed we didn't want to flip the switches to give ourselves away.

It smelled extra musty here tonight, and the floor glinted with water, much bigger puddles than last time. It sounded like there was a trickle, a leak somewhere.

The metal gate was ajar, and the dim light appeared to shine from the recess at the back of the vaults where the secret room was located.

Neil shook his head at me.

I scowled and nodded vigorously.

He mimed getting struck on the head.

I flexed my muscles to show I wasn't afraid. Though I didn't have much to flex.

After this went on for at least a minute, he finally rolled his eyes and shrugged. But he put a hand out, keeping me behind him, and went first.

We slipped through the gate. I pointed toward the back. Nothing was moving in front of the light, which meant the clanker had to be in the secret room. So we advanced slowly. The puddles here had become more like a small pond, joining forces and leaking through the sides of my sneakers. I didn't like the cold squishiness settling into my socks. I started to get a bad feeling about this.

But we were almost to the alcove. We crept closer and peered through the ragged hole in the brick wall. I couldn't see anyone, but they might've been hiding just inside the opening, behind what was left of the wall.

Neil once again took the lead, inching closer, half-crouching. And then he stuck his head all the way in the secret room. "No one is in here," he whispered. "There's a battery lantern. I can't tell what's making the clanking noise, but I hear water, too. It's ankle-deep in there."

Behind us, a much louder clank shattered the musty quiet of the vault, and we whirled.

"The gate!" I said, and we dashed to the center of the main room. But it was too late. A figure in a bulky, dark Dickens-era cloak, complete with hood, turned away and dashed up the stairs. The big, shiny padlock was again secured on the gate. We were trapped.

"They must've been hiding in the wine racks or something," Neil said. "We missed them in the dark."

The trickling sound was getting louder, more like gushing, and water swirled above my ankles now, getting right into the sneakers.

Neil looked down. "This isn't good."

"Where's all the water coming from? And what's the noise?"

"Let's look and see." He led the way back into the secret room. We waded in and looked around at the exposed niches in the walls. Closer to the floor, I noticed a new gap in the bricks, with plumbing visible inside.

"Metal pipes," Neil said. "They're being pushed together, and that's what made the noise."

I didn't want to ask what pushed them together because I didn't want Neil to confirm what I saw with my own eyes.

Water gushed through the opening in pulses like waves, pushing the pipes against each other so they banged out an eerie rhythm. The water wasn't from the pipes. It was from somewhere else.

And it was rising.

Chapter Thirty-Two

"Is the water rising faster, or is it just me?" I asked Neil, clutching his arm in the middle of the secret room. The rushing water swirled around my calves now.

"That's what flash floods do. Rise fast. But maybe it's a little deeper in here than out there in the main room," he said with false optimism, picking up the battery lantern that had been left on the floor. Waterproof, apparently, so at least we had some light. We waded out into the main vaults. The sound of gushing water echoed through the connected chambers.

It seemed like only a minute or so had gone by before the water sloshed around my knees. Granted, I was short, but I started to freak out.

"Let's call for help. Call Mark. Call 999." I pulled my phone from my bag and tapped. "No signal down here."

"Let me try." Neil set the lantern on a high shelf and pulled his phone from his back pocket. "Same." He kept the gadget in his hand, holding it high. Planning ahead for when the water reached our butts.

It was above my knees now. "Let's try the gate."

We both knew the padlock looped through the gate, but we slogged through the water anyway and pulled on it and got nowhere.

Squeaking sounded behind me. "Oh God."

"What?"

"Rats," I said. Was that movement in the water behind us? "I'm scared."

He put an arm around me and gave me a squeeze. "I called 999 already, remember? They're coming."

"They'll never hear us. And the clanking stopped. Why did it stop?"

"Maybe the water's deep enough now to muffle it or stop the pipes from banging together."

"Great." I held my bag on top of my head as the water reached the seat of my jeans. So cold. I thought back to Alastair saying there'd been a real flood here before he took over. What was a real flood, exactly? How high would it get?

Neil started wading around, inspecting the walls. "Maybe there's another way out."

"Didn't Alastair say there was only one way out?"

But Neil had moved deep into the vaults, into the shadows where it was hard to see him.

"Are you OK?" I called out.

"I'm OK." His voice reverberated through the space. "Coming back."

He made his way to where I stood by the gate. "Maybe we should yell."

So we yelled for a couple of minutes, to no avail. We settled into silence. And then I jumped and screamed in terror.

"What?" Neil exclaimed

"Something just slithered past my ankle."

"Awesome," he said grimly. "Maybe it was Nessie."

"That's Scotland. This is London."

Something touched my back, and I spun and shrieked, smacking at the water with my free hand as Neil jumped out of the splash zone.

"What the hell? What is it?" he shouted.

"I think a rat touched my back!"

"That was my *hand*." Neil gripped my shoulder so there was no mistaking him. "I am not a rat."

Well, that was true enough. I'd known plenty of rats in my time. "Sorry. I'm just a little jittery, that's all."

"Understandable," he said, releasing his grip on my shoulder. "But take it easy. If we have to, we'll climb up on something."

"But the ceilings are only so high."

"The water won't get that high," Neil said, but even he didn't sound convinced.

We moved closer together, quiet now, though my breaths came shorter. I looked at my good-luck bracelet and hoped it hadn't run out of magic. My fear rose with the water, now up to my waist. I scanned our skunky swimming pool, then lifted my head up and listened to the darkness above. I didn't hear anyone upstairs. But as the music beat thumped dimly from above, I heard something else. A crashing sound? It was over almost as soon as it started.

The battery lantern flickered and went out. Maybe not so waterproof.

"Shit," I whispered into the inky blackness.

"I know," Neil said. "Hold tight." He activated the light on his phone, but it threw about as much light as a match in a cavern.

"That reminds me. I have a flashlight in my bag."

"Save it. We might need it."

Well, that wasn't very encouraging. How long did he think we'd be down here?

The near-darkness didn't help my mental state. I had all kinds of awful thoughts the higher the water got. In a few minutes, it had climbed above my belly button. "I didn't even get to talk to my Aunt Celestine today. What if she's not OK? What about the hurricane? What if I never see Astra again?"

"I talked to my people tonight after their cell service came back online. Everything's OK," Neil said in a soothing voice. How he could be comforting at a time like this, I had no idea, but I appreciated the effort. "The storm blew a few palm fronds down. A lot of rain. Glancing blow. Nothing major."

"That's good news, anyway." I sounded pathetic, and I sniffled.

Neil pulled me close with his free arm as the water crept up my torso. "It'll be all right, Pepper," he murmured into my ear. "When we get out of here, we're going to have a grand old time."

I nestled closer to him, though we were both soaked and cold. "Someplace dry and warm, OK?"

"It's a deal." He lifted his head. "Hey, do you hear something?"

Noises filtered down to us. Something other than the music. "I think someone's up there!"

We started screaming again and paused after a minute to see if anything had changed. "They can't hear us over the damn disco," Neil said.

"Wait a second." I grabbed my bag off my head and reached inside, finding the Corgi-shaped squeaky toy I bought for Astra. "Think this will work?"

"They'll probably think it's rats."

"Very funny."

The music stopped, and we looked at each other. And then we started yelling, really hollering, our shouts bouncing around the stone walls and off the water. I squeaked the toy for good measure.

The water reached the bottom of my bra. My sweater had turned into a heavy sponge.

And then I heard footsteps on the stairs. Someone hit the switches. The ceiling lights blazed to life, revealing the terrifying lake the vaults had become.

"Pepper! Neil!" Mark appeared at the bottom of the steps, trailed by two cops. "I thought I heard something." He jumped right into the drink, pushing through the floodwater, holding up a key. He had to swish a hand through the water to locate and get a grip on the submerged lock, but in a moment, he had the shackle free, wrenched the gate open and helped us get to the staircase. From there, the officers led us up.

The spiral stairs again.

I was kind of happy to see them. We weren't in the water anymore.

"Thank you," I said to Mark once we reached the hallway at the top, all of us dripping. I tried to catch my breath and willed my panic to recede.

"Is Alastair OK?" Neil asked.

"See for yourself." Mark gestured us toward the main barroom. Neil went ahead, followed by the officers, who asked Neil if we needed to see the paramedics.

"We're OK," Neil told them.

I tried to tell myself that. *We're OK, Pepper.*

Mark gave me a one-armed hug and kissed my forehead. A tear came to my eye as we followed the others. Relief. Gratitude.

In a moment, we were in the main bar, where a few cops milled about and an ambulance crew had Alastair on a stretcher, checking his eyeballs with a bright penlight.

"I'm fine, damn you," Alastair said. "Just a bit of a headache."

"We should take you in, sir," a female paramedic said.

"You will not." Alastair struggled to a sitting position. "You!" He pointed at me. "What have you done to my bar?"

"What are you talking about?" I asked. "It's not like the flood is my fault."

"That!" Alastair said, pointing up behind the bar, next to the ladder we'd seen leaning there when we came in. Two newer barrels still perched up there by the clock, but the two old ones were missing.

I moved behind the bar to look and saw what was left of the barrels in pieces on the floor, along with an axe. An axe?

Someone came prepared. Someone figured out the letters might be in the barrels and came prepared and busted them open.

I spotted the remains of a ribbon amid all the pieces of wood and leaned down and grabbed it. It was pale peach, silk, and it had the remains of a wax seal on it.

Marked with an "N."

"Nelly," I breathed.

FIFTEEN MINUTES LATER, the cops and ambulance crew were gone. We'd told them only that a vandal had hit the barrels, struck Alastair and locked us in the cellar. We didn't know much more than that, anyway. Except for the bit about Charles Dickens's invaluable lost letters to his secret mistress.

"My head hurts," Alastair said, pocketing the vault key Mark handed to him. "The vault is flooded, the bar is a mess, and I can't do anything about it till tomorrow anyway. I want to go home."

"You shouldn't drive," Mark said.

"It's not far. And it will be easier without passengers." Alastair glared at us. "You smell like wet dogs. And you're dripping all over my floor."

"Don't you mean *our* floor?" Mark gave him a sidelong look, pulled off his sopping sweater and draped it over a chair. I saw his rain jacket on another chair—he must've taken it off when he arrived.

His very wet, now virtually transparent white T-shirt was plastered to his muscles.

I squeezed my eyes shut for a second. This was not the time to think about Mark's muscles.

"Stay," Mark told Alastair. "I'll get you a cab. And a whiskey. And I can probably scare up a few Dandy Tipple T-shirts if you two want to change into something dry." He nodded at Neil and me. "Can't do anything about the trousers."

Mark went behind the bar and rummaged. First he pulled out black T-shirts and threw them at Neil and me. Then he came out with another shirt, four glasses and a bottle of Bohemia Beachside Bourbon—a little taste of home that he poured for each of us. It was wonderfully warm going down. And I felt even warmer when he yanked off his wet white T-shirt—*holy abs-ville!*—and pulled a Dandy Tipple shirt on instead. But not before taking an extra second while he was topless to catch my eye and quirk his mouth, showing me a dimple.

"Excuse me a minute," I said, scurrying off to the ladies' room so I could recover my breath and change. My wet sweater and T-shirt came off first. I stuffed them in the trash bin, knowing I'd never be able to get the stink out of them. Or the idea of rats and snakes.

I took off my bra, rinsed it, wrung it out, and ran it under the heated hand-dryer for a minute, then put it back on with the Dandy Tipple T-shirt over it. I stepped out of my jeans, squeezed them over the sink to get more of the water out and pulled them back on. They were still clammy, but at least they weren't actively dripping.

I went back out to the bar, where Neil had already changed into his dry T-shirt. Good. Everyone had clothes on.

I sat next to Neil and took another sip of bourbon. "Thanks for this," I said to Mark. "So ... you're not under arrest."

"I'm not under arrest, thank God," Mark said. "I got your text when they were wrapping up, and then I heard something about the Tipple on the police radios, and D.I. Ibsen had someone give me a ride. Oh, and I told her that Stephan Sully, whose name was on the certificate she was so interested in, was a very suspicious character, and they dashed off to his hotel to pull him in for questioning."

I laughed. I couldn't help it. "Well done."

He smiled. "It's the least he deserves for breaking your heart, Pepper. They'll let him go soon enough. Now what's all this about a poem?"

We quickly explained our thoughts on the poem and my theory that Ben had been looking for the Dickens letters in Mark's library. I showed him the ribbon and the wax seal.

"But none of you saw who was here tonight?" Mark said.

"Unfortunately not," Neil answered. "We must have surprised them. Did you see anything, Alastair?"

Alastair shook his head. "They struck me on the head with my favorite bottle of scotch. All I saw was a cloak, like some kind of reenactor."

"Same here. One of Ben's theater group?" I asked.

"Maybe," Mark said. "But if the letters were here in the barrels, they have them now. And if they were still buried in the vaults, they were probably destroyed two floods ago."

Neil turned to me. "Didn't you say Ben's *Lawless* book had several pages about the poem with notes? We didn't look at those."

"You're right!" I pulled out my phone. At least my bag and phone were dry. I pulled up the pages and stumbled across one of the last photos I took, one of the last pages I'd captured. "Oh my."

Neil looked at me sharply. "What is it?"

"A few lines on one page, crossed out, then rearranged. *Darkness was cheap, and Scrooge liked it.*"

"*A Christmas Carol,* obviously," Mark said.

"Also, *He would make a lovely corpse.*"

"Another Dickens quote?" Neil said. "Wait—"

Alastair piped up. "*Martin Chuzzlewit,* I think."

"Yes," Neil said, "but that sounds like your threatening note."

"Exactly," I said. "He wrote it out here before, apparently, copying it to another page, ripping it out and leaving it in my pocket. *You would make a lovely corpse. Death is as cheap as darkness. Walk away and live.* Ben traveled a dark road."

"You're all right now," Mark said. "Thank God. Now go on and look at the notes on the poem."

I turned to images of the pages that had followed the poem in Ben's book. "He made notes on each stanza."

"Here." Neil leaned over the phone and pointed to the notes on the first stanza. "He wrote, 'Dickens called Nelly PATIENT in his letters. Disguise.' Then next to the line about derailment, it says, 'Ask A. about this.'"

"Ari seemed to know a lot about the train derailment. Could that be her?" I asked.

"Maybe," Mark said. "But I have a bad feeling about Albert. Where was he all evening?"

"Could Ben have gotten him involved when he started working for you?" Neil asked.

Mark shook his head. "I'd hate to think so. Albert has been with me forever. What else do we know?"

Another page of the journal was devoted to the "palace vault." Ben had written "Gin!" here. There were other notes, too, pretty much all stuff we'd already talked about. And then I came upon a kind of checklist.

It was titled "What to do next."

And it listed:

1. *Find a buyer.*
2. *Pay debts.*
3. *Talk A. into going public.*
4. *See if other Dickens will get tested.*
5. *Publish book.*

"What does that mean?" I asked.

"What does it all mean?" Alastair said, sounding bored.

"Obviously, if he got the letters, he planned to sell them," Mark said. "He could pay his debts then, the debts he was trying to pay by stealing and selling books and rare liquor. And he mentioned working on a Dickens book."

"Why would he talk Albert into going public?" Neil asked. "Wouldn't they want to hide their identities somehow? Sell the letters anonymously?"

"If Ben felt he had a right to the letters as a Dickens descendant and he'd recovered them without anyone finding out about his illegal activities, he could go public," I said. "He could claim they were handed down to him. It sounds like he wanted to milk them for notoriety, at least."

"He wanted other Dickenses to get tested," Mark said. "For what?"

I took another lovely sip of bourbon. "He was into genealogy. Assuming he was Mr. Mixy's supposed expert, he knew about DNA analysis or at least how to get it. Do you think he sent in a sample, found a Dickens and spotted some common DNA?"

"Some people make their results public or discoverable on those services so they can track down long-lost relatives," Neil said.

I nodded. "So maybe he thought he'd get tests just to prove the connection to distant cousins, if you can do that so many generations later. I don't know anything about genetics."

"And he wanted to get 'A' on board." Neil looked puzzled.

"Albert wouldn't have a reason to go public, not if he was busy stealing things, too." A lightning bolt fired in my brain. "Ari—do you have employment records here? Like personnel files?"

Alastair frowned. "For Ari? Whatever for?"

Mark cast a steely gaze upon him.

"Oh, all right," Alastair relented. "In the office."

"One moment." Mark disappeared through the staff door and came back two minutes later with a folder. He opened it on the table where we sat.

I stood and looked over his shoulder. "There."

He read where I was pointing. "Arabella Burton Fernsby."

"She was married before," I said. "Fernsby is likely her married name. Burton has to be her maiden name. I'll bet anything she's Ben's brother."

Chapter Thirty-Three

We all looked at each other.

"*Ari* hit me over the head?" Alastair squeaked in disbelief.

"And she might have killed Ben." I shivered, partly due to my damp clothes and partly from horror. *Her own brother!* What a terrible thing.

"Arabella sounds vaguely familiar," Neil said.

Alastair perked up. "Benjamin and Arabella were siblings in *The Pickwick Papers.*"

"Bingo," I said. "Their parents knew the secret too. Maybe passed on to them the letter about 'Mr. Tringham' and the baby."

Neil looked around the table. "We need to report this. She could be the killer."

"We don't have a lot of evidence," Mark answered. "Not really."

"But if she took the letters," I said, "she has all the evidence we need to prove she's involved."

Neil shook his head. "Haven't you had enough excitement for one night?"

"We could go to her home," Mark said, completely on board. *Go Mark!* "Her address is in this file."

"For Christ's sake," Alastair said. "I'll tell you exactly where she is." He pulled a phone from his pocket, tapped a few times and pulled up an app. "Here."

The screen showed a map with a slowly moving dot. I looked at him in disbelief. "What the— Do you track your employees?"

"I track *my* phones. I bought them. If the employee happens to carry it, then I know where they are, too." Alastair greeted all of our stares with hostility. "Oh, don't look at me like that. I've never used it before now. Except that one time someone left theirs at a restaurant in Bethnal Green."

"Then let's go," Mark said. "Oh, come on, Neil."

Now this was interesting. I watched the thoughts play across Neil's face. Neil couldn't *not* respond to a challenge from Mark.

"OK, fine," Neil finally said. *Go Neil!*

"Alastair can drive," Mark said.

"No, I can't!" Alastair's voice hit a high pitch. "I drove the Roadster."

"Not that tin can," Mark said. "Why didn't you drive the Ford tonight?"

"It's a classic," Alastair exclaimed.

The more he said it was a classic, the less it seemed true, but whatever.

Mark's phone rang, and he glanced at the screen. "It's Albert!" He picked it up. "Yes? ... Really? ... Actually, that would be grand. The Dandy Tipple. ... Yes. In a jiffy." He disconnected. "That was Albert. Mrs. Pidgeon told him the police hauled me off, and he went to the station to pick me up, only I'm not there, obviously. He's five minutes away. He can drive us."

I downed the rest of my bourbon. "Excellent!"

Neil looked less than thrilled. But hey, at least we weren't riding in Alastair's "classic."

ALBERT SHOWED up in a dark gray Range Rover and greeted us politely, though he seemed confused by our matching shirts.

Alastair rode up front since he had the tracking app. Mark and I got in the middle seat, and Neil, still unhappy, in the third row.

"How many cars do you have, Mark?" I asked as the SUV rolled away from the curb. I didn't care, really, but I was curious.

"Oh, I don't know. I lose count," Mark said offhandedly.

That's how you know you're talking to a rich guy. He doesn't know how many cars he has.

"Where does it look like she's going?" Neil called to Alastair.

"The dot seems to be somewhere around Piccadilly Circus. She must be walking. Nowhere near where she lives."

Odd, I thought.

"That's not far at all," Mark said. "We'll catch up to her in no time. Keep us updated."

The car got pretty quiet. We really didn't know what we were in for, and if Ari was a killer ...

"She's in the theater district," Alastair said in puzzlement.

"Steady on," Mark said.

And Albert, the other *A,* was driving us there.

"I think she's stopped," Alastair said. "At Charles Street and Haymarket?"

I leaned over the front seat so I could follow along. We were almost there, so I looked out the front window, trying to see her. It was a lot busier here than it had been near the Tipple.

"Albert, drop us here, all right?" Mark said.

Albert didn't say anything. Just kept driving.

Uh-oh.

"Albert?" Mark said. "Albert!"

Albert jolted, then looked around. "Sorry, sir. Daydreaming. Haven't been getting much sleep. Stop here, you say?"

"That'll be fine," Mark said, his tone short. "Then wait nearby but not too close, all right? And stay awake."

"Of course," Albert said sheepishly, pulling up to the curb by a movie theater. I exhaled a long breath and looked at Neil. He shook his head slightly and smiled. OK, I wasn't the only one with a suspicious mind.

The four of us climbed out of the SUV, and Albert drove on. The rain had let up a bit. Now a cool mist swirled around us. And so did people.

"Lot of clubs and restaurants around here," Mark said. "We can blend in."

I burst out laughing. "Sure. Squad Dandy Tipple."

Neil chuckled, and we turned around to face the direction where the app showed us the Ari dot.

Alastair pointed. "She appears to be just ahead of us on the left side of the street. If you don't mind, I'd rather not get all that close." He rubbed his forehead, where a bump had appeared. *Ouch.*

"No problem," Mark said. "We can go all ninja in our black T-shirts. But stay near enough that I can ping you if I need you, all right?"

"I'm a bit peckish. There's a pizzeria right there." Alastair pointed behind us. "I'll grab a slice. Text me when you're done." And he walked away.

"Doesn't he want to know what's going on?" Mark asked no one in particular.

"This might be one time when I agree with him," Neil replied.

Mark shrugged. "We're just going to talk with her. We're in the middle of the bloody theater district. What could happen?"

"Pepper!" The shout came from behind us, and I turned to see Blue Eyes and a cohort of his hot footballers swaggering down the sidewalk, waving at me. "We won! Want to celebrate?"

"Uh—I'm busy." I gestured to Neil and Mark.

"Oh, I see. I'm not jealous at all. The Dandy Tipple?" Blue Eyes ogled my T-shirt. Or my chest. And let's just say I wasn't a hundred percent sure he said *Tipple.* "Adore that place. Catch you later, love!" He and his friends wandered off.

When I turned around, Neil and Mark just stared at me. Gobsmacked, as the Brits say.

"What?" I shrugged and headed across the busy street behind a double-decker red bus, and they followed. "So why do you think she's *here?*" I asked more quietly.

We moved with the crowds toward where Ari, or her phone, might be. I took off my glasses and used my T-shirt to wipe away the mist, then put them back on. It was a toss-up whether they helped keep the rain off or impaired my vision in this nasty weather, but they were comforting, somehow. Like a shield.

Pedestrians weaved around us, happy, sloshed, oblivious. It smelled like someone might be grilling somewhere.

Ahead of us, on the left side of the street, a beautiful cream-colored building glowed in the mist, fronted with grand columns. *Theatre Royal Haymarket,* the gold letters above the columns spelled out.

And sitting cross-legged on the sidewalk under its porte cochere was a sad little figure in a dark cloak. Its hood had fallen around her shoulders, and her pale blond hair shone golden in the lights. An antique copper bucket with claw feet—the one from the Tipple's hearth; I recognized it—sat in front of her, as if she were busking. Or begging. In fact, as we watched, someone dropped coins into it with a muted *ka-clink.* She didn't even flinch, paid no mind to the pedestrians walking around her, seemed oblivious to the neon-trimmed pedicabs parked nearby that cast her down-turned face in a pale blue glow.

In her lap was a pile of papers, and she seemed completely immersed in their contents.

We looked at one another, and then we walked up to her, slowly, and stood around her—a few feet away, just in case she had a brick handy.

Finally, she seemed to sense our presence and looked up. Tears streaked her cheeks.

"Ari?" Mark said. "May we talk to you?"

Anger replaced the grief on her face. "You may not." She looked up at Neil and me. "What is this? Team Tipple?"

"Squad, actually," I said. Though Team was pretty good. I cleared my throat. "What are you reading?"

"You'd like to know that, wouldn't you?" She gathered the papers close, straightening them into a neat pile.

"Letters to Ellen Ternan?" Neil's tone was kind and steady. "You won't be able to sell them now. They're evidence."

"You know what? They *are* evidence." Ari clutched the papers tightly as she shifted to her knees. I took half a step back. "They're evidence of a crime. Of what Charles Dickens did to her, to her life. Do you know what this is?" She made a wide gesture behind her.

Mark appeared baffled. "The Haymarket?"

Ari smiled grimly. "The last place Nelly ever performed as a professional actress before Dickens squirreled her away in his secret love nest. She was only twenty years old."

"And you and Ben are her descendants?" I asked.

She looked at me, her ice-blue eyes bright and glossy. "I knew you had brains, Pepper. But I wish you didn't know that. I wish no one knew that." A wild note bubbled in her voice.

I tried to sound reasonable because she did not. "But you were going to sell the letters. Wouldn't everyone know then?"

"*I* wasn't going to sell the letters. *Ben* wanted to sell the letters. And he ruined everything, stealing those books. Stealing the bottles. Drawing attention. I wish he'd never got the idea in his head. We knew who we were for years. Our mother told us before she died. But Ben didn't get obsessed until those Dickens letters sold for all that money and he started researching what might have happened to Nelly's."

"Why The Dandy Tipple?" I asked.

"He found a journal in the museum's papers. Her journal. And he ripped out the page with the poem. You found his book, didn't you?" I nodded, and she looked unspeakably sad. "He figured she hid them at a gin palace, one of Dickens's haunts, and the Tipple seemed likely; she'd mentioned it more than once, its old name. So I got a job there. Ben asked me to. But I didn't do it for the letters.

I did it to stop him. He was one step behind. I had an idea of where they might be, but I hoped he would forget the whole thing."

"In the barrels," Neil said.

She nodded. "And when he didn't find them and figured out you were one of the Tipple's owners, a renowned collector"—she looked at Mark—"he got a job at Fairyland Distillery to see if you'd already taken them. He ingratiated himself."

"He was good," Mark admitted.

"He did well in that job. He was smart. He did well at everything he did. He could have been happy. But instead he finagled a way to get into your library, and it all went downhill from there." She looked back at me, her voice cracking as she spoke. "He had a weakness. He gambled. He lost a lot of money. That drove him. I tried to help him. I tried so many times." She looked down and sobbed.

Out of the corner of my eye, I saw Mark step back. He pulled out his phone and tapped on the screen. So I tried to draw her attention to me.

"You didn't have to kill him," I said quietly so passersby wouldn't hear.

She lifted her head again. "He was out of control. Nothing could stop him. Even you—he followed you, you know? He was mad. He would have done you harm." *Like hitting Alastair on the head or locking us in a flooded cellar, as she did?* "I tried to get him to stop tonight. Turn around. Turn himself in. He could've returned the things and been all right." Her voice became more strident. "But he wanted the letters at all costs. Even worse, he wanted the *glory*. To further the glory of the illustrious Dickens name. To ride on his coattails. I couldn't let him do that! To ruin both our lives. And Nelly wouldn't have wanted that either."

"We think maybe she did," Neil said. "We think she hid the letters on purpose, hoping they'd be discovered."

"Well, that's up to me now, isn't it? As the last true heir," she said bitterly. Ari held up one of the papers so we could see it. It was covered in writing, dark blue scribbles—clearly a letter, with a bold signature underscored by a flourish that looked kind of like a squashed tornado. I realized I was looking at a real-life letter written by Charles Dickens. Even knowing this whole Nelly story, I was a little dazzled.

"That's history you have in your hands," I said. "You could stay anonymous—no one knows your connection to her, outside of us. Why not let them be published?"

"Because *he* doesn't deserve it." Her voice was low and angry. *"He* doesn't deserve a new round of fame and love and modern understanding of his quaint Victorian foibles. There've been rumors about these letters, about how they would reveal his soul, how all would be forgiven. But all I see is a manipulative, powerful man with an idea of love that was never really true. Not for her. He became one of his own villains. He took her baby away from her!"

I felt her pain and wondered if we could pull her back from the edge. "You're here, though," I said. "You wouldn't be here otherwise. And Nelly, your great-great, um ... whatever great-grandmother ... it seems like she was ready for the world to embrace her legacy."

"Her legacy? What a joke. Do you think I'm proud to be her descendant?" Ari scoffed. "She was a liar, too. She just wanted a conventional little life. Joined the anti-suffragette league after *he* was long gone. She didn't want the rights denied her, didn't want any woman to have them. She was part of the damned conspiracy."

The blue neon lights from the pedi-cabs changed, started to flicker. We all looked up.

It wasn't the pedi-cabs. Police cars, their blue lights flashing, poured down Haymarket Street and into the intersection. Ari blinked as if in shock, then seared us with an accusatory glare. She jammed the papers into the copper bucket and pulled something from under her cloak.

A weapon?

She stood, and then I saw what she had. "Whoa no."

Mark took a step forward.

Neil croaked out a "Wait!"

And I put out a hand, as if I could stop her.

But it took her only half a second to light a match and set the tiny flame to the Dandy Tipple matchbook in her hand. It caught and flared bright.

She dropped it into the bucket.

A blossom of fire roared up from the vessel, splitting the night with a crackle and a whoosh, intense and hot. I gasped and faltered backward. People nearby screamed and jumped away. There must've been more than a couple of coins in that bucket. *That* was the smell I'd noticed—lighter fluid.

Ari stood there, a triumphant smile on her face, lit like a demon by the flames, her cloak billowing in the breeze. The blaze was too hot for us to grab the bucket, and there were no fire trucks among the police cars.

And it was already too late. With a fire that hot, the letters had to be destroyed, gone almost instantly. Embers rose up as the old papers burned. Bits of charred paper caught on the wind, whirling around us, all that remained of the story—or half the story—of a long-ago affair between a literary lion and an invisible lamb.

Ari laughed at our expressions as the flames dwindled and the officers eased up to her, including D.I. Ibsen, who exchanged a glance with Mark to confirm their target. She offered no resistance as they cuffed her and led her away.

D.I. Ibsen watched the officers put her into a car, then looked at the fire. "What have we here?" she asked Mark. "And thank you, by the way."

"She had a little campfire going," was all Mark said. "And she confessed to killing Ben."

"Well, that's a start. I'll be in touch." She looked around at us with a wry expression. "Look at you. The Tipple Triplets." Then she headed back to her vehicle and left.

The Tipple Triplets!

Maybe not. It made us sound like a circus act.

"You didn't tell her," I said to Mark.

"She'll figure it out. Or maybe she won't. Ari might talk. Or she might not."

"It won't be much fun for you and Alastair if she does, all the attention," Neil said.

Mark sighed. "We'll take what comes. I really appreciate what you two have done, though I wish it hadn't ended in this awful way."

Alastair strolled up to us, a big cup in his hand, a confused expression on his face. He looked at the flaming bucket—the fire now low, with its fuel mostly spent—and then curiously at us doing nothing about it. And he stepped over and dumped the contents of his drink over the blaze. It sizzled and popped and belched out a puff of steam, and in a minute, it went out.

The police all seemed to have left.

We looked at one another.

"Might as well just make sure," Mark said.

"Wait a second." I sifted through my bag and pulled out the Union Jack oven mitts I'd bought for Aunt Celestine. "Use these."

Chapter Thirty-Four

I woke up with a warm body next to me. Victoria, of course. But Albert didn't wake me up to get her.

In fact, no one woke me up for once. After getting back to Mark's from our second cold, wet adventure of the evening, I'd taken a hot shower and collapsed into bed, and by the time I opened my eyes, my phone said it was around ten, with gauzy sunlight filtering through the curtains.

The puppy sat up and whimpered at me when she realized I was awake, and then she climbed onto my chest. I scratched behind her ears, and she licked my hand.

"I'm going to miss you, girl, but you're going to have to stay here with your buddy Mark," I told her.

Her long ears perked up, and she cocked her head. And then she barked once.

"Will you miss me?"

She scooched up my chest and licked my nose.

"Oh my goodness. Astra would love you. I think. Maybe Mark can smuggle you over when he visits his condo in Bohemia Beach. Would you like that?"

She barked louder.

"OK, OK! You're hungry or you want your master. Or a vacation in Florida. Give me a few minutes, sweetie."

It actually took about fifteen for me to find dry clothes that I liked: black jeans and an oversize, soft green sweater. I'd need it, given that my phone showed the promised cold front had moved through last night. At least it wasn't raining. My sneakers were a total loss, and my boots weren't much better, so I put on my chunky black comfy shoes. And this was why I brought the big suitcase to London: You never knew when you'd need an extra outfit. Or three.

The hallway outside my room was empty, so Victoria and I headed downstairs. Albert intercepted me.

"You're just in time, miss. Meet us here by the fireplace in ten minutes." His face was wreathed in smiles as he leashed Victoria and took her away for her morning ritual.

I found my way to the breakfast room. Most of the food had been taken away, but there were scones, jam and clotted cream, along with hot coffee, so I was all set.

Except, where was everyone?

I ate hungrily, downed some caffeine, then headed back to the fireplace.

Mrs. Pidgeon and Albert appeared. And then Mark, with Victoria trotting happily alongside him.

"Pepper!" Mark called out, looking more perky in his casual duds than he had a right to be after last night. "Good morning! Your people seem to be rather scarce. They all vanished after breakfast. Did they go out?"

"I have no idea." Dang. Did I miss another chance at London tourism? We had one more full day after today, then our crew would be heading home on Tuesday.

"Well, Mrs. Pidgeon and Albert want to show me something. Would you like to come along?"

"They do?" Clearly, the caffeine hadn't supercharged my bloodstream yet. But I shut up entirely when Mrs. Pidgeon's eyes got so wide, I thought they might pop out. She was clearly giving me the DON'T SAY ANYTHING signal.

Only I really didn't know what to say. She gave me more credit than I deserved. Maybe Neil and I had solved one mystery, but I still didn't know why the help had been skulking about all week.

So I tagged along, following mindlessly as Albert and Mrs. Pidgeon led the way up lots and lots of stairs.

"Victoria's going to miss you," Mark said.

"That's what she told me this morning," I said. "But she loves you so much, she'll be fine. Maybe you can bring her across the pond sometime."

"Not a bad notion, as long as I can keep her out of the mouths of alligators."

"Hey, did you ever go back and look at the bottles in the niches around your secret staircase?"

Mark shook his head. "No time, but I hope it's something tasty. Or collectible."

"Your collections are going to get you into trouble."

"You're probably right. Speaking of which, I have a little something for you. Catch me later. I say, Albert, where are we going?"

"Almost there, sir," Albert replied.

We were in a corridor I wasn't familiar with. This place had enough rooms to open a resort. But in a moment, we stopped outside a closed door labeled *Nursery*.

"This is it," Albert said in an absurdly loud voice. Then he looked at Mrs. Pidgeon. She smiled—*she actually smiled!*—and gave him a nod.

And Albert opened the door.

As soon as we stepped inside the dark space, lights popped on and the sound of horns and noisemakers and clouds of confetti filled the big room, and a rock song cranked up on a killer sound system. It was like being dropped into an insanely loud snow globe. I realized the source of the horns and confetti was my bartender crew, who were all standing there grinning.

"I hope you like it, sir," Mrs. Pidgeon said. *Still smiling!*

I had a sense that I was on the wrong side of things, though I supposed I'd been a good distraction while Mrs. Pidgeon and

Albert lured Mark here—to what appeared to be a glorious dog playground with modern decor and lots of light from large windows.

I went across the room to join my friends in the merry audience, answering Neil's questioning look with one that said, *First, I had no idea about this circus. Second, I was in bed. Third, I was in bed alone, if you don't count Victoria. And fourth, I'm not here as the lady of the manor.*

I think he got it, because he nodded at me and smiled as I sidled up next to him.

Victoria, electrified by the noise and light, barked and barked. And then she started running around. She ran through the dog tunnel. She ran up and over the seesaw without balking for a second. She ran up a ramp and onto a day bed that could double as a couch, and she spun around, picking up the toys piled there one by one, shaking them and tossing them. The sensible, colorful carpet seemed to be made of removable squares. Good thinking.

A big basket held more toys, alongside food and water bowls. A short sliding board with wee steps could hold a dog or even a small child. And there was still plenty of room.

Mark gaped. "You—you did this?"

"Yes, sir?" Albert sounded hesitant. "With Mr. Stout's help."

So that's what Samuel Stout didn't want to tell us at Eltham Palace.

"We thought you might want an alternative to the library when you need to relax, sir," Mrs. Pidgeon said. "Someplace bright where you can play with the little miss."

Aw. The little miss. The little miss still tore around the room, her long ears flapping.

"I love it! Victoria loves it! This is fantastic!" Mark said. "And it was so kind of you to think of me as well."

For in addition to the dog playground, there were two large, comfy chairs. A massive television hung on the wall. A billiards table had its own space in the back of the room. A sleek, well-stocked modern bar stood in one corner. Plus, there was room to add more accoutrements. Which gave me an idea ...

"It's a man-dog cave," Neil said wryly.

"Yeah," Luke said. "I wonder if he's taking applications for any dog positions at the moment."

Unfortunately, Mark did have an opening, but it wasn't for a dog. It was the first time I'd really thought about Ben this morning, and I tried not to dwell on his sad fate.

"This is wonderful," Mark said. "Thank you so much."

It really was thoughtful of his staff. Even though he no doubt paid for all of it.

"And I have a surprise for all of you as well," Mark continued. "We're having a picnic out in the gardens in about an hour. I've invited some of our friends. I just want to thank you for all you've done."

"I think maybe we should thank you," Neil said, only a teeny bit grudgingly.

"Then let's call it even, all right?" Mark looked around, his gaze settling for an extra second on me before he scooped up the happy Victoria. "It's always a pleasure to see you."

Chapter Thirty-Five

It must be nice to have a staff. It took a staff to throw together a "picnic" this quickly—really more of a garden party, with a large tent filled with delicious food.

Sure, I had a staff back home—in my bar. They were awesome but not nearly as numerous as Mark's.

Speaking of Nola, Jorge had texted me that all was well with our bar/restaurant in Bohemia post-hurricane. A huge relief.

Given our festival job was done and our mystery was solved, if tragically, I could walk around the exquisite gardens with a light heart. So I strolled by myself for a little while before the party got under way.

As I was breathing in the crisp, cool air laden with floral scents, I ran into Diana Silva, the botanist, poking around one of the flowerbeds. She wore another khaki outfit.

"Anything interesting?" I asked her.

She stood up straight in surprise. "Oh, I say. Pepper, isn't it? Mark's a sly one. He's got chicory growing here behind the *fuchsia hatschbachii.*" She pointed to small, blue flowers hiding behind a bushy profusion of green plants accented by dangling, deep pink blossoms.

I chuckled. I doubted Mark made decisions that granular about his garden. "Chicory? I used to like chicory coffee, but that was when I lived in New Orleans. Now I don't touch the stuff. My aunt grows some, though. She's big into herbs and plants."

"You're with the group from Bohemia, is that right?"

"That's where my bar is. I live in Bohemia Beach. I share a duplex with my Aunt Celestine."

Diana's eyebrows shot up. "Not Celestine Fontenot?"

I gaped at her. "Yes! Do you know her?"

"Why, we're on an online discussion board together. I've read her books. I had no idea you were related. I really will have to come explore the swamps thereabouts."

I grinned. "You're welcome anytime."

We exchanged contact information, and I headed toward the fountain to enjoy its peaceful bubbling.

"Do you like it?" came a deep voice behind me.

I spun to find Mark. "It's beautiful. Everything here is beautiful."

"Yes, it is." He smiled and stepped forward, something in his hands. "I'm so grateful to you, Pepper. And Neil, too. D.I. Ibsen sent a package over this morning. *The Sword in the Stone*. She's found other books in Ben's flat, too, but those will come later. I'd told her this was the one I cared most about."

"You mean you have it right there?" I eyed the package wrapped in brown paper in his hands. "Can I see it?"

"I'll be happy to show you my *private* collection anytime." His eyes twinkled as he handed it over. "But no, this is something else. A little souvenir of your trip. I hope you only remember the good parts."

"There were definitely good parts. And some not so much."

"It was the best of times. It was the worst of times. Enjoy, darling Pepper." Mark winked, turned and strolled away.

I looked down at the package in my hand, tied with twine. I pulled the string off the corners and gently unfolded the paper wrapping. And gasped.

It was a beautiful, leather-bound book that reminded me a little of Ben's notebook. Only this was a real book, with gold designs stamped into the brown cover and spine, which said "Dickens's

Works" and under it, *A Tale of Two Cities.* I gently thumbed through the pages. It was illustrated, too, and a bit rough on the corners. I had a feeling this was a precious book. When I got around to reading *A Tale of Two Cities,* I'd put this up on a high shelf and get the ebook from the library.

As I turned it around in my hands, I barely caught the tiny piece of paper that fluttered out of the pages, encased in a small, clear plastic envelope. The fragment was dark around its irregular edges. Burnt?

Oh my God.

I hadn't seen the bucket after Mark took it into the house last night. I didn't even think to ask him about it. The burned contents looked like an irretrievable mess to me. But could this be—?

Only three words were legible on the scrap of paper, in a difficult-to-read script. I squinted at it and finally made it out: *friend to Temperance.*

I laughed out loud, imagining Dickens writing about taking it easy on the booze. I supposed if most of his letters to Nelly were burnt to ashes, one couldn't be too picky. But I did wonder what else Mark might have saved.

It would be difficult to prove this scrap was anything at all, but I carefully put the clear envelope back in the book, rewrapped the volume, and flagged down Albert, who was hustling by with a case of gin, presumably from the distillery.

"Hello. Where are you heading?" I asked him.

"To the tent and then the house. Mark has thirsty friends. If you'll pardon me for saying so."

I grinned. "You are absolutely right. Would you mind taking one more thing to the house? Maybe drop it by my room?" I held up the book.

"Of course." He nodded at the box, and I set the wrapped book on top.

"And thank you for everything you've done for us. For your kindness." I still felt bad for suspecting him of dastardly deeds.

"You're welcome, miss. Least I could do for a good friend of Mr. Fairman's." Was it my imagination, or did he emphasize *good?* "And I hope you weren't put off by Mrs. Pidgeon. She feared you'd give away our little surprise."

"No problem." Though I thought her hostility was a little more personal than he suggested. "Hey, one more thing—I have something for Mark's man-dog cave. I set out a soccer—er, football jersey on my bed, and it's autographed. I think it would look great framed for his new playroom. Can you take care of it?"

Albert smiled broadly. "What a lovely idea. Glad to."

"Thanks! Take care of yourself, OK?"

He bustled off, and I turned and almost bumped into Nigel and Lottie, both looking merry with cocktails in their hands.

"How are you doing today?" I asked. "You looked—wet last night." I was one to talk—but Nigel had been soaked and ghastly pale.

"Some dashed drunkard knocked me into the moat!" Nigel exclaimed.

Lottie nodded at my shocked expression. "We were in the garden—with an umbrella, thank you—enjoying the light show when someone sprinted past us and bumped Nigel from behind. It was so dark and happened so fast, I couldn't even tell you who it was, but he lost his balance and fell in. Thank goodness the water wasn't deep. Scared him silly."

"Not much of a swimmer," Nigel confessed, taking a sip from his drink.

"I'm so glad you're OK." *And not a thief or a killer,* I thought, wondering if Ari was the one who'd knocked him in the drink when she left the scene of the crime. "When will we see you again?"

"Not sure," Nigel said, "but that cooper-distiller fellow says he's having a big bash to launch his bourbon, so we might wangle an invitation. Write about it on the blog."

"Oh!" I said. "I hope we'll see you there, then."

Nigel declared he needed a hot toddy, and we said goodbye.

Once again I had a touch of envy for bon vivants with invisible means of support. But I missed my peeps, so I went looking for them in the food tent.

Dozens of full platters, a punch bowl and plenty of interesting bottles were laid out on tables draped in white. On one small table, a pile of blankets sat, awaiting picnickers who wanted to take their repasts into the garden and eat al fresco.

I found Neil lurking by the trays of yummy-looking tiny sandwiches.

"There you are. I was hoping I would run into you," he said, looking pretty delicious himself in blue jeans and a dark-blue sweater over a white collared shirt.

"More like he was waiting for you to show up," said Luke, whose plate would be as tall as the London Eye if he added any more shrimp.

Barclay, who was scooping up fish, elbowed Luke for his indiscretion, and the tower of crustaceans teetered.

Luke yelped and did a little dance to balance his booty, but a fat shrimp slid off the pile and to the ground.

Victoria leapt out from under the table and scarfed the shrimp down. Then she sat with a doggy grin at Luke's feet, gazing up at him expectantly.

"Now you've got a friend," Gina said while adding salad to her plate.

Melody stood next to a punch bowl chatting with Cray, William Buttersby—who smoked an aromatic pipe—Oleanna and Mark.

Hmm. Oleanna Lee and Mark Fairman. I looked for any special spark between them—and saw nothing obvious. I'd like to see both of them happy, even if it wasn't with each other.

I had a new appreciation of Mark after this trip, and not just because he rolled out the red carpet. We were better friends, and he'd saved our butts. He was still hotter than a tiki torch, but I felt OK about stepping away from the flame.

I felt Neil watching me and turned to him.

He held up a blanket. "Want to have a picnic?"

A slow smile took over my face. "Sure."

We gathered plates full of food—I went for sandwiches, fruit and an assortment of cheese—and carried a couple of cups of gin-champagne punch out into the formal paths of the terraced garden. We strolled around the fountain, deeper into the plantings, and found a shady spot next to fat, cylindrical topiaries, big green bushes that gave us a little privacy.

"I didn't see Alastair here," I noted after we'd spread out our blanket and cozied up to the food.

"He's dealing with the aftermath of the flood," Neil said. "I don't envy him. Mark says it will cost a fortune, but he's going to button up those vaults tight to minimize the chance of that happening again."

"I suppose he has a fortune to spend." I took a bite of my tasty chicken salad sandwich.

"I know." Neil looked a little glum.

I sipped my bright, bubbly punch and smiled at him. "If I was going to be trapped in rising floodwaters with anyone, I'm glad it was you."

"Uh, thanks?" Neil grinned at me.

"I mean, I don't ever want you to be trapped in floodwaters! Or me, for that matter."

"Let's not do that again," he agreed. "Mr. Mixy isn't here, either."

"Forgive me for being happy about that. Would Mark have invited him?"

"He told me he took pity on him and asked him to come, but Mr. Mixy was too busy filming something about his adventure at the police station."

I rolled my eyes.

"Besides," Neil said, "you'll see him soon enough in Kentucky."

"That's *great!*" My sarcasm mode was cranked up to eleven.

Neil laughed. "The fall colors should be nice." Then his face sobered. "I keep thinking about Ben."

"And Ari. And something's bothering me. Ben had a photocopy of that letter about his ancestor in his journal. Could she still have the original?"

"Given how she felt, I doubt it," Neil said. "But who knows? The truth is likely to come out anyway, and she'll have to suffer the consequences."

"It's all so awful, isn't it? I feel sympathetic toward her, but I'm not sure why. Maybe because of all her failed expectations."

"Especially because she couldn't save her brother." Neil shook his head. "Watching him founder—it must have driven her to the edge. It's such a helpless feeling when you love someone who is hell-bent on destroying themselves."

"The gambling?" I asked. "Or the obsession?"

"Both, I suppose. Any addiction." His eyes went dark. He looked so troubled for a moment.

"Neil?"

He seemed to shake himself. "Just remembering something I'd rather not."

I reached out and laid a hand over his and squeezed. He blinked, and the light came back into his gaze. He leaned closer. My breath hitched. My heartbeat sped up, and I closed my eyes ...

"Neil? Pepper?"

We snapped apart faster than a racquetball and a wall.

Royce Doucet had appeared between the topiaries and walked in our direction. He wore a tan jacket over a button-up blue shirt, with dark brown pants, and his hair was as rumpled as ever. I figured it was a deliberate look involving hair gel. Hard to tell.

"Royce!" Neil clambered to his feet, and I joined him.

"How are you two?" He gave us both a warm smile. "I'm sorry to interrupt your lunch, but I wanted to make sure we could talk today about your Kentucky trip and what I need you to do for my event. Find me, OK? I have to fly back home tomorrow."

"No problem," Neil said.

"I'm sure it'll be a barrel of fun," I added.

The cooper groaned and grinned. "Like I've never heard that before. But I hope it will be. I'm so grateful to Mark for introducing me to this crowd. I'm making friends and networking, and I know it's going to help me launch my bourbon." His tone turned more serious. "Hey, I heard you guys had some trouble last night. I'm glad you're OK."

"Me too," I said. "Thanks for thinking of us."

"Of course. Take care. See you later!"

He moved off and vanished between the bushes.

Neil looked at me and smiled. "Should we grab another cup of punch and enjoy the afternoon? I don't think there's any rush."

I smiled back. "I like the way you think."

Stay tuned for
Beguiled by Bourbon,
the next Bohemia Bartenders mystery!

WANT TO GET NOTIFIED WHEN THE NEXT BOOK COMES OUT?
Subscribe to my fun, occasional newsletter—and get a free Bohemia
Bartenders story—or follow me on BookBub.

I also have a Facebook group where we hang out and chat about life
and books — please join us in Lucy's Lounge. And you can always
find me at LucyLakestone.com.

READ ON FOR A LOOK BEHIND THE SCENES IN THE
ACKNOWLEDGMENTS AND A COCKTAIL RECIPE!

WILLIAM HOGARTH'S "GIN LANE"

Acknowledgments

I knew I wanted to include a storyline involving Charles Dickens in *Jiggered by Gin,* since he was a well-known imbiber and wrote such memorable words about the terrible impact of subpar gin's takeover of London and the false allure of gin palaces back in the spirit's bad old days. You can still find a handful of these glittering gin palaces in London, though The Dandy Tipple is a complete invention.

Gin was once the plague of the city, and the Hogarth print of "Gin Lane" that Cray buys at Buttersby Books is a real thing, depicting the sordid deaths and depravity wrought by the Blue Ruin. If you want to read more about gin's ignoble beginnings and its rise to popularity and sophistication, I recommend *Gin Glorious Gin: How Mother's Ruin Became the Spirit of London* by Olivia Williams.

I read several other books as research. One was Claire Tomalin's *Charles Dickens: A Life,* which led me to conjecture, *What if Dickens and his mistress had a child who survived?* This thought led me to her biography of his mistress, Nelly. She writes that no known descendants of Dickens and Ellen Ternan have ever come forward, but I thought the idea might make for interesting fiction. I apologize to Dickens's descendants, of which there are many, for any fanciful inventions that might offend them. Dickens was a complex man—hugely talented, a champion of the poor and even of "fallen" women, if not so good at writing realistic women—who betrayed his own ideals in his affair with Nelly. I highly recommend Ms.

Tomalin's *The Invisible Woman: The Story of Nelly Ternan and Charles Dickens* if you'd like to learn more. It's a kind of mystery, too, and the author is a savvy detective.

If you want to learn about what Charles Dickens drank and how, dig up a copy of *Convivial Dickens: The Drinks of Dickens & His Times* by Edward Hewett and William F. Axton, which includes, among other things, a list of the impressive contents of Dickens's cellar when he died—including wine, champagne, gin, genever, rum, brandy, scotch, curaçao, and chartreuse.

And the "friend to Temperance" fragment Pepper finds in the book Mark gives her? That's taken from a real Dickens letter from 1842 in which he claims emphatically that he is a "friend to Temperance" and writes: "As to denying myself my cheerful glass of wine because other men get drunk, I see no more reason for doing so."

I've taken liberties with London in small ways, whether it's geography or bar hours (my best to Trailer Happiness; you rock). And, of course, I've invented places, too. All inaccuracies (or creative renderings) are my own.

It's been some time since I've visited that great city, and the ongoing plague, which doesn't exist in the same timeline as the Bohemia Bartenders Mysteries (perhaps after, before or never?), has been hard on the city's beautiful drinking establishments. It may sound corny, but a tear came to my eye as I researched one setting in the book and saw that the gorgeous bar was closed until further notice. This lovely world of craft cocktails is on the bubble there, here and everywhere, and I only hope we come out of these dark times soon and can all enjoy a dandy tipple together again.

Heartfelt thanks go to my various writer groups and friends, including Star, the Harbaugh Literary Salon, and my online motivational buddies Ann Chaney and Jill Wallace. Thanks to Whitley Cox for her sharing and encouragement. A shout-out to Debbie, Karen and Cathy T. for their first reads. I treasure Naomi Bellina for her wisdom over coffee and Maria Geraci for her brilliant advice. Thanks to my storm-chasing support group, for want of a better term, who've helped me stay sane, especially Alethea Kontis for sharing the adventure. And my deep appreciation goes to Holly Martin, who cheers me on and lends my books her editor's eye.

Thank you to George Jenkins, my in-house mixologist, for, well, everything.

Cheers, my friends.

Cocktail Recipe

THE RESURRECTIONIST

The Resurrectionist is the pretty gin cocktail Neil makes for his seminar at The Dandy Tipple. It's a variation on Harry Craddock's classic Corpse Reviver No. 2. As Neil explains, a resurrectionist was what body snatchers were called in Dickens's time.

This is a lemon-forward, friendly cocktail. Your choice of gin will affect the final flavor, of course, depending on how herbal it is. And you might choose to substitute Cointreau for the high-end dry curaçao, for which I used Pierre Ferrand.

For the syrup, I used the very nice Hibiscus Elixir All Natural Flower Syrup from Floral Elixir Co., which adds tang as well as the beautiful ruby-red color. And I gave a nod to Mark's estate-based distillery by using gin from the setting of *Downton Abbey*, Highclere Castle. Your dash of absinthe is up to you; for a mild touch, about five drops should do it. Add more for boldness.

For the garnish, you might try a flower from a jar of Wild

Hibiscus Flowers in Syrup, either with or as a substitute for a lemon twist, or even dried *Hibiscus sabdariffa* (Roselle) petals.

Add to a cocktail shaker:

> 1 1/2 ounces gin
> 3/4 ounce quality dry curaçao
> 1/2 ounce Lillet Blanc
> 3/4 ounce freshly squeezed lemon juice
> 1/2 ounce hibiscus syrup
> 1 dash absinthe

Scoop in ice and shake vigorously. Strain into a coupe glass. Garnish with a lemon twist and/or a Roselle hibiscus blossom or petals.

BOOKS BY LUCY LAKESTONE

BOHEMIA BARTENDERS MYSTERIES

These funny mysteries star Pepper Revelle and a team of mixologists who travel to colorful gatherings where life is a cocktail of fun — until it's shaken into madcap mayhem ... and murder.

RISKY WHISKEY

BAFFLED BY BITTERS - *story free to subscribers*

WRECKED BY RUM

VEXED BY VODKA

JIGGERED BY GIN

FUN SUSPENSE

DESIRE ON DEADLINE

An original novel of light romantic suspense set in the Barefoot Bay World

Rival reporters ... the scoop of a lifetime ... and an attraction that can't be denied. Working together against a dangerous enemy might be the only way to survive, but can they get the stories they need when what they really want is each other?

The BOHEMIA BEACH Series

Award-winning hot contemporary romance

Within a beautiful small city on Florida's east coast, artists struggle to make their way. Where creative minds meet and restless hearts yearn, where emotion and ambition vie with lust and dark secrets, romance is impossible to resist. Welcome to the seductive tropical escape that's home to drama, humor and lots of heat . . . Bohemia Beach. Though these steamy novels have a common setting and the characters travel from one story to the next, each features a different couple and can be read as a standalone novel.

BOHEMIA BEACH

BOHEMIA LIGHT

BOHEMIA BLUES

BOHEMIA HEAT

BOHEMIA NIGHTS

BACK TO BOHEMIA - *story free to subscribers*

BOHEMIA BELLS

BOHEMIA CHILLS

The STORM SEEKERS Series

Writing as Chris Kridler

FUNNEL VISION

TORNADO PINBALL

ZAP BANG

About the Author

Lucy Lakestone is an award-winning author who lives on Florida's east central coast, among the towns that serve as an inspiration for the hot romances of her Bohemia Beach Series and the jumping-off point for the Bohemia Bartenders Mysteries. She's been a journalist, photographer, editor and video producer but prefers living in her imagination, where the moon is full and the cocktails are divine.

She also writes storm-chasing adventures as Chris Kridler, and in her spare time, she chases tornadoes.

Learn more at LucyLakestone.com

facebook.com/lucylakestone
twitter.com/lucylakestone
instagram.com/mslucylakestone
amazon.com/Lucy-Lakestone
bookbub.com/authors/lucy-lakestone
goodreads.com/lucylakestone
pinterest.com/lucylakestone